Intention's Folly

STEN RETHAGE

Published by: Epic Kawaii LLC

ISBN-13: 978-0692400586
ISBN-10: 0692400583

1st Edition - 2015

Death is better, a milder fate than tyranny.

- Aeschylus (525 BC - 456 BC)

STORY I

VINCENT LAYMON

★ CHAPTER 1 ★

It is hard to imagine a thing which more adequately proclaims the relative insignificance of a man than an order to dig a canal between America and Canada - by hand. But orders are orders. And, from where Vincent stood, there seemed little choice but to obey them.

A small circle formed in the dry dirt beneath Vincent Laymon's feet. Another drip of sweat fell beside it, and then another. The circles crept ever-so-slowly towards an earthworm, half of which had been exposed by his digging. An additional bomb of sweat rolled off Vincent's nose and hit the ground about a centimeter from the worm. Another miss.

"Keep that shovel moving!" The foreman's shout was enough to snap Vincent out of his trance. But it was a command easier said than done. The shovel had grown heavy in Vincent's hands as he neared the end of his shift. The sweat that dripped from Vincent's face now managed to reach his eyeballs, which stung with pain.

As the Canadian foreman moved on, Vincent gazed upon the endless rows of steel dragons that were working beside him. They stretched out along the sloping hills as far as he could see. The roaring of backhoes had become a part of his life. Now, after working in northern Michigan for almost three months, Vincent didn't even notice them anymore. It was like breathing. He wondered how this was even possible as he watched the enormous vehicles, built for moving loads of dirt across the terrain. The machinery was gigantic. Cranes piercing the sky in every direction, towering over what looked like ants scurrying around beneath, many of which, like Vincent, were digging with shovels. Trucks the size of small houses moved across the bare earth. It was hard to imagine that the Canal Project stretched from coast to coast. But it did.

Half of the digging equipment displayed the bright red maple leaf that Vincent had grown up his whole life singing to. The other half was owned by private American companies, who were under contract by their government. Usually Vincent went to bed dreaming of the girl he had left in Montreal, but that night all he could think about was how such a large-scale effort could be coordinated between two countries on such bad terms.

* * *

As usual, the Canadian workers were awakened from their slumber by an obnoxious officer of the Global Civic Order.

"Get up! Your government isn't paying you to sleep all day!"

As Vincent came to his senses, he wondered which government the officer answered to. He sounded Italian, or maybe Spanish. At any rate, the timing of the daily wake-up call had become so consistent that Vincent's internal alarm clock usually had him sitting up in bed before the officer even entered the living quarters. But for some reason, not today. Today Vincent felt like rolling over and falling back into a warm oblivion of sleep.

The shelters that housed the tens of thousands of Canadians who worked on the Canal Project were really no more than recklessly constructed shanties, enormous in size. Or, if you were lucky, large, government-issued tents. Vincent and his brother, Frank, had been assigned to a tent. Each shelter housed hundreds of workers who slept in small beds layered for efficiency. Despite the cramped living conditions and the monotonous work involved in digging dirt every day, there were few riots – few cases of disobedience. This was largely due to the fact that the Canadian workers were being paid very good money by their government for services rendered. It was not a job, Vincent contemplated - it was a career. A profession.

The same could not be said for the Americans, however. To Vincent, they always seemed dirty. He often worked side by side with such men. They drank heavily and smoked their lungs into black mush - actions which would never be tolerated by the Canadian Union. Sure, the Americans he knew worked just as hard as the Canadians, but they were much more unruly. Very unpredictable. Regularly, Vincent would look up from his digging in time to see a pair of resentful eyes gleaming at him. Yes, there was bad blood between the two countries, but it didn't run through the veins of Vincent Laymon, he liked to think.

Every morning, after an early breakfast, the Canadians met in small groups, usually outside of the entrance to their housing units. If it was raining, the meetings were held inside (although rain never stopped a shovel handler from his hard day's work). At these gatherings, a foreman would assign each worker to a specific group, usually designated by color. Then another foreman would assign each group to a specific area, which were mapped out by sectors. The sector map was to be memorized by all workers. At first Vincent thought such a task would be a pain, but after a few weeks on the job, he had memorized it out of routine. Each sector covered about three hundred square meters and had a specific letter assigned to it. Canadian workers were not referred to by the names given to them at birth, but instead by numbers.

Today Vincent would be working in Group Yellow, Sector G, as the worker number 4299 that had been granted to him upon his arrival three months earlier and sewn onto the chest of his uniform.

This particular morning, after the meeting, Vincent started on his long walk to Sector G. Although disappointed that his brother had not also been assigned to Group Yellow, Vincent was particularly happy that he had been ordered to work in Sector G. Sector G meant one of the longest walks to the worksite, and it was turning out to be a beautiful morning. The sun was rising over the horizon and attempting to cut through the morning fog layered over the dug-up earth around him. It was cool out, but Vincent knew that he would be sweating by eight o'clock. The currently-unmanned backhoes and cranes peeked their monstrous necks up out of the layer of white as the rising sun painted their steel bodies a magnificent hot pink. Vincent stopped to take a mental picture as he breathed in a deep gasp of the fresh Michigan air. By eight o'clock, when he would be covered in sweat, Vincent knew that the same breath would reek of diesel fumes and smoke. For this reason, he cherished the moment.

As Vincent approached the site designated as Sector G, his face lit up with excitement. There before him, only half of his body revealed from the trench he worked in, stood a familiar, wiry figure – a man Vincent knew only as Saul. Saul was an American who had been working in Sector Q on Vincent's first day in Michigan. He was a smoker, fitting the little stereotype Vincent liked to apply to the Americans, but he was also one of the nicest men Vincent had ever met. Vincent had been assigned to Q early that inaugural morning, and Saul had been the first person he had really gotten a chance to talk to other than his brother, who had made the long trip from central Alberta with him. Immediately, they hit it off. Saul was one of those guys who was just coasting through life. He told Vincent that he had only two more years until retirement and then he could receive his pension. Whatever *that* was, Vincent had thought.

Saul had a very coarse look about him. His face was covered in black scruff, sprinkled with flakes of silver. It seemed amazing to Vincent how his facial hair never seemed to grow out into a beard while, on the other hand, his face on no account appeared to glow in the aftermath of a close shave. He had noticed this as they had worked together every day for the first two weeks of Vincent's stay. Saul's facial features reflected those of a man who had seen it all and just didn't care anymore. Thin wrinkles converged at the points of his eyes and mouth when he smiled. Saul looked like he was in his late fifties, and when Vincent had first asked him how old he was, this theory had been confirmed with the response, "Fifty-eight".

Now Vincent was in high spirits. Working with Saul was an unexpected treat and so he decided to have a little fun to start off what would be another hard day's work. He snuck alongside the trench towards the small mound of dirt that had been growing with every motion of Saul's shovel. It was not necessary to remain quiet, as Vincent knew that Saul's hearing was very bad. His back was now facing Vincent, and the noise of someone trying to fire-up a nearby backhoe made it even easier to make his way into position. Saul's head was facing down as he was digging, and Vincent filled his shovel full of dirt from the pile. As Saul threw the next shovelful of soil over his left shoulder and onto the pile outside of the trench, Vincent carefully tossed the dirt from his shovel right back down into the trench in front of Saul, where he had been digging. The playful stunt startled Saul a bit more than Vincent had planned. He flinched back and let out a gruff yell, "Hoah!" The cigarette he had been smoking ejected from his mouth and landed on the ground. As Saul whipped around, he saw Vincent's face and began laughing hysterically. Vincent joined in, and the two roared, Saul crying, for a good five minutes. The prank wasn't really that funny... It was mostly because the two were so happy to see each other again.

Vincent and Saul got along like old high school buddies. This despite the gaping age difference. Saul was easily old enough to be Vincent's father. But this type of situation was not uncommon for Vincent. His young face glowed with wisdom, and his personality had the innate ability to transcend age. The older man had absolutely no problem in seeing Vincent as his peer.

"So what the hell have *you* been up to?", asked Saul, as he poked at the #4299 patch sewn onto the chest of Vincent's uniform with the handle of his shovel.

"Same old..." Vincent thought about that for a split second. The life of a Canadian Union worker was not all that exciting - it was a good life, but not all that exciting. But just for a split second. "You?" he returned with a subtle grin.

"I left that hill we were working on together about a day after you. Boss has had me here ever since."

"How are the kids?" Vincent asked.

Two weeks - six days a week - ten hours a day... that's a hundred and twenty hours. You learn quite a bit about a person's life by talking to them for a hundred and twenty hours. You learn about the jobs they've had, the car they drive, their love life, and you learn about their kids. To Vincent, this had just seemed like the best one to ask about.

"Simon just got accepted into grad school – he'll be going to Yale. I'm so damn proud of that kid." He paused for a second, choked up. "We all are," he managed to whimper.

Saul was the most emotional man Vincent had ever met. But it wasn't a weak, vulnerable "emotional". It was simply passion. Even in this slice of time, as he muttered only a few words about his son, it was blindingly obvious what was more important to him than anything else in the world - his job, his retirement, or even his own life. Saul was passionate about the love he had for his family.

"Well, congratulations!" Vincent said, trying to be as cheery-sounding as possible to lighten the mood.

It worked.

Saul and Vincent worked together all morning, exchanging stories and laughing with one another, just like they had two and a half months before. By eight o'clock, they were both soaked in sweat, and at a little after ten, a Canadian Union overseer broke the two up, sending Vincent to dig in a different portion of Sector G, about seventy-five meters further down along the ever-growing gully. This was a fairly standard maneuver. It had happened several times during those first two weeks in Sector Q, but never since, probably because Vincent hadn't really talked to anyone other than his brother, Frank. Vincent figured that they did it either because they presumed that it made for a less productive day of work, or because they had seen one too many scuffles break out between Canadians and Americans working so closely together. Of course in this case, Vincent knew neither reason applied. But he would follow the orders, and, as he had done before, he would wait until the overseer was out of sight to make his way back to

Saul.

But as Vincent walked to the new position with his shovel slung over his shoulder, now about half way there, the harmonious purr of engines – not diesel – made him stop in his tracks.

It was not uncommon for a Canadian military envoy to drive through the worksite during the day. They would usually be driving jeeps, the forerunner occupied by a Canadian officer of some type. Although Vincent had never known much about the military, the barrage of colorful ribbons on an officer's chest could be seen half a kilometer away. It was obvious, and it usually meant trouble. While Canadian officers would be willing to jump down into the mud to help a fellow Canadian dig a ditch, they despised Americans with a deep hatred that could only be radiated by a man carrying a deadly weapon. The problem was that they often acted on this hatred. And if there was one thing that Vincent had learned about Americans during his three months in the country, it was that they were suicidal when it came to their dignity... their "patriotism", as he had heard it called in a book.

Normally, the Canadian military would never have access to a state like Michigan. No more than the American military, as powerful as it was, would have access to a Canadian province. But the Canal Act, which had started as a piece of American legislation but was since carried out under the supervision of the Global Civic Order, had temporarily designated a certain portion of northern Michigan, along with other bits and pieces of states and provinces, as neutral – a vast no-man's-land of what had become a world of endless dirt... or mud, on a rainy day. The Global Civic Order had taken it upon itself to emit officials into these areas to ensure that "peaceful and cooperative operations" would ensue. The GCO officials were not big fans of either country sending military units caravanning through no-man's-land, but on this day there was not an official in sight.

The sun, now almost directly overhead, radiated waves of air from the bodies of the vehicles as they slithered like a shiny snake over the horizon and across the terrain from the direction of the housing sites. It was the same route that Vincent had walked earlier that morning, on his way into Sector G. The snake came to a halt about fifty meters from Vincent, directly on the other side of the trench that Saul was working in. There were five jeeps altogether, and out of the first stepped a man with a powerful-looking physique. All Vincent could see, however, was the barrage of colorful ribbons on the man's chest.

Vincent had seen it all before. It was a scene acted out by the Canadian military quite often. The whole thing made Vincent sick. It was a haughty display of power – that was all. The routine began with an officer exiting his vehicle and walking to the nearest trench. An onslaught of privates, probably in training, would follow him. It looked like a mother goose leading her young. The officer would then walk along the trench complimenting Canadians on their hard day's work... muttering something about how they were making Mother Canada proud. But the real reason for their little tour of the desolate digging fields was much more vindictive. Any American the officer would come upon would be subject to the most malicious verbal abuse that could be imagined coming from the mouth of an officer plastered in such brilliant medallions. And Vincent knew it was all for that sense of supremacy, that little rush of clout that he would feel by being so cruel in front of all of the wide-eyed neophytes lined up behind him. Officers loved performing such flashes of what they considered power – simply because they could. And of course too often the Americans, so foolishly proud, would react with violence. The Global Civic Order had made known in the Canal Act that, while in the new no-man's-land designated by the text, both Americans and Canadians would be subject to the criminal laws of the law-breaker's native country. It was actually a lot more complicated than that, but really, that was what it boiled down to. This was of course what the Canadian officers banked on, but a presiding GCO officer would usually break things up before they could get started. However, there was still not an official in sight.

Although Vincent knew that Saul was one of the last Americans that would ever be prone to such violence, he equally weighed in the immense quantity of passion that flowed through the man's veins. Something made Vincent want to be with Saul at that moment. Maybe it was because he noticed that Saul hadn't heard the convoy of automobiles pull up behind him. Vincent started walking faster, not running so as to avoid alarming the line of soldiers that was now creeping along the trench towards Saul, as he had done playfully that morning. Vincent saw the huge outline of the officer bend down and compliment a Canadian Union hand working in the ditch as he continued his approach towards Saul. Realizing that he wouldn't make it to the spot in time, Vincent took advantage of the officer's momentary distraction and waved his hand at Saul trying to get his attention. It worked… sort of. Saul glanced up and smiled, waving back and then put his head back down to continue his digging. Vincent stopped as the officer looked up at him with a cold stare. He was now about thirty meters from the line of soldiers and his muscles froze stiff. The officer then nodded to him with a wide grin and continued his walk.

As the officer approached Saul, for an instant in time, it looked like there wasn't going to be a problem. The man didn't even seem to acknowledge Saul. And Saul himself, with his poor hearing, still had not even noticed the procession of military uniforms that were now about to pass him by. Vincent studied the scenario, and for a second, he even chuckled as he thought to himself about the great care he had taken while sneaking up on Saul that morning, and how it had been so unnecessary. Then it happened.

Although Vincent had never believed in God, or Allah, or any other divine power, it was instances like these that made him think about those things. How intricately lives could be woven together by the smallest of actions. Immense changes in history brought about by the life of a single man or woman. And how the life of a single man or woman could likewise be changed by a simple, seemingly meaningless action. Take for instance, throwing a shovelful of dirt over your left shoulder without looking.

While the scene smoothly unfolded before Vincent's eyes, his heart leapt into his throat. The dirt rolled off the officer's finely-pressed trousers, as his massive head very slowly, methodically swiveled around to meet the offender. Saul, standing in the ditch, only stood up to the officer's knees. He had immediately realized what had happened, and began frantically mumbling apologetic remarks which were inaudible from Vincent's standpoint. The Canadian officer gradually squared his body up so that he was now facing Saul, looking down at him with a look of hatred that Vincent would never forget. The officer then made a quick glance to his right, which Vincent later figured was to make sure that all of his young privates were watching. Turning his evil gaze back down upon Saul, he proceeded to punt

16

him in the head with all of his might. The shiny, black Canadian-issued boot struck Saul square in the face, shattering his nose and left cheekbone, and sending his limp body into the ditch, and out of the sight of Vincent Laymon. All told, Vincent was actually relieved at this. He knew the wrath of such officers and, honestly, had expected worse. This, however, did nothing to tame the rage that was building up inside of him.

What happened next, Vincent didn't see coming. The Canadian officer barked out an order to the two nearest uniformed troops. At first they just looked at each other, but hearing the fury in the officer's voice the second time, they quickly leapt down into the trench. Vincent knew Saul's body couldn't weigh more than a little over seventy kilograms, and it showed in the way the soldiers were able to hoist him out of the gully with little trouble. Saul was not yet unconscious… instead, he was choking on his own blood – spitting it all over the dirt around him. He was now standing before the Canadian officer, but bent over half way, holding his face in his hands. Other than the spitting, he wasn't making a sound.

By this time, every worker in Sector G had noticed that something was happening. Those close enough to see what it was stood in shock, both American and Canadian. Vincent was the only one moving. He was walking towards the commotion, unsure of exactly why. When the officer removed his pistol from the holster on his side however, Vincent froze like the rest of them.

Vincent would never forget the next words to come out of the officer's mouth. His mother, when he was younger, had scolded him for listening to his music too loud. The basis for her argument was that Vincent, by doing this, would acquire a condition which would leave him with a ringing in his ears for the rest of his life. And so it was with the officer's words, but his mother had never given him advice on anything like this.

Pressing the end of the barrel against the top of Saul's head, firmly enough to cause it to bow down, the officer spoke… "So die all who dishonor the red and white of our Mother Canada."

The blast of the firearm echoed through the landscape. The force of the shot was enough to send Saul's corpse hurling back so far that it rolled down into the trench where he had been digging. Immediately Vincent's body turned to ice. The chill of death ran through his spine as his eyes narrowed with ultimate concentration. He casually walked up beside the officer who was now huddled with his neophyte followers looking down over the edge of the trench. Vincent knew that Saul was dead, and he wondered why the soldiers had to prove this to themselves. They were, after all, trained to kill.

The officer now swung his massive head around, peering into Vincent's eyes. It was the look of a schoolyard bully who was just waiting for the younger, weaker, noble boy to make a move of defiance. But Vincent did nothing to alarm the Canadian officer. Instead he smiled a broad smile. It was a smile that would later be interpreted, by those who would come to know Vincent, as a warning signal. But the officer, blinded by his own false sense of dominance, only saw a fellow Canadian that was proud of the fact that justice had been served.

Vincent glanced at the nametag which shared the officer's chest with his many medals. It read "Capt. Lunsford". With the smile remaining on his face, Vincent looked down at the gun that the officer still held in his right hand. He had a way of talking to people without saying a word, and the officer realized that he wanted to hold it. Without a moment of hesitation, Captain Lunsford extended his arm offering Vincent the gun. There must be something about the security of having a dozen armed troops standing at your service that makes one feel untouchable.

"That is the tool of righteousness, son."

The words almost made Vincent throw up. But he kept that chilling grin gleaming on his face. His body now felt completely cold. His veins had frozen solid, and for a moment Vincent Laymon felt invincible. The only thing he could feel, other than the ice of death in the air, was the barrel of the officer's pistol in his hand. It was still warm from the shot he had fired into Saul's head.

Vincent knew so little about guns. And considering all of the books he had read, he found this hard to believe. He hadn't even seen a movie in which they had been used. In fact, watching Captain Lunsford kill Saul was the first time he had ever had such an experience. He remembered how Saul had laughed when he had learned of Vincent's inexperience with firearms, and Vincent remembered how shocked he had been when Saul had told him that he actually owned guns himself.

Saul had such a beautiful laugh.

Vincent, with all of the strength that his young, built stature could muster, suddenly swung his right arm around, ramming the butt of the pistol into the officer's head. The action was like that of a viper, with a swift flash that allowed the Canadian officer no time to react. The contact occurred on the officer's left eye, causing an explosion of blood. He collapsed immediately. To Vincent's surprise, not one of the young soldiers who had accompanied the captain to the worksite even moved. They stood in shock, many of them with mouths and eyes wide open. Vincent took advantage of their frozen status and dove onto the officer's immobile body that was now lying flat on its back. As Vincent continued to batter the officer's face with the pistol, he didn't even think about the twelve Canadian Army soldiers who stood around him, clasping Canadian-issued machine guns while watching their superior officer being reduced to a bloody pulp. Vincent Laymon knew he was - at that instant - still invincible. By the time he was flooded with resistance coming from multiple troops, Vincent had counted four hits that he had gotten in on the bastard, not counting the initial blow.

Now two of the young men restrained him, lifting Vincent to his feet. Each had a grasp on one of his arms. Another soldier tore the firearm from his hand. He had been crying ever since he had taken his position straddling the officer. It was the first time that Vincent could ever remember crying. It was simply not in his character. And now that he thought about it, he wasn't crying for himself or for what would become of him. He wasn't crying out of pure emotion or blind passion. No, Vincent Laymon wept for Saul, and the family of his good friend. Saul would never be able to spend time with his wife after retirement. He would never see an ocean, would never visit the Gulf of Mexico, both of which Vincent could remember Saul talking about with the anticipation of a child. Saul would not witness his son, Simon, finish graduate school. This was why Vincent Laymon wept.

And now, as he gazed down upon what remained of Captain Lunsford, his spirits were lifted by the hand of justice. He was no physiologist, Vincent reasoned, but when a man's brains could be seen through his forehead, it was a

20

pretty good sign that he was dead. And a most righteous death at that. For Vincent knew that, had the officer lived another day, he would have wasted no time in issuing a military court order proclaiming that he had acted against Saul in self-defense. He knew that none of his mindless followers, the young men who now restrained Vincent, would have dared testified otherwise. In fact, the Canadian officer would have probably pressured a couple of the more vulnerable young troops into speaking out in his defense. No workers, even American, would speak a word of the matter now... realizing that a similar incident could easily befall them – on another day, at the hand of another Canadian military envoy. The outcome of such a trial would inevitably be the destruction of Saul's family name, and the acquittal of Captain Lunsford. For this reason, though the captain's demise did nothing to avenge the murder of Vincent's friend, he was sure that, at the least, it had prevented Saul's death from becoming one wrapped in malicious rumors of injustice.

These thoughts were the last thing that Vincent remembered going through his head as he tried to regain his bearing, sitting up in a hospital bed. A young woman dressed in white now gazed down upon him with a look of both dread and awe.

★ CHAPTER 2 ★

Vincent had spent the first twenty years of his life living in the small rural town of Drayton Valley, about three hundred kilometers north of Calgary, and three thousand from the work site. His father had died when Vincent was ten. Pancreatic cancer. He was only forty-four years old. Forever ingrained in Vincent's mind was the picture of his mother, his brother Frank, and himself crowded around his dad's hospital bed. The sheets were white with a pattern of very small flowers – blue and red – sprinkled over them. And hospitals have a certain smell, or at least this one did. Vincent hated that memory.

The worst part about his father's death was that it was practically the only memory he had of the man. His work had forced him to spend all of his time away, supporting the family. And Vincent's mother always seemed too sad about it to discuss. But Vincent could remember the phone calls. They were major events. Huddling around the receiver, tears of joy in their eyes. Frank had not been old enough to understand the frailty of the human body, but Vincent could remember his mother's voice. She understood. If only Vincent could have spent more time with his dad, maybe he could have done something. But really none of them expected death. Not at forty-four years old. Then again… *Really* does anyone?

It seems that death has only two states. It is usually so distant and impossible, like a dream. But fatality has another guise – and so different it is. Death can immerse the human being into another world. It can burst into such a reality that life simply becomes a challenge to avoid it. Vincent had felt this way for quite some time after that hospital visit. Much later in his life he would take some classes at the university on electricity and simple circuit design. It was during one of these lectures that his mind wandered into figuring out the meaning of life according to Vincent Laymon. He reasoned that human beings were identical to resistors that were placed in a circuit. Current was death. Resistance is added to circuits to control the flow of current. Death will continue, with new resistors being soldered into the circuit every day, and others being taken out. A week later, Vincent had forgotten about his little theory, his little stroke of genius. He had since slipped back into the dream of mortality.

And now Vincent had experienced another account of death, this time at the will of his own hands. And he felt nothing. No remorse. Death was not residing in a fantasy state. No, the blood and brains of that Canadian officer had seemed very real. But, on the other hand, Vincent was not running from his end. The invincibility which had surrounded his person during the murder had never left him. And that is exactly what it had been – murder. Vincent had no grand delusions of righteousness. He just didn't care. It was justified murder. And so his new life began – one which would not discriminate between life and death, but instead between that which is justified, and that which is not. But it had not always been this way. Vincent had not always believed himself to be invincible.

By the time he was old enough to begin his secondary education, Vincent Laymon had already settled into a daily routine – part of which was good, and part not so good. In the morning, Anna, his mother, would set an alarm on her clock so she could rise so very early in the morning. Once she was done putting lunches together for

Vincent and Frank, it was time to wake them up. Getting her sons ready for school had been the happiest part of Anna's day. She loved them in a way which could only be reflected in her interaction with them, not in words. It was love that moved her to set her own alarm, so Vincent and Frank would be able to awake to her soft voice instead of an aggravating buzzer. It was out of love that she had prepared their lunches every day and walked them out to the school bus. She would stay with them until the bus had come and left, even when it was running late. This despite the harsh penalties that would be placed on Anna's resulting late arrivals to work. And it was this same love that caused Mrs. Laymon to weep every time her son, Vincent, would come home, clothes ripped, cut and bruised, but despite this, never crying himself.

It was simple. The most important thing was to never fall apart in the presence of mom. Vincent loved her too much to cause her that grief, and besides, he knew that boys don't cry. His father had taught him that at a very early age. The grind would begin as soon as he and Frank were out of the protection of the home. Vincent would usually hear a comment or two before he even sat down in his assigned window seat on the bus. However, this did not stop him from wearing a loving smile as he returned a wave from his mother, who would watch the bus drive out of sight. In retrospect, Vincent was later better able to grasp the reason for the abuse he had endured during those years.

First of all, he was the runt of his class. So much so that, as Vincent entered his homeroom on the first day of secondary school and the class laughed, the teacher chuckled along with them. She thought Vincent had made a mistake and wandered over from the elementary school section. It was not until the teacher accompanied Vincent to the school office that she had realized the truth, despite the calm pleas of Vincent Laymon. Such a case was not at all uncommon anymore, and it didn't even faze him. What really ate away at Vincent was the idea that he could never be accepted by his peers. When he was thirteen, he looked eight or nine. But by the time Vincent was twenty years old, he just looked like a young twenty-year-old. It was over. Those grueling years of his childhood had, in the end, actually taught Vincent to appreciate those friends he did make, not hold a grudge against those who harassed him. Vincent had a certain way of deriving good from a seemingly bad experience.

The other problem was that Vincent loved to read books. Such an activity did not rank among the upper echelons of male popularity during high school. He played no sports but, for some reason, had developed a relatively athletic build by the time he was in college. Vincent always assumed it was genetic. His father had been the same way. During his time in Drayton Valley, Vincent read hundreds of books. He read everything he could get his hands on. And in Canada, as it would later become more obvious to him, the selection was rather limited. Books on politics and war seemed hard to find. Those that were accessible were usually historically-based – very little original thinking. Non-fiction books ran rampant on the shelves of the public library. And Vincent read all of it - biographies of Canadian heroes and documentaries of Civicism among his favorites. But Vincent paid a price for his hobby. It was in the defense of his books that he was usually beaten by his peers. Vincent thought that if his mother found out the cause of the beatings, she would take away his pastime, his books.

And so the routine went on. Go to school, get teased, get beaten, come home, and continue reading. Not even Frank, looking about right for his age and never tormented in this way, could get any information on the beatings. Vincent refused to rat on the kids who mocked and tortured him. Little did Frank know that Vincent was only trying to imitate what he thought was Frank's saintly nature. It would always be a mystery to him, but Frank could tell that his older brother looked up to him in a way that mimicked a naïve grandson listening to stories told by a war-hero grandfather. Maybe it was because Frank never got into trouble. But then again, this was because trouble never found him like it did Vincent. Or maybe it was just that Frank was one of the only children who never teased him. In fact, Vincent could not remember his brother ever reproaching him with even one word of malice. There was too much love between them. There was no one else to love.

Vincent graduated high school at the top of his class. He decided to let the next-in-line give the speech at graduation. He had never really gotten over the abuse he had taken years earlier, and Vincent truly believed that many of the students who had acted cruelly towards him then still carried their contempt for his book reading and young looks. Vincent thought he would be booed for anything that he said at the podium. But in reality, he had since become the most popular kid in school.

Upon graduation, Vincent attended the University of Montreal. It was expected that any student with a shred of potential attend college in Canada. Good government jobs were out of the question without a degree, and Vincent decided to pursue architectural engineering.

It was during his time at college that Vincent Laymon met Laura Welsh. He had seen her around campus from time to time. Dark hair – brown, glimmering. She had the greenest eyes Vincent had ever seen, and she was gorgeous. Her face was innocent-looking, and her body was a ten, though usually veiled with a conservative outfit. Vincent had very little experience with girls. He had dated a few times in high school, but it never lasted more than a few dates. He didn't know how to talk to them, didn't even know how to look at them. Vincent had always hated seeing guys gawking at girls as they passed by, so blatantly that it seemed disgusting to him. This was the reason that one evening he had become so embarrassed of himself.

Vincent was sitting in the lounge of his dormitory, plugging away at a book on elementary structural design, when she walked in. It was the first time that Vincent had really gotten a good look at Laura, and he was fascinated. She wore a tight-fitting navy blue shirt, complemented with gray nylon pants that outlined her lower half, forming a picturesque silhouette of the female physique. It was the look of a girl who, no matter how hard she tried, could not prohibit her image from flooring young men like Vincent. And it was Laura's lack of concern for her appearance that finally did him in. She spun around and sat herself on a sofa so that her right side was facing him. As he watched her read, Vincent noticed her green eyes scanning each line of the prose. As she came upon something that was obviously funny, he witnessed her face light up with interest, as a tiny grin grew on her sweet lips. At that moment, Laura must have sensed Vincent's stare, and she looked right into his eyes. He knew he was busted. An animal caught in the headlights. Vincent just smiled, with full knowledge that his face was flushed with red. Laura smiled back. Although they both simply returned to their books (at least Laura did – Vincent could not think straight), there was a noticeable change in the atmosphere of the room. Vincent felt compelled to call her the next day, and so the two began the process of dating.

What kept the relationship together for Vincent was how great of a friend Laura became. The girls he dated in high school were never on this level. Honestly, he dated them just to say he had dated - just to fit in. Or, maybe it was simply a matter of giving in to the adolescent lusts of the female anatomy. Either way, Vincent had never had a girl for a friend, certainly never to this extent. But now it seemed that everything just clicked. Soon after the dating began, Vincent found that Laura held almost all of the same interests as him. They read the same books, they listened to the same music, and one day Laura even told Vincent that she had been picked on for her size when she was younger (though now she was almost as tall as Vincent, who stood at one hundred and seventy-eight centimeters). It was his relationship with Laura Welsh that made Vincent ponder so deeply the idea of one's fate. How else could he be dating Laura? It would have to be quite a large coincidence – one the percentages did not favor.

One evening, after Vincent had been going out with Laura for nearly a year, he decided to share with her his feelings on fate. The two aficionados were lying on their backs in Laura's bed. Laura's dorm room had become a safe haven for Vincent. It was now the only place that Vincent could feel truly right. Laura's presence was an escape from the cruelty of the world and the realities of stress. Just laying together with his girlfriend had become one of his favorite pastimes. It was so inexpensive, so simple, and yet so perfect. And this day, this nap, was no exception.

"Do you believe in fate?" Vincent was known for his straightforwardness in conversation, and he was not about to disappoint.

"I suppose… I never really thought about it before." Along with her presence, Laura's voice was magical to Vincent. So soft, so soothing. A conversation with Laura could be likened to a warm bath with relaxing music. It could change his worst day into his best.

Vincent continued, "I do. I think everything happens for a reason. I think every little incident in someone's life has purpose." He paused. "The purpose is rarely known by those involved however. Otherwise everyone would share my theory, and it would no longer *be* a theory, but a fact."

One of the qualities that Vincent most admired in Laura was her ability to listen. Not just hear, but listen. Vincent knew the difference like no one else. He had always had a problem in school, ever since he could remember. A teacher would be lecturing on economics or explosives, it didn't matter. Vincent's mind would wander off to other subjects, other worlds, other universes. He had always thought to himself that it was a good thing that he liked reading, because he really sucked at listening. But now he watched Laura. How he envied her. She was eating up and digesting every word from Vincent's mouth, her beautiful green eyes gazing into Vincent's sea of gray.

"Honey?" Laura said worriedly.

Vincent now realized that not only could his mind be diverted during a lecture, but also when he himself was the speaker. That's pretty bad, he thought.

"Sorry. Anyway… I mean…. OK take this for example… I once read a speech written by one of the former presidents of America. In it he says 'Men are not prisoners of their fate, but only prisoners of their own minds.' I mean, how ignorant is that? Who is he, or anyone else for that

29

matter, to believe for a minute that he is above fate? It was his fate that had him give that speech, and it was his fate that would later deal him a deadly cerebral hemorrhage. What do you think?"

"I believe in God." Laura said it both to settle Vincent's nerves and finish off the conversation, and she succeeded.

"Call it what you will," Vincent said, voice trailing off.

Vincent had been raised a Catholic, but it seemed that with him none of the priests' sermons had ever really stuck. His mother was devout in the faith, and he knew that she prayed for his soul every day. Vincent never brought the subject up. It was always her. He hated talking about religion. Of course Laura knew this, and used this information as a vice to end an uncomfortable conversation from time to time. This never bothered Vincent though. What did nag him was Laura's Protestant upbringing.

But in spite of the incompatibility of their religious backgrounds, Laura and Vincent were incredibly happy together. Their harmonious existence was due, in part, to the fact that they both shared the same system of *basic* values. Vincent had, more than anything, a sincere respect and honor for women. As a teenager, he had vowed to save himself for one woman. He believed any male sexual promiscuity to be dishonorable to the female gender. And he thought that, because he couldn't be sure of his commitment to Laura Welsh, he would remain abstinent. This of course was perfectly fine with Laura, as her strong Presbyterian roots would have it no other way.

Vincent had created his own standards on which he would live his life. As a voracious reader, Vincent had devoured the entire Bible, the Koran, the Characteristics of Existence and Noble Truths of Buddhism, and countless books on Canadian law and sociology. By age twenty-two, he had, in his head, created a virtual doctrine of life. It was largely based on two principles – fate and love.

Love, Vincent had decided, was so closely intertwined with fate that often they were confused with one another. Like fate, he believed that love could bring the best out in a man, then turn around and butcher him. He understood that women were the most deadly weapon a man could face, and he always handled them as such. He also knew that women, too, had a weapon of their own. It was the concoction of love and sex.

Biology had always been one of Vincent's favorite subjects, and, after an entry-level high school class, he had decided to read as much as he could about the subject. This reading had gone on for months. In his comprehension of the material, Vincent had been fascinated by a certain aquatic creature known as the Betta fish. He had followed up this discovery with a visit to the local pet store. The fish were small and beautiful. Their vast, paper-thin fins delicately trailing in a magnificent hue as they dashed around the water in what seemed to Vincent a choreographed dance of expertise. So innocent, so delightful – by themselves. For these fish had another aspect to their identity, and it was this quality that intrigued Vincent Laymon. When one is placed in a bowl or tank with another of its kind, death ensues. The fish attack each other and one must fall to its doom. Like love and sex, so harmless apart, yet so deadly together. Vincent was so contented with his analogy that he made a deliberate mental note of the occasion – which lasted until he read one day that it was only the male Betta that attacked, and it was only the females who were victimized.

Either way, Vincent had early on identified the deadly mixture of love and sex, and had purposefully separated himself from such danger. In fact, deep down, he knew that if he were to be completely honest, he could not deny that it was at least partially for this reason that he had never made love to Laura.

And so the two principles of his doctrine remained. Fate and love. Fate, Vincent could handle, but love, he thought... love is a funny thing.

★ CHAPTER 3 ★

When Frank Laymon heard the news, he staggered in disbelief. He had realized something was wrong when his brother did not show up for dinner at the Union barracks that night. Frank had spent the whole day working on Sector E, as had been his assignment. He had barely noticed the medical emergency vehicle flying across the barren landscape. It happened all of the time. With so much heavy machinery rolling around and working amongst the miniature vessels of fragile human life, accidents on the job were simply unavoidable. Any more, such instances failed to reach the inner workings of a man's sensitivities. But when Frank saw that Vincent's chair in the cafeteria, the one he had been assigned by the Union, remained empty at supper time, the entire scenario replayed through his brain in vivid detail.

The emergency vehicle had been escorted by a Canadian Army jeep in the front, and followed by a GCO military escort. The train of camouflage and flashing lights was on the main vehicle inlet to Sector G, a dirt road used mainly to accommodate incoming digging equipment. At that moment in Frank's mind, this information became permanently fused with his memory of Vincent's working area assignment that day. All of the evidence added up to trouble, and the emptiness that Frank was beginning to feel in his body was only further fueled by rumors that he was hearing around the tables which filled the Union cafeteria.

It was almost six-thirty in the evening, and those men who had labored through the sun's merciless heat all day now sat in the mess hall enjoying their Canadian issued "hot packs". It was the name assumed by most of the

33

workers for the foil-covered cuisine that they were served every night. Such food portions were used by the Canadian Union because of their efficiency in preparation and their ability to suit the needs of each worker. Over the past several years, the Canadian government had invested a very sizable amount of time and money into the research of food products. The research had been a huge success, and the end result was a major cost reduction of government-purchased rations coupled with a breakthrough that the nutrition scientists coined as "individual nutritional adaptation", or INA. The premise was that by using the new INA technology, the government would be able to order the meals that would make their employees the most efficient workers that the limits of their natural bodies deemed possible. The individuality of the order would be based on the worker's height, weight, metabolism, and largely the conditions in which he or she operated. All that was needed to be done in preparation was the filling out of a five page survey – a new requirement that was implemented at the initiation of a worker's employment with the Canadian Union. The Canadian military, however, had been the real reason for all of the research, and now that INA had been proven in the workplace, the government was ready to install a similar program within the bounds of its armed forces.

This night, Frank Laymon wasn't hungry. Although the food before him was theoretically the best thing he could eat for his body, Frank knew that INA technology had not yet been able to create an interactive food based on the emotional state of the consumer as he or she ate it. And at this moment, he felt an emptiness that even all of the technology of the hot pack couldn't fill. He was thinking back to the times he had spent working with Vincent in the yard back home. Over the years, Frank and Vincent had developed a bond, one that had formed in the same way a grain of sand forms into a pearl while residing in the oyster. Layers of episodes that had been shared by the brothers sealed them off from all others. Frank remembered all of the times in the more recent past when they had shared wings and twenty-five cent drafts at the local bar back in Drayton Valley. They could spend an entire night talking about the most trivial things, but twist them around in a way which could lead to some truly thought-provoking discussions. There was no doubt about it, Frank loved his brother.

"Francis R. Laymon?" – the sound broke Frank's train of thought. As Frank looked up from his blank stare that had been affixed on the hot pack before him, he saw the insipid face of a young man, clad in the typical entry-level Canadian military attire.

"Yes," he replied quietly. Frank hated it when people called him that.

"Brother of Vincent F. Laymon?" the soldier inquired.

"Yes." Frank was becoming a bit impatient with the interrogation, and he stood up as if to receive what he already knew was going to be dire news. The Canadian soldier now let out a quick smile of relief, as if he had already asked a hundred workers the same question, only to be told no. The smile coming at a time like this bothered Frank, but he allowed it to pass, more concerned with what this messenger had been sent to tell him.

"Francis, your brother is in some serious trouble. He is being held at the Union hospital. If you wish to contact..."

"What the hell happened?" hollered Frank, his voice loud enough that a swift hush rippled across the cafeteria.

All was quiet.

The Canadian soldier was now a little irritated himself because of the scene that had come about due to Frank's inability to control the inflection of his voice. He said softly, "Sir, I think it would be best if you came with me."

Frank, although overflowing with a sense of panic, figured the quickest way to solve the problem was to follow the soldier's advice. As the two young men walked through the darkness which was now falling over the worksite, the soldier explained to Frank that his brother was going to be OK. At this, Frank felt the emptiness in his body subside. His spirits were momentarily lifted. Had anything happened to Vincent on the worksite, Frank would never be able to live with himself. For it had been Frank's suggestion that the two brothers take the job as Union diggers in the first place. However, when the soldier explained that Vincent had killed one of the most prominent officers in the Canadian National Army in Michigan, Frank threw up.

* * *

Vincent Laymon, still coming to his senses, swung his legs around and placed his feet flat on the floor. The nurse that had been standing beside his bed was now quickly moving towards the door, mumbling something to herself in a panicky murmur. This was the first time that Vincent had ever worn handcuffs, and now he was disappointed that the books he had read had never made note of the pain that handcuffs, if put on too tightly, could induce upon their captive. He examined his body. Everything still seemed to be attached and properly functioning. There were no bruises, cuts, or broken bones.

However Vincent knew he was delaying the inevitable. He knew he had a head injury. And he knew it was bad. The pain felt like a knife constantly being driven into his face, just above his right eye. His head throbbed with every beat of his heart. When he extended his fingers to touch the area, he sensed a cloth – a bandage no doubt. But Vincent's head didn't sense the probing of his fingers in return. Anesthetics. As he lifted himself out of the flurry of white sheets, Vincent made his way across the small hospital room to a narrow, full length mirror hanging on the door that the nurse had slammed shut upon her swift exit.

As Vincent gazed at the reflection, he broke down into an uncontrollable laugh. The ribbons of gauze that were wrapped around his head had increased its size by a factor of two. With his white hospital robe and excessive head bandages, Vincent imagined himself as a colossal piece of cauliflower. And every time he looked back at the mirror meant another fit of laughter.

The noise must have raised some eyebrows outside of his room, because it took no more than thirty seconds for Vincent Laymon to find himself surrounded by three brawny soldiers of the 32nd Canadian Infantry - as he had been made aware by a patch on one's shoulder. The man at Vincent's twelve o'clock was the first and only to speak. He was about the same height as Vincent, but built like a tank. His eyes were dark slivers of granite, seated in a narrow face which hinted at no emotion whatsoever. His face, like Vincent's, had obviously been tanned by the hot sun. This man was no pencil pusher. The soldier had the look of a warrior. One who had killed a thousand men in battle, and who wouldn't feel the slightest bit of guilt knocking off the large piece of cauliflower that now stood before him.

"I am 2nd Lieutenant Clay Somers of the 32nd

Canadian Infantry." The voice was a perfect match for the man's burly appearance. "It is my duty to inform you that you will receive a fair trial in the Global Civic Order's military justice system upon the completion of the following medical examination."

One of the other two soldiers broke away from the circle and reached for the door. As he pulled it open, the doorway revealed the outline of an older man. And as he stepped into the light, Vincent could see the imprint of fear on the doctor's aging face. This was the first time Vincent had ever seen such a reaction to his presence, but it would not be the last. It was true - Vincent Laymon was a killer. But a feeling of sympathy flowed over Vincent at that moment. All it took was a warm smile, and the doctor seemed to relax and let down his guard. Vincent found it funny that such a small expression of joy could so disarm a man's judgment – just like it had with Captain Lunsford.

The man had Vincent sit down as he began the process of unraveling the strips of gauze from his head. The anesthetics seemed to be wearing off now, and Vincent began dealing with a tremendous, splitting pain in his temple. As he waited for the wound to be revealed, he tried prodding the soldiers for information.

"So, any of you know what happened to my head?" he asked with a curious charm.

The soldiers took turns looking at each other and Vincent realized they didn't know. They probably didn't even know why they were at this hospital guarding this patient. For a moment Vincent even wondered if anyone had told them that he had just killed one of Lt. Somers' fellow officers.

When the doctor glanced back towards the three troops, however, Vincent grabbed his arm. The doctor looked horrified.

"You know, old man. What happened here?" Vincent ripped the remaining bandages from his head and pointed to the area which was radiating pain. He could see into the mirror on the door over the shoulder of the doctor. The gash was very deep and crossed his forehead at an angle just above his right eye. Vincent wasn't sure why exactly the hospital felt the need to use so many bandages on such a cut, but now he turned his gaze back upon the doctor for an answer. By this time, even the soldiers seemed interested in what the old man would say, which made Vincent realize that they had probably not yet heard about the captain.

The elderly man nervously stuttered, but Vincent spoke. "Don't worry, old man, you're safe. I am just a patient who can't remember why he woke up in a hospital bed." Again his smile was the clincher.

Finally words - "They told me it was one of the army boys that witnessed the whole thing. I guess he figured they could manage getting you in a little easier if you were unconscious. He used the butt of his rifle."

Vincent truly appreciated the nonspecific speech pattern the old man had chosen to use in front of the guards. He could have said more, been more precise in his description of the incident, especially about what had happened with the captain just before. Vincent put his hand on the left shoulder of the old man and said with the utmost sincerity, "Thank you." The doctor gave a little nod, notifying Vincent that he had understood the double meaning which had laced the phrase. Vincent realized that the doctor was no fool after all. Perhaps this is why he trembled in fear when in his presence. But Vincent had already ruled out taking the civilian doctor hostage at the point of the pen sticking out of his front pocket. The soldiers would have had no hesitation in his swift execution, and three armed men at once was a bit much. No, now was not the time for escape. It seemed now that Vincent may have to go through a great deal of bureaucratic red tape before the whole thing was over.

* * *

Vincent's eyes opened to a blur of railroad ties and the sound of Russian opera. He leaned back into a faded blue vinyl seat, peeling his face from the train's window. Oil from his brow had created a mark on the glass. Vincent studied the blotch, likening its shape to America's state of Michigan. Michigan made him think ever-so-briefly of his beloved friend, Saul, a reflection which was swiftly decimated by the cloud of pain swelling in his heart.

"Vincent Laymon." The voice came from the aisle to Vincent's left. Vincent stared blankly at what seemed like a moderately ranked Canadian official. The officer's slender, fragile stature, combined with a pale complexion and topped off with a small pair of reading glasses, quickly gave away his role as a part of the Canadian army's administrative division. The T33 Tokarev 7.62x25mm pistol grasped firmly at his left side was a bit sobering, however. In the officer's other hand was a military document of sorts.

"You *are* Vincent Laymon… correct?" Quickly calculating the officer's strength, speed, mobility, and experience, Vincent made no hesitation in expediting his escape. With all of his might (which ended up being much less than he had assumed at the time), Vincent lunged towards the officer's sidearm. Hardened-steel cuffs dug into his ankles and right wrist as Vincent did what could be described in no other way but a face-plant in the aisle seat to his left. It seemed to Vincent, at that moment, so ridiculous that upon waking up he had overlooked the military-issued hand and ankle cuffs which bound him to the seat's framework. He was quick to chalk up this obvious oversight and his lack of strength to sedatives which must have been administered to him for his transport. And now, lying with his face buried in a faded blue vinyl seat, Vincent Laymon laughed out loud at his helpless state.

Of course, all of this commotion proved quite traumatic for the gaunt officer standing above Vincent. He now stood, pistol extended before him, trembling at the unexpected sign of aggression. The officer had released the document which had been held by his right hand, and was now slowly slipping the hand into his front right pocket. Vincent, still chuckling and prostrate on the train's seat, failed to even notice the movements. Instead, his eyes were affixed to an official-looking document that had just touched down beneath the seat on which he lay. Its title read "Military Court Summons – Global Civic Order, Honorable Judge Brenson Terat Residing".

A high-pitched shrill blasted just above Vincent's head. While Vincent's attention had been devoted to the paper on the floor, the Canadian officer had managed to draw a small, metallic whistle from his pocket. Now a veritable flood of infantry men were rushing into the train car, but Vincent had already slipped back into unconsciousness, his drool forming a tiny pool on the blue vinyl.

* * *

After eight weeks of the longest kind in Manitoba's Transrek Correctional Facility, Vincent actually looked forward to his hearing. The living conditions that he had endured over the past two months were almost unbearable. The Transrek facility was, even from its exterior, quite a dismal sight. Walls of cement block standing twenty meters high were marked by water stains and moss - a testament to the region's sodden climate. And what the dreary fortifications surrounded was no better. The prison itself was no more than a dungeon. With a topographically rectangular shape, Transrek was laid out like a long hallway, with cells on both sides of a two-level walkway running through its center. This allowed for every prisoner's chamber to share an exterior wall – except there were no windows at Transrek.

Upon Vincent's arrival by train, he had to be brought in on a stretcher. After his little outburst towards the Canadian officer, Vincent had been injected with a large dose of another sedative. The result of the act was a near-comatose state, lasting two days. This ensured unconsciousness for the rest of Vincent's train ride and a full day and a half of immobility in Transrek's medical unit.

Years ago, each cell at the Transrek prison had been designed to hold a single prisoner. But in light of recent mass arrests, typically involving political activists and "revolutionary types", the chambers were now packed with humanity. It was not uncommon for five or even six prisoners to be living in a cell together. Killings and attempted suicides were a daily occurrence. To make matters worse, the number of prison guards had not increased to match the demand for prisoner control due to an inordinate amount of government money being used for military purposes of late. This concoction constantly led to a very violent and unmerciful state of affairs between prisoners and their guards at Transrek. At the time of

Vincent Laymon's arrival, there were over thirty-three hundred prisoners and only sixteen guards at the Transrek Correctional Facility.

Luckily, the prison's warden had been blessed with enough common sense to allot Vincent his own cell until he regained consciousness and strength. Otherwise, his stay (and life) would have been undoubtedly cut short, and more than likely in a way involving sexual acts and brutal violence. Even after three days in the recovery room, Vincent was not looking forward to joining what was commonly referred to as "the horde", the swarming prison cells making up Transrek's east wing. This wing, or the E-Block, was reserved for the most malicious and evil offenders. Designed as a maximum security prison, there was a time in which the whole of Transrek was filled with this type, but now over two thousand revolutionaries and political refugees occupied the west wing, pushing the violent offenders into a condition of overcrowding more than twice as bad as it used to be, and dividing the prison at its center.

"CLANG... CLANG... CLANG..." Vincent rolled over on the floor of his cell to make visible the source of the aggravating clamor. At his gate, a prison guard stood, striking his security baton against the rusty steel bars. "Rise and shine F473, time for the tour..." The words didn't even register in Vincent's mind. His headache was too strong. Before he could respond in any way, two other guards lifted Vincent to his feet and led him from his cell. It would be the last morning that he would awake in a chamber of his own, Vincent thought to himself.

The three medical cells at the Transrek facility were positioned near the entrance at the far west end of the building. Because of its location, E-Block prisoners were led through the entire west wing to their destination. It was the first time Vincent had experienced the inside of a prison, and he hoped it would be his last. The procession through the west wing was a long one… a two-hundred meter walk in shackles. Vincent kept his gaze forward, as the two guards who had picked him up from the floor of his cell now directed him down the long corridor towards the E-Block, and the horde that awaited him.

On either side of him, the hum of nearly-inaudible murmuring arose. By the time Vincent and his escorts were about one hundred meters through the west wing, someone, a revolutionary no doubt, broke into song. Soon it seemed the entire wing was chanting along. It was a song which parodied the Civicist party of Canada. As far as Vincent could tell, it was trashing the Canadian President, Andrew Marcell. It didn't matter to Vincent Laymon. His headache was now returning, and the slicing pain in his head was becoming excruciating, seemingly pounding away to the rhythm of the song. They were all so safe behind their metal bars, and they found strength in numbers, he thought. As Vincent now approached the center of the compound, and the end of the west wing, he snapped his head around to his left side and focused on a single prisoner who was singing along with the group, a wry smile on the captive's face. As soon as the prisoner's eyes met the glare of Vincent, his smile melted. He was no longer singing. Vincent held his stare as he walked by, slowly turning his head to remain locked at the eyes. Only now could the captive really see Vincent, and he was petrified by the figure before him. Since his captivity following the Canadian officer's death, Vincent had changed – both in appearance and countenance.

Weeks of not shaving yielded a scruffy reddish

beard on his face, and his hair was unkempt to say the least. The unwavering constant, however, were those cold gray eyes... even now partly hidden by his matted locks of hair. An unknowing soul might have cast him as a madman, but Vincent was more than sane... more than aware of his surroundings.

In between the west wing and the E-Block, at the geometrical center of the Transrek Correctional Facility, several doors, on both sides, lined a relatively well-lit hallway connecting the two wings. On the solid steel construction of the doors hung polished brass plates. Specific labels had been stamped into the plates, and as Vincent walked through the access strip he was able to make out "Prison Staff" and "Warden" on two of the doors.

The singing prisoners in the west wing had sparked the attention of many of the E-Block residents. It was obvious to Vincent that this half of the building received much less attention as far as cleaning and maintenance were concerned. The captives here were filthy, much less enthusiastic than their west wing counterparts, and had both attitudes and statures that were infinitely more hardcore. But one thing that Vincent did appreciate was that none of them were making even the slightest of sounds. In fact, there was dead silence with the only exception being the resonance of shuffling chains as he walked.

The guards managed to prod Vincent along until he was approximately one-third of the way down the E-Block corridor. There they drove his body to the ground and began removing his ankle shackles. As Vincent lay face down against the damp concrete, his eyes scanned the premises. His heart began to slam against his chest as he anticipated his first move upon the release of his handcuffs. As one of the prison guards pulled the ankle shackles free, the other began fumbling for the appropriate key for the cuffs which bound Vincent's wrists. At that moment, Vincent's eyes met with a prisoner's. He was a short man with a dirty complexion and a great muscular frame. He looked at Vincent with fear in his eyes and he was subtly shaking his head. The suggestion was enough to send snapshots of certain scenes through Vincent's mind. He pictured the semi-automatic pistols holstered at the guards' sides, he pictured the two guards, one at each end of the corridor, each firmly grasping a Canadian issue 5.56 caliber rifle across his chest... and finally he pictured his family. The reflections instantly decreased Vincent's heart rate. He now realized that he must have been nothing short of mad at the thought of making such an escape. Vincent Laymon was now prepared to accept his fate as a member of the horde.

The next eight weeks in Transrek felt like eight years. Plenty of time for Vincent to dwell on life's blessings. Laura's tragic car accident. The economic collapse. Now this. Vincent was awakened every morning by the ghostly howling sound of wind that emanated each time the guards changed shifts. The ventilation and geometry of the prison was such that a gust of air flow was produced when either of the end doorways was opened. Such a terrible, empty sound. On the fifty-seventh morning of his stay, however, Vincent's sleep was broken in a much different way...

The rusty, steel latch of Vincent's cell swung upward, clanging against the metal stop. As the barred door swung open, Vincent rolled over in his mattress and squinted through tired eyes at the sounds. It was still night time, or at least dark, and Vincent could barely make out the figures entering his cell. It was two of the E-Block guards, and they moved directly and with great purpose towards the bed of Vincent Laymon. Before Vincent had time to react or even fully awake, the guards had fastened his wrists and ankles with the steel cuffs that were always associated with a trip out of the cell.

Each prison guard grasped an arm and quickly half-dragged, half-led Vincent out of his cell and down the E-Block corridor towards the center of the Transrek facility. The guards never bothered to say a word to him, and Vincent never bothered to ask a question. He was too busy cautiously wondering what lay at the end of this little early morning stroll. And it didn't take him very long to find out.

As the three entered the hallway between the two main wings of the prison, one of the guards pushed Vincent down onto the ground, firmly planting his shiny, black, Canadian-issued boot into the center of his back, pinning him down. The other walked to one of the doors and removed a set of keys from a clip on his waistline. An embossed plate of brass on the door read "E-1 OVERFLOW". The first guard swung the door open, and they each grasped the metal chain which spanned the shackles between Vincent's legs and slid him into the room. Vincent, lying on his stomach, was being dragged backwards across what felt like filthy cement. It was completely dark in the room and as the dragging stopped, Vincent heard the jingle of the guard's keys once again. The creaking metal door which then opened was enough to assure Vincent that he had reached the destination of his move. The shackles on his legs and arms were removed, and with a push from one of the guards and a slam of the cell door, it was over. As Vincent slid himself across the rough floor and into a corner, the door to the hallway banged shut, and he sat in complete darkness and silence. Vincent fell back asleep.

As morning came, rays of faint sunlight made their way through the grimy line of glass block which lined the upper-back corner of the cell. This morning, Vincent was not awakened by the howling of wind through a corridor, or even by a guard for that matter. In fact, Vincent had been awake for several hours before the hallway door was cracked. In that time, the sunlight had lit the room enough for Vincent's analysis. He had determined that he was in some kind of temporary holding chamber. The room was divided into two. The front half, which was connected to the hallway, looked like a waiting room with a steel bench on each side against the wall, and a tile floor which was much nicer than the floors in the E-Block cells. The back half of the room was Vincent's holding cell. But this cell was also quite nice compared to the one he had come from. Even the bars which separated the cell from the exterior section of the room were painted a pleasant sea green color, in contrast to the rusty, pitted steel bars that Vincent had grown accustomed to. There was no bed in the cell though. In fact there was nothing other than an aluminum chair resting in one of the corners. But when the door to the hallway swung open, Vincent was sitting on the floor, his back against the wall of the cell.

The opening of the door did not startle Vincent. After the events of the past couple of months, nothing really did. He slowly turned his head to watch two of the Transrek prison guards walk in. Vincent couldn't tell for sure, but he thought they were the same two who had transferred him early that morning. The guards were at full attention, and in a methodical and perfectly symmetrical fashion, they both took one step inside of the door, shoulder to shoulder, and then one step away from each other so that they were standing on both sides of the opening. They each held a rifle across their chest. Vincent remained seated as a larger figure now emerged in the doorway between them.

This was a mountain of a man, his head towering over the guards and his body almost too wide to make it through the door facing forward. Vincent quickly figured that he must be close to two meters tall and about a hundred and fifty kilos. This man was not wearing military clothing. A massive black robe adorned his immense stature from his neck down to his feet. As the man approached, Vincent noticed that he was much older than he had initially estimated. The gray scruff, which was barely noticeable, combined with his wide face reminded Vincent of a big old bear. His hair also looked unattended to. Once the large man had passed between the guards into the room, he raised his right hand over his shoulder, casually dismissing their presence. Despite his old, burly complexion, the man had a look of purpose in his eyes that told Vincent that he was most definitely still all there.

The Canadian guards shut the door behind them, and the big old man was left alone in the room with Vincent, who was now standing and staring through the bars at his new company. The man pulled a cigar from somewhere underneath his black robe, and stuck it in his mouth as he plopped himself down on the bench to Vincent's right. The cigar was huge, very fitting of the man sitting before him, Vincent thought. As the man lit a match and held it to the end of the cigar, he spoke out of the side of his mouth, all the time concentrating on what he was doing.

"Vincent Laymon..." His voice was gruff, but a bit higher in pitch than Vincent had anticipated. Vincent just stood, still studying the man... particularly the lighting of his cigar. The cigar was lit, and a plume of smoke burst from the man's mouth, filling the room.

"My name is Brenson Terat. I handle all of the major military judicial cases in this district." For the first time, the judge turned and looked at Vincent.

"I'm your judge, Vincent."

Vincent was not impressed. A moment of silence passed…

"Congratulations?" Vincent muttered.

The judge let out a bit of a forced chuckle, and was clearly not in the mood.

"It would seem that you've gotten yourself in some serious trouble, Mr. Laymon. You've been charged with murdering a Canadian military officer… A *captain* no less. That is a serious charge." The judge rocked himself up off the bench and made his way towards the steel bars which constrained Vincent to the back of the room.

"Quite serious, Vincent…"

Vincent had begun to realize what was going on here. Ever since the rise of Civicism in Canada, really ever since Vincent could remember, the judicial system had become a cesspool of corruption. Money… power… threats… These were the things that drove the system. Justice and honor had been swept under the carpet of paranoia and fear. There was a lot of dirt under that carpet. A lot of dirt. And there were a lot of Civicists in power to make sure no one dared lift up the corner.

Vincent now stood at full attention, hands firmly gripping the bars of his cell. He positioned himself close enough to the dividing bars that his face all but touched them. The bulky judge was now standing only centimeters from Vincent on the other side of the cage. With his giant stature, the judge actually looked down upon Vincent to some degree. The man's countenance was very serious now, and he removed the massive cigar from the side of his mouth to speak.

"Do you know what the penalty is if you are convicted?" His face wrinkled with pain as he let out a gruff cough.

Vincent, coolly cocked his head a bit to one side. He was staring deeply into the judge's eyes.

"Death," whispered Vincent, as a bit of a smile rolled across his face.

The judge continued to stare at Vincent, letting out a quick "Hmmff," then slowly spun around and began walking towards the doorway. He came to a stop about half way there and took another large puff from the cigar, his back still facing Vincent.

"There is another way, you know," muttered the judge. It almost seemed like he was disgusted by his own words.

Vincent remained silent.

"We all have our problems, Vincent. You... well, yours is pretty obvious..." The judge turned his head around about half way over his left shoulder.

"I also have problems, Vincent." His voice was lower now. The judge sighed as he pivoted around.

"One, in particular..." The judge's voice had now been reduced to little more than a whisper, and he once again crept closer to the metal bars. Vincent could now see that Judge Terat seemed a bit warm. His old, weathered face glistened as a beam of sun caught him in the eyes. Sweat was beginning to bead on his brow.

"One of our guards..." he paused. "One of the guards here at Transrek needs to be dealt with."

Vincent showed no emotion.

"I am getting old in my years, Vincent. I don't get my hands dirty anymore. I am a judge now."

Vincent spoke softly. "Tell me more…"

"There's a lot that you don't need to know, but it breaks down like this. You are going on trial in an hour and a half for the murder of a Canadian officer. I can help you in this trial. Vincent, you don't have to face execution."

Vincent just listened. The judge fidgeted a bit. He seemed uncomfortable with the one-sided conversation.

Vincent felt the need to help him along. "What do you want from me?"

"I need you to take care of one of the guards here. Understand? We will make it look like self-defense. I can delay your trial. We'll set the whole thing up tonight. We can make it easy for you. He won't have a weapon… You will."

"It will cause a stir. I will have to put you on trial again, but like I said, I'll have you off on self-defense right away."

Vincent looked at the judge's cigar… He hadn't smoked it for a while, and it had gone out. Noticing the slight distraction, the judge looked down and tossed it on the ground.

Vincent spoke, "What if I say no?"

"Death," the judge said as though he were lightly mocking Vincent by reciting the word that he had spoken moments before.

"Why are you telling me all of this?"

The judge seemed happy to respond, "Because, by tomorrow night, Vincent, you will either be a dead man or you will be involved." He kicked the butt of his cigar into the cell and began walking out. "I'll be back in fifteen minutes. All you will have to say is yes or no."

Vincent spoke quietly, "Don't bother…"

The judge spun around, "What??"

In the same quiet voice, Vincent returned, "Don't bother stopping back. The answer is no."

Vincent began to smile a bit. "...oh, and you're a fat, old, shit-eating, Civicist bitch."

Imagine a train with a steam engine going full bore, the engine churning so hard that the train is almost coming off the tracks. Now imagine that the train is bright red... and sweating. This was the judge's face. Vincent knew he had hit a homerun with the comment.

Needless to say, the judge was not happy. In fact it seemed that a fury of poison shot through his every artery. The wrinkles in his face became even more pronounced with a grimace of hate. The bear had become rabid...

"Fool!! ...I thought you'd be at least a bit more intelligent than your father! I guess peasant trash births peasant trash..."

Vincent's heart stopped. Although the judge was still bellowing out condemnations, only his first statement echoed in Vincent's ears. Vincent's father had not crossed his mind in some time, and the very mention of him dropped Vincent to his knees. Tears that had not flowed since he had witnessed the death of his friend Saul began pouring down his face. In that moment, emotions that had been stored up in Vincent's soul over the past weeks were released. Not having a father figure for most of his life had proven difficult for Vincent, and this was perhaps the catalyst of his current breakdown.

The judge was still yelling and pacing about when Vincent spoke...

"You knew my father?" His voice quivered with instability.

Only now did the judge notice the distress that his statements had caused Vincent, and he appeared quite pleased with the result. He stepped forward, crossing his arms over his wide chest. The judge peered into Vincent's broken eyes with great interest, and spoke as though curious of the effect his words would have on the weeping man.

"Yes, I knew him... Terrence Laymon... your father. Like you, he was a prisoner here once. But I met him before I was a judge, on other business..."

Vincent was fixated on every word. Although his mother had told stories of how his father was a war hero, she had never said a word about prison.

"What did he do? Why was he here?" Vincent was speaking with a hint of skepticism.

"Your father was a brave man, Vincent. But he wasn't exactly a smart man." The judge pulled another cigar from beneath his robe and jammed it in his mouth. After lighting the cigar and taking a large puff he spat on the floor.

"Terrence overstepped some boundaries... Much like yourself." The judge seemed irritated and began speaking with passion, "It's not black and white, son. It never was. Sometimes you have to use your head instead of your damn instinct. There are consequences..." He paused. "Look, your father was a good man for the most part, but he got what was coming to him..."

Vincent was incessant, "What are you talking about??"

"I had your father killed, Vincent."

Hate in its purest form filled the inner being of Vincent Laymon. "My father died of pancreatic cancer... I watched my father die of cancer... In a hospital... I remember..."

The judge sighed and took another puff of his cigar.

"Your father died from lead poisoning, Vincent. He was stationed here at this prison for two years. Probably when you were just a kid. Back then the government had all of our prisoners take vitamin pills... A pill a day. Your father was given lead pills instead... It was my order. I was compensated well... It was a government job. The agency that the orders came down from doesn't even exist anymore... heh..." He continued, "We planned it so that he would be released with enough lead in him to do the job, but over a long enough period of time so as not to seem suspicious."

Vincent managed some words, "But the doctors... they said..." Vincent was cut off by the judge's laughter.

"Back then if it wasn't a heart condition, the doctors diagnosed it as cancer. All they knew was that he was dying." The judge paused and looked at Vincent.

"And what's it matter, you'll be with him soon enough..."

During the judge's explanation, Vincent was sick. As the information streamed into his mind, he tried to keep up with the conversation... all while processing its validity. There was no reason for this man to make up such a story. The man before him knew that Vincent would soon be dead, and at any rate, a Civic judge with such tenure was all but politically and socially invincible.

Vincent's stomach was in knots. His vision was dimming. There was nothing but genuine rage that fueled his movements and thoughts. In an instant, in one sharp motion, Vincent leapt against the bars thrusting his arm out between them, towards the throat of Judge Brenson Terat.

It was not the judge's lighting quick reactions that saved him, but rather the length of Vincent Laymon's right arm. As his swipe carried past the judge's face, Vincent could barely feel the man's facial scruff on the tips of his fingers.

In response the judge jumped back, his cigar falling from his mouth to the floor.

"Shit, son! You think assaulting a judge is the answer?" He was breathing hard from the sudden scare.

Vincent fell to the floor and vomited. As the judge covered his mouth with an embroidered, white handkerchief he spoke...

"You are in no condition for court, son. I am postponing your hearing until tomorrow at one thirty. I hope by then you will have collected yourself a bit."

The judge walked to the door. As he swung it open he turned around, "We'll make it a quick death, Vincent... It will be an injection. You'll just fall asleep. And when you wake up, you'll be with your father."

More vomit spewed from Vincent's mouth, and the judge, now simply disgusted with the whole incident, slammed the door behind him on the way out.

That night, as Vincent lay slumped over in his own vomit, nearly in the same position that the judge had left him, he thought of his mother. He often wondered how she was dealing with the news of his imprisonment. Vincent could only hope that, after the brief phone call Frank had made to him at the hospital, he had laid it on her tactfully. He loved his mother so much. Vincent then thought of Judge Terat. He thought of all of the experiences this man had stolen away from his mother. He never knew a time when his mother and father had been both healthy and together... But memories that never happened danced through his head, and photographs which were never taken pierced his mind.

Vincent spent that night remembering what never was.

★ CHAPTER 4 ★

The courtrooms of a military prison like Transrek didn't have all of the amenities of the district courthouses that you would find in the Canadian cities. Another key component that they lacked was jurors. Military courts were under the control and ruling of a single judge. Government-issued prosecution and defense lawyers were present in such cases, but prosecutors were merely there to pass on the appropriate information to the judge, and defense attorneys simply made sure that it got there. Typically, an officer of the Global Civic Order would also attend to ensure that the sentencing was "in accordance with the current international standards of punishment".

This was, for the most part, the case at Vincent's hearing as well. The courtroom was actually located in a building situated a few hundred meters outside of the walls of the Transrek Correctional Facility.

That morning, Vincent received his first shower in his now two months at Transrek, though it was little more than a cold blast from a water hose held by one of the prison guards. He was also issued a fresh shave and haircut, and a new, clean set of prisoner's clothes. The smell of the clean clothes was refreshing.

At one o'clock, the door to the room cracked open, and four prison guards walked in. Two of them took the positions of the guards who had escorted the judge into the room the day before, while the other two proceeded to open the barred door of the holding cell. Vincent was quite submissive in his actions. From a kneeling position, with his head down, Vincent extended his arms straight forward as the guards again secured shackles to his wrists. This time the guards did not constrain his feet as had been the case during his transport into the holding cell. Perhaps it was because of the amount of walking that was about to take place. Each of the guards in the cell took one side of Vincent, locking an arm, and hoisted him to his feet. The two guards that were still watching the door led the procession out into the hallway, as the others, still clasping Vincent's arms, followed.

The group turned left heading out of the door, away from the E-Block and back into the west wing through which Vincent had entered the facility weeks before. Dead silence crept through the air, as the guards began marching Vincent down the corridor of cells. There were no murmurs from curious prisoners. No, this time, the prisoners simply watched. In the little time that Vincent had spent at the facility, rumors and tales had circled about. Vincent had become marked as the man who had taken a stand against the military by brutally murdering one of its high-ranking officers. Obviously, such information had a very powerful effect on the political outlaws occupying the west wing of Transrek. Thus, despite Vincent having no defined protest against the Canadian military itself, the masses of political dissidents that filled Transrek's west wing had already rumored him right into the status of "revolutionist hero".

As Vincent and those who guarded him reached the middle of the wing, several of the inmates began singing. Soon every prisoner in the west wing was bellowing out the lyrics. It was a much different song than the one that they sang to mock the guards upon his entrance two months prior. Vincent actually knew this tune. Almost every Canadian did. His mother had sung it to him as a young child, often while tucking him in at night. The song was called *"Dum vita est spes est"*. Through his voracious reading, Vincent had learned that the Latin words translated to *"While there is life, there is hope"*. It was a sort of folk song, decidedly more popular among the working class of society.

As the group continued its walk, the singing became louder and louder. All of the prisoners in the west wing that were physically able were now on their feet, and many of them were beginning to salute Vincent. Vincent himself was a bit overwhelmed by the tribute and a little saddened, knowing that their faith in him was misplaced. In a way, to him, it was even more heartrending than if they had lost their hope altogether. In any event, by the time they had reached the end of the wing, the prison was in a complete uproar.

Vincent was now at what would be considered the entrance area of the facility, and as he looked to his right, he noticed the medical unit where he had once been revived, and the cell in which he had spent his first couple of days at Transrek. Ahead of him was a gated door with more metal bars, and, once the convoy passed through it, further down the hall, they reached the end of the facility.

Sunlight showered through the glass doors which marked the prison entrance, and Vincent squinted as his eyes adjusted to the change. With no windows in Transrek and poor lighting, the blocked glass lining the top of the room he was in that morning had provided the only bit of sunlight that Vincent had experienced in many weeks. As the guards led Vincent through the doors, the chilly Canadian air struck his face and he breathed deeply.

Vincent was escorted first by foot, then, once outside the walls, by military jeep, to the prison's courthouse. The courthouse, which proved to be no more than a small, plain building constructed of cement block, rested along a gravel road less than half a kilometer outside of the walls of

Transrek. Between the prison and the courthouse was nothing – just rolling terrain, and as far as Vincent could see beyond the courthouse was more of the same. A few very luxurious cars lined the front of the building in a gravel parking area.

It was nearly one-thirty in the afternoon as Vincent entered the court through its large oak door. Upon being ushered in, Vincent found himself in the cleanest room that he had seen in quite some time. But despite its condition, the room lacked the ornate structure and permanent fixtures often found in a standard court of law. Empty wooden fold-up chairs filled the room to his left and right, leading up to two metal tables, one on each side of the room. At each metal table sat a man in a suit, presumably the prosecution and defense. Beyond those tables, spanning across the front of the room, was a heavy wooden desk, possibly the largest desk that Vincent had ever seen. On the smooth lacquered finish of the desktop sat only a judge's gavel and a few papers, while a massive brass plate was screwed to the front of the desk facing the courtroom. Engraved on the plate in large, bold letters were the words "Honorable Judge Brenson W. Terat". The only other notable feature of the room was the enormous Canadian flag which adorned the rear wall, behind the wooden desk. Not a cement block on that wall could be seen, as the massive maple leaf stared down upon the courtroom. Other than the two lawyers, only the four military guards who had served as Vincent's escorts remained in the courtroom, each positioning themselves in a corner, standing upright with rifles slung over their shoulders. Vincent did not see a representative of the Global Civic Order anywhere, and the judge was not in the room.

As Vincent was seated at the table on the right side

of the courtroom, the suited man was quick to greet him with a kind smile and introduced himself as Vincent's defense attorney, as assigned by the Government of Canada, under Article blah blah blah. Vincent knew it was all just formalities from here out. This man was no more on his side than the other suited man who represented the prosecution. This was sure to be more of a performance than a lawful and just hearing.

Five minutes passed before the judge entered the room. He entered from a different location, in the back left corner behind the desk, near the edge of the Canadian flag. Before his entrance, Vincent had not even noticed the door there. The judge looked tired. He did not look happy to be there, and he may have even seemed a bit rushed. Upon seeing his face, Vincent began to feel somewhat queasy. Vincent Laymon had not forgotten the words that were spoken to him the day before. Quite the contrary, the words of the judge were burning very brightly in his memory. Vincent had not slept for even a minute since their meeting, but his lack of sleep was not an issue that day. For that day, Vincent's thoughts were very clear, his every instinct and wit was at its peak.

A trained eye may have noticed that, ever since entering the room, Vincent's mind had been at work. He was very aware of the guards, each standing in a corner. He was well aware of the shiny 5.56 caliber rifles slung over their shoulders. He was likewise aware that the prison staff of the Transrek facility had gone to great lengths to remove any sharp objects that could possibly be construed as a weapon. The lawyers who sat at the metal tables lacked even jewelry and writing implements.

"All rise, this court is now in session." The judge's voice was listless. Although the judge looked just as he did the day before, his emotion was absent. The same robe, the same wide face, the same wrinkles, the same scruff. Just no cigar, Vincent thought. Again, the old age of the judge showed, as he slowly made his way to his place. Judge Terat's massive figure was well proportioned with the enormous desk behind which he now stood.

"I think we all know each other here... Prosecution if you could present the case... The rest of you may now be seated."

As Vincent sat down beside his lawyer, the attorney from the table across the room made his way up to the judge's desk and plopped a few papers down before him. While the judge began skimming the documents, the attorney returned to his table and seated himself. During the formalities, Vincent just stared at the judge's face. He, even more so than the judge, showed absolutely no emotion. It was as if he was looking right through the judge to the polyester, red maple leaf hanging on the wall behind him. His gray eyes were a sea that lacked care or even feeling.

The judge pushed the papers aside and leaned back in the black leather chair which was mostly hidden by his desk. His right hand reached behind his head as he leaned back, as his left lightly stroked the circular base on which the gavel rested. It was the first time the judge had even looked at Vincent the entire time, and his line of sight quickly honed in on the defense attorney to Vincent's right.

"Has the defense prepared anything for me?"

"Yes, your Honor," the defense lawyer was quick to respond.

The judge extended his hand, "Please..."

The same routine followed... attorney handed over paperwork, judge skimmed paperwork while attorney was again seated... Vincent did notice, however, that his "defense" had obviously been boiled down to a single page. And the amount of type font on that page was suspect, as the judge seemed almost through reading it by the time Vincent's attorney had sat down. Breaking out of his zone for a moment, Vincent leaned towards his lawyer and whispered...

"I hope you didn't have to work too hard on my defense... You weren't up all night were you?" The attorney fidgeted a bit and was about to speak when Vincent cut him off with another whisper...

"...I was."

Judge Terat had noticed the little exchange and was quick to restore order.

"Vincent Laymon."

Vincent's head snapped back towards the judge as he regained his blank stare.

"Please approach the bench."

Vincent rose to his feet and began walking towards the judge's desk. His attorney also stood, but the judge held out his hand so as to stop him... "David..." The judge calmly shook his head and the lawyer sat back down. Everyone here knew each other alright.

Vincent lowered his head and approached the desk with his hands clasped in front of his body, shackles still chaining his wrists together. The judge leaned forward and, with a slight movement of his head, beckoned Vincent to do the same. As Vincent leaned across the desk, the judge spoke very softly.

"Have you thought any more about our conversation yesterday, Vincent?" Judge Terat's breath smelled like coffee and burnt cigars.

Vincent's reply was cool and calm. "All night."

The judge continued, "You can still change your

mind, you know… but this would be your last chance."

Vincent straightened his back and stared at the judge for a moment. The judge looked up at him, curious for an answer.

Vincent had not had much to drink over the past twenty-four hours, and his mouth was quite dry as a result. But he made sure that every bit of saliva that he could conjure up in that moment spewed forth onto the judge's face.

The guards rushed in to contain Vincent, who now displayed a broad smile. The judge procured a handkerchief from his robe which he now used to wipe the spit of Vincent Laymon from his eyes. He motioned with his right hand…

"It's fine… It's fine, I'm ok… It's fine." The guards stopped where they were for a second, analyzing the situation, and began to return to their posts in the corners of the courtroom. Both attorneys sat wide-eyed at their tables, dead silent.

The judge was hot. Although there were no words immediately, anger poured from his eyes, and his face was beet red. Wrinkles emerged across his forehead and it looked as though he were about to scream. Vincent's smile had all but disappeared now, and a blank stare once again rested on his face. The judge was able to gather himself somewhat, although there was no mistaking his true emotions…

A murmur crept from his lips as he grasped the wooden gavel. It was just barely loud enough for Vincent to make out, but Vincent heard every word…

"Like father, like son…"

Vincent's heart stopped, adrenaline raced through his bloodstream. A tingling sensation coursed over his body, and a chill ran down his spine. It was a chill that

Vincent had not felt in some time.

The judge spoke aloud, "I have been presented the case of both the prosecution and the defense. I have reviewed said documentation and have hereby come to a conclusion in my judgment. All rise."

The attorneys stood to their feet, while Vincent remained still, staring right through the old man in front of him. He felt the touch of his mother on his cheek. He felt the firm handshake of his brother Frank, and the warm hug of his friend Saul. He felt the grief of his father's death. And yet, in this moment, Vincent Laymon felt nothing. Nothing at all.

"By the order of the Sovereign Government of Canada, and with respect to the punitive ordinance of the Global Civic Order, I hereby find the defendant, Vincent Laymon, guilty of murder in the first degree of an Official of the Canadian Army. My sentence is execution by military firing squad."

As the judge raised the gavel above his head and swung it down to punctuate his decree, Vincent thrust his shackled hands forward and clasped the judge's wrist. With a tremendous swiftness, he drove the judge's hand down, ramming it into the solid oak desk. The impact caused the head of the wooden gavel to snap off and the post fell from the judge's now broken fingers. In a single motion, Vincent leapt onto the desk and, with both hands, scooped up the post which was now no more than a sharp wooden shard. With all the force he could produce, he lunged forward, driving the pointed shard of wood through the front of Judge Brenson Terat's throat.

The force of the thrust was more violent than even Vincent had anticipated, and his momentum sent Vincent tumbling over the desk, knocking the judge back over his chair. Both men rolled to the floor, settling in a position in which Vincent straddled the torso of the judge, who now lay flat on his back.

The entire sequence had played out in a matter of mere seconds. The guards, having lost sight of the action as the two men fell behind the desk, sprinted towards the commotion with rifles in hand. Vincent, now on top of the judge, stared down deeply into his eyes as he leaned his whole weight onto the post which protruded from the judge's neck. Blood was everywhere. The little life that was left in the judge allowed him to feebly grasp the chain which bound the shackles around Vincent's wrists. The judge's eyes were wide open, his red face accented with the blood which was now leaking from his mouth as well. Vincent made a final push. He could feel the post drive completely through, crunching into the vertebrae of the judge's spine. And it was over. The judge no longer stared in horror with his wide eyes, which now rolled back in his head. The bubbling of blood and hissing of breath which had been leaking from around the post ceased. The judge's grip on Vincent's wrists loosened, and his arms fell limply back to the floor. His lifeless head rested to the side.

Hunched on the judge's chest, Vincent leaned forward, pressing his lips against the wide, wrinkled brow of what was now only a corpse. Had the guards made it closer by that time, they may have seen Vincent's lips moving. They may have even heard the lightest of whispers which graced his mouth.

"Necessitas non habet legem." Necessity knows no law.

Vincent Laymon did not die that day. Not in that courtroom. Not by a 5.56 caliber bullet fired from the rifle of a guard. Some would consider it luck. Others may say that Destiny had a greater, more important part for Vincent to play. In either case, or neither, one thing was for certain... It was not yet Vincent's time.

It would seem that there are a number of traits that God has allowed Satan to instill in the human's being. The most obvious of these, as seems apparent from the very day of a child's birth, is selfishness. It is not always so apparent – and the sight of it not nearly as disturbing as the sound of the word itself… but that is only because it seems so natural. How could something so natural be so bad? In fact, to denounce a trait so innately tied to man is to say that man himself is bad…

Perhaps he is, or maybe not "perhaps"…

The opposite of selfishness is a word that almost mirrors its very textual content… selflessness. There is no doubt of this – that selflessness is the most unnatural of human traits. And certainly, for this very reason, it is the most difficult to obtain. Selflessness is an ascendance. It is one of the greatest of gifts. But empathy… Empathy must be the younger brother of selflessness, or maybe its cousin. The ability to feel what others feel. The ability to understand. It would seem evident that anyone possessing the latter would automatically touch the robe of the prior. …But this assumes that humans are capable of overcoming themselves.

Perhaps they are, or maybe not "perhaps"…

STORY II

MARCUS PRATT

★ CHAPTER 1 ★

Marcus Pratt had always been rather proficient in mathematics. He was notorious among his cohorts for expressing his belief that "everything is numbers" - as he seemed to always remind them. And now, wading through a reservoir of steaming blood, it was math that plagued his mind.

"Six pints of this life fluid in every one of our boys... three quarts of blood." General Louis Riccard just listened, as the chief of his country stood before him. The eyes of Marcus burned with passion – green embers amidst an ocean of white. His dark hair ducked out from under the red beret on his head and fluttered in the cold November breeze. As Marcus stood and stared down into the deep tomb that was the Border Canal, his body formed the silhouette of a great statue.

A buzz resonated through Marcus's spine. The reverberations shot into his brain and swelled up behind his eyes. He fell to one knee, his right hand clutching his left forearm with all of his might – a failed attempt to stop the shaking. Flashes of the putrid scenes flickered before his eyes and the air was sucked from his lungs.

"How many men did we send in here today, Lou?" As he spoke, wisps of steam slipped from his mouth.

"Eleven thousand, four hundred and thirty one," the general replied solemnly.

Marcus rose to his feet and lightly swayed the toe of his left boot through the swamp of crimson liquid. Bursts of gunfire and flurries of light on the horizon acted as a grave reminder that the carnage was far from over. It was nearly midnight, but because of a full moon and a light dusting of snow on the ground, the landscape was lit up as if it were only dusk. The illumination was such that lines of aid officers could be seen for hundreds of yards carrying away corpses on stretchers. At thirty four years old, Marcus was the youngest man to ever lead the nation of America, but as the general studied his grave countenance, he noticed the Commander in Chief now looked much older.

"And we only lost what…" the words so lightly formed by his lips.

"Nine hundred and fifty yards, sir."

Marcus admired the general's attention to detail, and, for that slightest moment, a smile of approval may have crept across his lips, were it not for the smell of death around him, quickly thwarting the instance of appreciation.

"Was it worth it, general?" Marcus was not asking with any contempt or cynical doubt… He was truly interested in the general's assessment.

"Sir…"

"Call me Marcus, for God's sake, Lou… This morning I was Sir. Right now… Right now, I'm not sure what…"

The General broke the thought… "Today, American soldiers held a chunk of land that will be critical to the defense of our territory from the hands of the enemy." The general paused, noticing the blank stare covering the president's face. "Wars these days are not easily won, Marcus."

"How did it ever come to this?" Marcus muttered exhaustively. He partially knew the answer to this question. He could have gone on all night about the restrictions of the Global Civic Order – no military aircraft, no weapons of mass destruction, no biological weaponry, etc. – and how these restrictions set the stage for massive land wars with heavy casualties on both sides. He knew full well about America's one hundred and twenty-six PX7 fighter jets and nearly two hundred Strikefire missiles hiding in the mountains of New Mexico, only awaiting his beckoning. But not yet. It was not the time. The GCO was still much too strong, and Marcus could ill-afford every GCO-affiliated nation coming to the aid of their banner country... Canada. Not now. Marcus was truly pain stricken for all that had happened earlier in the day where he now stood. He knew the horrors of war. He now lived them daily.

That night, as Marcus lay in the bed of his secured emergency location, fifty miles south of the canal, he felt the weight of thousands of casualties – both American and Canadian – resting on his shoulders. Marcus Pratt was a man who cared dearly for human life. He was a freedom fighter. He knew in his soul that every man, woman, and child in the world deserved, if nothing else, their freedom. Marcus Pratt was a revolutionary hero... a true patriot. But he hadn't always been in a position of such authority... of such responsibility.

* * *

Marcus Pratt was born in a suburb of Pittsburgh, Pennsylvania. His memories began at the Hendrickson Community Center. Marcus was an orphan. When he was old enough to know to ask, he was told by the Center that his mother had passed away before he was born and his father had "problems with the law". Marcus later found out that his mother had died during his birth and that his father had lost custody of him when he went to prison for armed robbery.

At eleven years old, Marcus was adopted by a

family of little wealth. Truthfully, as he had often reflected on, the new living conditions were probably worse than he had faced at the Community Center. But Marcus had been ready for a change of scenery, and he seemed to like both of his new guardians. They were a husband and wife, unable to conceive because of certain medical conditions, but truly in love with one another. It was here that Marcus first began the saturation process that would melt and mold his lifelong journey... a saturation of love, and one of independence. While the Community Center had taught him independence as a necessity for survival, it was here in his new family that Marcus learned how to both give and receive love.

It is common knowledge that the best way to become skilled at speaking a foreign language fluently is to immerse oneself in a culture which depends on it. If one is forced into a position in which the language is necessary for everyday life, one hardly has a choice but to learn it. And so the same held true for Marcus, but the language was not one of words. In his earliest of years, it was one of finances. When Marcus entered into the Pratt family, they lived in a small, two bedroom apartment just east of Pittsburgh. There was very little money to spend on entertainment. Mr. Pratt worked two jobs, as a custodian of a nearby high school and as an automobile mechanic in a garage under the apartment. Mrs. Pratt was a substitute teacher, struggling to get a job in a market which overflowed with young women in the same situation. Little did either know that their adoption of a young boy named Marcus would prove to be one of the best financial investments in American history.

From early on in his childhood, Marcus began to uncover the most predominant of his God-given gifts. This gift was that of success. Looking back on his life, he could not conjure a scenario in which his life would have turned out any differently than successful. But he never took this for granted. The truth was that Marcus was an extremely thankful person. Every night, before lying down to sleep, Marcus would kneel beside his bed and thank God for everything he had been given… from the air he breathed to the country into which he had been born. But despite his deep convictions in giving thanks where thanks was due, Marcus was often prone to using somewhat unconventional means for his survival. Marcus's family was not rich in material things, and he had realized this from the beginning. At eleven years old, however, Marcus had already found ways to greatly contribute towards their finances. As it turned out, his most successful "job" at that age was one of selling raffle tickets door-to-door.

It was a fairly simple operation really. Barely any start-up costs, and almost no foreseeable repercussions, if done correctly. In the summer of his eleventh year of life, Marcus had an idea to start his career. He knew he would need a roll of about five hundred generic raffle tickets, which cost less than three dollars at the local department store. To get the three dollars, he spent about five hours scouring stores and video game or vending machine change-return slots until this goal was fulfilled. Granted, he could have probably gotten the money in fifteen minutes by begging, but in Marcus's eyes it would have been unfair to the giver, as they would receive nothing in return. The next morning, after buying the roll of tickets, Marcus set out on a journey, roaming door-to-door, neighborhood to neighborhood. He would present himself simply as he was – a boy selling raffle tickets. The prize was a "thirty-two inch television" and the cost of a ticket was two dollars. Sure, there were many who shooed him away or lied that they didn't have a couple of dollars, but there were also many who bought tickets, and those who did had their names and addresses faithfully scribed onto a notepad which Marcus carried under his arm. Marcus was surprised how few people actually bothered to ask what group or situation the fundraiser supported. When someone did ask, however, Marcus would simply reply, "This is for needy families," or "the SNF organization... Supporting Needy Families," a name he had contrived himself.

After three days of ticket sales, Marcus had grossed three hundred and twelve dollars, as a result of one hundred and fifty six sales. Now it was off to the department store again. It would have been very easy to pocket all of the money he had earned, but that would have been bad business in Marcus's mind, and even worse... dishonest. So he scouted out the cheapest thirty two inch television he could find... a purchase of one hundred and eighteen dollars. Marcus knew full-well that the winner of the television would be so overjoyed by their success that it would hardly matter that the television was not of the best name brand. After buying the raffle prize, Marcus went to his notebook. He had devised a sort-of code throughout the pages, which consisted of a series of checkmarks beside the peoples' names. During his door-to-door sales, Marcus had been a busy young man... not only was he there making a sale – his mind was occupied with other things. He would strike up conversations, or at least try, with all of those individuals who did not immediately send him away. Through these conversations, he would develop a true sense of sadness and pain for certain individuals, mostly based on their life situations. From his experience with these encounters, Marcus would place a series of checkmarks beside the names of those who generated this pity in his soul... between one and ten, depending on how bad their situation and how good their heart. Now he stood in the parking lot of the department store, the television at his feet, leafing through the pages of names. The winner, receiving eight check marks, was an old woman named Ann Glestwick. Marcus had felt an affinity for her from the very beginning of their conversation the day before. She had seemed lonely, and, like Marcus, not of great wealth. He had even come close to giving her back the two dollars at one point, but had decided that she would probably be the one getting the television anyway. Something happened to Marcus that day. It was the greatest feeling he had ever experienced in his life – the byproduct of a concoction of tears, words, and hugs.

Mrs. Glestwick opened her door with a big grin on her face, but quickly Marcus noticed that her gaze was not affixed on the brand new television, but upon him. Marcus proclaimed, "You won!" hoping she would disclose her true happiness. But Mrs. Glestwick was already smiling – she was already happy.

The two talked for hours... mostly about her life, her situation. She had raised three children, two of which had been killed in wars, and her husband had passed away a year ago. Apparently, her third child never even called her anymore, and Marcus was taken by the impression that he was the first person she had actually *talked* with in a very long time. He left Mrs. Glestwick's house feeling as if he had just spent the most important two hours of his life. Of course she hadn't accepted the television, stating that "an old lady like her has no use for such a thing" and Marcus had felt compelled to at least give her back the two dollars that she had spent on the ticket – along with a big hug.

Marcus now sensed that he was seeing things in a

new light, and a world of possibilities had opened up to him. That evening, as he walked home along the dusty street pushing a wheelbarrow filled with a thirty-two inch television, Marcus Pratt felt like he was on top of the world. He had just made Mrs. Glestwick's day, learned countless life lessons from a variety of experienced people, and walked away with one hundred and ninety two dollars and a new T.V. – not bad for three days, he thought.

However, Marcus's adventures with Ann Glestwick were not the end of his business career, but instead the very beginning. Although his mother was quite persistent in forcing a "normal" career path on Marcus, there were hurdles that she faced. For one, he would not read anything. Marcus didn't believe in reading. Through his childhood years, he developed the idea that reading books somehow tainted one's perspective on the world. That the only pure personality, the only pure life, is one that has not been exposed to literature. Instead, Marcus had become obsessed with talking to people – learning from people – learning from life itself.

* * *

By the time he was eighteen, Marcus was already a millionaire… and not by a little. Moreover, during the past seven years, the name "Marcus Pratt" had been carved into the foundation of the greater Pittsburgh community – or at least among those who understood the inner-workings of it. He was the leader of the local chapter of Ascendacism, a political school of thought which was quite new to the scene, and one fiercely consumed with personal liberty, freedom, and private enterprise. Marcus was quite involved in the Ascendants' movement. The party had only existed for ten years or so, and Marcus maintained a close relationship with its founder, Robert Nochman, who was now sixty-three years old and living in Seattle. The two corresponded quite often through phone, email, and written communications. Marcus was also writing a weekly column for one of the major Pittsburgh newspapers. His articles were known to reflect those of a creative visionary, with critiques on the American government that were almost prophetic in nature.

Marcus, from within a populace of complacency, observed that the government was constantly being pressured by foreign powers, all under the rule of Civicism. President Drake and the People's Congress were drowning in attempts at diplomacy, and were walking a line which was beginning to draw rather thin. America was the single remaining nation which had not given into the steady influences of Civicism, and the country was not a member of the Global Civic Order. This was only made possible by two things... 1. America was probably, militarily speaking, still the single most powerful country in the world (*still* because this ranking was nearly in contention), and 2. Americans were happy for the most part and therefore, in most cases, passively rejected large political alterations. Despite their contentment with the current political forecast however, an increasing percentage of Americans were slowly opening up to the ideals of Civicism. Ascendants, like Marcus, were a much smaller contingent, often referred to as extremists, and sometimes even terrorists (initially due to some quite untimely associations with a few "bad apple" violent offenders). This group fully rejected the notions of what they considered a one-world government, spreading like a disease across the earth. They passionately opposed the founding principles of Civicism. Ascendants believed that the American government had already grown much too large, and that the country was slipping in the wrong direction.

Despite his unashamed affiliation with Ascendacism, Marcus was revered in his community. He had blazed through high school, excelling on the debate team, leading the local Youth and Government chapter, and topped it all off by becoming Valedictorian of his class. If there was a thing that Marcus sacrificed for his success, it was romance. With his money and looks, there was no shortage of fish in the sea. But, though he was known to dabble from time to time, the chances of a long term relationship were nil. Love would have to take a back seat to his career.

Upon graduating, every top Ivy League university in America, as well as many foreign schools, actively sought to recruit Marcus. Letters from Harvard, Yale, and Stanford filled his mailbox. Princeton had actually sent representatives to Pittsburgh to take him and his parents out to dinner. But despite the best efforts of virtually every prominent university in the world to recruit Marcus Pratt, he had made the final decision to educate himself. And it began with a class on finance.

By the age of twenty-four, most of Marcus's assets were buried in the American stock exchange. His skills in math had carved out quite a niche for himself in the world of stock trading. Marcus had derived algorithms for many of the various patterns which had emerged from his incessant studying of the influence of free will and greed on the economy. These algorithms were the foundations of a set of hack-and-slash software programs which Marcus had developed for his own personal use. Those programs banked him a substantial amount of money in the stock exchange.

The remainder of Marcus's wealth found its place nestled in small foreign investments throughout the world. These investments were mostly quite risky. The majority were not in company stocks, but rather in entrepreneurial ventures. At any given time, Marcus Pratt was sure to be funding multiple endeavors under binding contracts that he would make with independent factions – both American and foreign. He was incessantly being solicited by think-tank groups, research scientists, and inventors for funding, and eventually his name became virtually synonymous with venture capitalism.

On the day that Marcus met Antonio Benza, he was already funding projects that ranged from human embryonic research to oceanic treasure hunting...

* * *

It was a stifling mid-summer's night, and now it seemed that a new breed of entrepreneur had emerged for Marcus Pratt's solicitation. Marcus sat back in his chair with his legs resting on his brushed-aluminum desk, staring across its surface at the man seated in front of him. The barely audible hum of air conditioning accented the cool chill of the room. The man was well-dressed, in a dark, European designer suit. His jet black hair was slicked back, and his freshly-shaven face emitted the aroma of expensive cologne, flooding the crisp air. It was apparent to Marcus, from first sight, that the man was Latin American, a notion only solidified when the first words, thick with the Latino accent, rolled off his tongue...

"It is truly a pleasure to meet you, Mr. Pratt. My name is Antonio Benza... I come to you from Columbia and bring all of Her respect with me."

Reaching into his briefcase, the man withdrew a sealed box of imported cigars and placed it on Marcus's desk. While accepting the gift, Marcus studied the Latino for a moment. The man was dressed exquisitely. He was of average height, with a strong frame and a square jaw. His accent was heavy, and for a second, Marcus wondered if that was the only line he knew how to speak in English.

"Columbia, eh? Last time I looked I was in no way tied to Columbia... What can I do for you, Mr. Benza?"

The Columbian smiled slightly and gazed deep into the eyes of Marcus Pratt.

"You are one of these Ascendants, no?"

Marcus's attention was thus set. He placed his feet on the floor and sat up in his chair, staring at the Columbian before him. Marcus's ties to Ascendacism, while somewhat public knowledge, were rarely discussed with anyone besides his closest colleagues and, occasionally, Robert Nochman himself. Certainly no businessman, which the man sitting in front of him professed to be, had ever spoken of such things in his presence.

"Surely you haven't come thousands of miles to discuss politics with me, Mr. ... Benza was it?"

"No, I *have* come to discuss an investment, Mr. Pratt."

Marcus forced the issue... "What would a businessman from Civicist Columbia know about Ascendacism?"

He leaned in towards Marcus and spoke with a lowered voice. "Mr. Pratt, I come to you as a representative of a small organization that you have never heard of. We are not bound by Civicism, Mr. Pratt. We are not bound by any political structure. We are The Desconocido... The

Unknown."

Marcus was following every word. Though beginning to feel a little uncomfortable with the situation, he decided to remain silent and hear what the man had to say.

Mr. Benza continued, "I am here to offer you an investment opportunity..."

He once again reached into his briefcase, this time extracting what seemed to be a very detailed, topographical map of Central America. Mr. Benza unfolded the map, covering Marcus's desk entirely. He carefully ran his fingers over the creases that were left from the folds and rotated the map to suit Marcus Pratt's view.

Marcus was used to this type of thing, but he had a feeling that The Desconocido was not a mining company, environmental science group, or treasure hunting team. And he was right...

"Panama." Benza said it with a sharp, confident tone, slamming his forefinger into the map to further emphasize the obvious location of the country.

"Panama..." Marcus echoed, waiting for more description.

Benza carried on, "My clients and I came to you because we believe that you are the only one who can understand our cause, Mr. Pratt."

Marcus quickly interrupted, "Cause? ... Mr. Benza, I am not sure what you may or may not have read about me, but I am not in the business of funding *causes*..." Marcus smiled, "They just don't yield the same kind of profit margins."

Antonio Benza slouched back into his chair and looked over Marcus Pratt. Mr. Benza was now restudying Marcus, almost as if he had initially miscalculated the man. Marcus represented his twenty-four years of age well. His

82

light frame was accented by fair skin and very dark hair, which now partially covered his deep green eyes. He was dressed very casually, as always, wearing a gray hooded sweatshirt and tennis shoes. All of the investing and networking that Marcus did was based out of his high-rise condominium, and he saw no reason to dress up. He had, however, felt a little remiss when he had first seen how well-dressed Mr. Benza was.

"Mr. Pratt..." the Columbian now spoke in a more serious tone, "...You would be surprised how profitable causes can be."

If for only an instant, the statement made Marcus think of Ann Glestwick. He spoke directly to his visitor, "What *is* your cause, Antonio Benza?" Despite what he had let on, Marcus actually had always been good at remembering names.

"Do you like stories, Mr. Pratt?"

Marcus, still not completely at ease with the situation, was eager to move the conversation on, "I prefer a more direct means of data transfer, but my gut tells me it doesn't matter."

Mr. Benza continued, "One night, long ago, when I was just a boy, I sat with my parents at the dinner table. While we were eating, my younger brother, Julio, reached under the table and fed a piece of his chicken to our dog. My father was furious, screaming at him that he did not work his hands to the bone to feed animals. My brother did not understand, so my mother, after supper, told us this story..."

"There was an old man who had many dogs. He kept them in cages behind his house. The dogs were mistreated. If they barked at night, they were beaten. If they growled at their master, he would pour boiling water on them."

"Every night, before going to sleep, the master would walk out to the cages, open them up, and dump a cup of grain onto the floor. He would pour dirty water into their bowls... Barely enough for the dogs to survive. The dogs were able to live like this for many years. They lived, bred, gave birth, and died in those cages."

"One night, long after the old man had gone to sleep, a young boy who was walking down the road heard the dogs whimpering behind the house. He curiously found his way to their cages, and was immediately filled with compassion for the animals. The next day, the boy ran to the butcher shop and bought the best cut of meat he could afford. That night, after the old man had gone to bed, the boy returned to the cages. He divided the meat and placed a piece in each cage. Immediately, the dogs devoured every bit of the food. These dogs had never tasted anything like this in their lives. Their ancestors had never tasted it, nor *their* ancestors. In that moment, the very flavor of that meat redefined what life could offer."

"Over the next several days, the old man noticed a change in his dogs. The dogs became much more hostile towards him, snapping and growling when they were fed. As the old man increased the beatings and the boiling water, the dogs' skin grew tougher and thicker. One night, as the old man walked out to feed the dogs, he noticed that the dogs had not even touched the grain that was left for them the night before. He opened the cages, thinking that the dogs may have died. But the dogs had never been more alive."

"That night, the dogs would eat the best meal they had consumed in generations. That night, Mr. Pratt, the hounds feasted on their master."

Marcus leaned back in his chair and stared at the ceiling. His mind was processing Benza's words.

Mr. Benza spoke again, "You have an English word that I like very much, Mr. Pratt. The word is *entropy*. Do you know what this word means?"

Marcus knew quite well, but cautiously listened.

Mr. Benza went on, "We have this word en Espanol as well, but the English definition sounds so nice..." Antonio Benza spoke as if quoting scripture, *"the degree of disorder or uncertainty in a system."*

"The Desconocido, much like your Ascendants, believe that there is too much order in the world, Mr. Pratt. We believe most humans who were dealt a life on this planet are living it with no real understanding, no real knowledge of what life really is."

Marcus responded, "You must have done enough research on Ascendacism to understand that we have chosen specific fights and specific goals. And were these specific fights won, and these specific goals attained, order would be achieved... But you are against order, aren't you, Mr. Benza?"

Benza remained cool, "Differences as we may have, I do believe our factions share a common and more *immediate* goal..."

Marcus grew restless.

"What is in Panama, Mr. Benza?" he asked, taking his feet off the desk and now staring the Latin American man in the eyes.

As Antonio Benza leaned back, a smirk crept across his face. His eyes gleaming with enthusiasm.

"A canal, Mr. Pratt."

★ CHAPTER 2 ★

And so it was. The Desconocido... *The Unknown*, were now known to Marcus Pratt. That night, Marcus lay on his black leather couch. The television was on, its flickering glow dancing on Marcus Pratt's shadowed, blank face. But Marcus was not watching. The sound from the speakers was lost somewhere between the reverberation of Marcus's eardrums and his brain, and his stare projected straight through the screen. No, Marcus Pratt was still very much consumed in deep thought over his recent visitor, Antonio Benza.

In those moments on his couch, something was changing in Marcus. Until now, or at least since he was old enough to care about global, international, and environmental issues, Marcus had understood the role of a single person to be supportively, constructively, and creatively bent on *collectively* sustaining an ideal. But what if the man himself could change the world? That man would have to make hard decisions. *That* man would have to make sacrifices. Sacrifices of pride, control, comfort... morals? The man would have to be a politician, no doubt.

Memories flashed through Marcus's mind. Memories of sitting in front of a television, the television that Ann Glestwick had refused to accept as her prize, watching non-profit infomercials with tears running down his face. The images still burned bright in his mind. Honest working families from all over the world starving to death on government-subsidized farms, factories, and offices. He would change the channel to see Civicist and GCO ambassadors dining together at diplomatic banquets or peace conferences. The images had the same effect on him then as they did now. Tears welled up in Marcus's eyes and began to roll down his cheeks.

Marcus knew that had he been born in any country other than America, his life would have turned out radically different. Most countries did not even recognize the institution of adoption, and those that did knew it only in the form of government assistance programs. These were no more than government agencies that took control of "stray" children and typically used them for things such as military projects, experimentation, and international espionage.

Not for a single instant in his life did Marcus Pratt take for granted the gifts he had been given. Of the one hundred and ninety-two dollars that he had made during the raffle ticket sale on the weekend that he had met Ann Glestwick, one hundred had gone to his parents. The other ninety-two dollars were sent to one of the non-profit charities that he had seen on television. Even now, Marcus Pratt was known both locally and internationally as a great philanthropist.

But Marcus also knew that America's back was now being unnecessarily broken by the weight of a needy international community. A community where administrative powers left their very own citizens drowning in a sea of depravity. At that time, America accounted for ninety-six percent of the world's private donations. And it had not been long into his fiscal career when Marcus Pratt realized one key truth – the transfer of monetary value from point "A" to point "B" rarely has a long term effect on a given society.

It was time for Marcus Pratt to have a real effect upon society – and the world.

The next morning, Marcus woke without the assistance of an alarm. His shower was neither hot nor cold. His breakfast had no taste. He could not even remember getting dressed. Marcus Pratt's mind was churning. He found himself staring out of one of the massive windows of his high rise condo. The streets of Pittsburgh below were buzzing with the activity of the early morning rush hour. A light fog separated the towering skyscrapers of the downtown region from one another.

The early morning sun shined through the large panes of glass, casting a glow on the determined face of Marcus Pratt. Marcus owned the whole sixteenth floor of the Macy's building. Solid glass walls separated level sixteen from the exterior of the building the entire way around the structure. It made for a stunning setting, each room boasting a magnificent view of downtown.

This level was filled with the best the world had to offer, from artwork to technology. Flat screen monitors, voice activated climate control, a roomful of contemporary art... But none of it mattered. Not right now. Not anymore.

Marcus knew what he had to do. He had some phone calls to make. Starting with a call to Robert Nochman.

* * *

It was a matter of only days and things had moved quickly into action. Robert Nochman was busy stirring support for Marcus among the Ascendant party (a task which proved quite easy, as Marcus was already a well-known advocate), and Marcus Pratt was on a flight to Columbia.

Upon arrival, the Columbian International airport was a complete mess. Marcus landed at three o'clock in the morning, and the place was vacuum-packed. Fifteen minutes before the scheduled landing time, the pilot had informed the passengers that the airport was on lockdown, courtesy of the Civicist Columbian military police. Apparently there was a disturbance at the airport which had to be "neutralized". The situation did not make the extra hour and a half of circling the runway a pleasant one for Marcus. Marcus had hoped for a quick, clean, subtle journey. Commotion of this kind was not welcome. Especially on a trip like this.

When the aircraft finally touched down, the flight time had exceeded nine hours. The pilot once again made an announcement. The military police were no longer allowing incoming aircraft to dock at the airport terminals. All passengers and personnel were being ordered to disembark the planes on the airstrip, by way of the portable emergency stairways.

It would take another half hour before Marcus set foot on Columbian asphalt (longer for those who did not have the benefit of first class). By this time, the airplane was uncomfortably warm and crowded, and the passengers had grown quite restless. The warmth inside the aircraft, however, was no match for the wall of heat and humidity that slammed Marcus as he stepped from the plane onto the rolling, steel staircase. The blistering, moisture-rich air was enough to spontaneously invoke sweat.

As Marcus's eyes adjusted, they made out green and red lights dancing across the pavement of the expansive air field. Behind the lights sat emergency vehicles, scattered among other airplanes which were also being evacuated. Military police marched about in small groups, in some cases running, and a mixture of murmurs and shouts presented the ears of Marcus Pratt with their first-ever dose of the authentic Spanish language.

Once off the plane, the passengers were being ushered in a single-file line into the ground level of one of the airport terminals. Leaning to his left and peering ahead towards the front of the line, Marcus could see three Columbian military guards making their way down the procession of civilians. The guards were being rough in their searches and thorough in their questionings. Many men and women were being forced facedown on the asphalt surface, and others were partially stripped.

Marcus looked around the airstrip as if searching for options. He knew that an American was at risk in such a situation, but the airport seemed in such a state of military lock-down that there was no choice but to take his chances with the guards. As the trio of Civicist guards approached the family in front of Marcus, the guard who appeared to be the superior officer of the three barked some orders in Spanish to the other two. The language barrier made it unclear to Marcus what exactly was said, but whatever it was seemed to confuse the guards at first, as they momentarily glanced at each other in an aura of uncertainty. The officer then shouted the same command, this time mustering even more vigor. Immediately, the two guards began running back in the direction of the airport terminals. The officer continued to watch his fellow soldiers until they were out of visual range. At that moment, his head swung around and his eyes focused. All of his attention was on Marcus Pratt.

Marcus stopped breathing. The Columbian officer was about the same height as Marcus, but he carried a much stronger physique. He also carried a Columbian-issued handgun on his right side. Every muscle in Marcus's body was tensed and his veins pumped with adrenaline. Just when it seemed time for fight or flight, the officer spoke...

"Mr. Pratt?" The words were spoken softly and wrapped in a thick Spanish accent.

It seemed like minutes before Marcus could even respond... Questions were firing through his head. The confusion was almost too much to process...

"Yes, but how..."

The officer abruptly responded, "Turn around."

Obediently, Marcus turned his back to the officer and felt the cool steel of handcuffs tighten down on his wrists. He was beginning to feel sick. He grasped onto the knowledge that he had nothing illegal or even controversial in his possession, and this did manage to comfort him to some extent. Marcus had not brought with him any luggage or even a carry-on. Only his wallet, passport, and a cellular phone.

With a hand placed in the center of Marcus's back, the officer forced Marcus out of the row of passengers. The two soldiers who had been sent away were now jogging back to their place in line. With confused looks, they shouted repeatedly at the officer, who snapped back and must have ordered them to continue their progression along the line of people, as they subserviently obliged.

"No questions, Mr. Pratt. Just walk." The words of the uniformed officer were spoken quietly into the right ear of Marcus Pratt. Marcus was in no place to launch the barrage of questions festering in his mind. And he clung to the safely-rationalized belief that, as he had at this point done nothing wrong by either Columbian or international standards, he would be fine as long as he followed orders.

The officer moved Marcus along the airstrip at a

quickened pace, all the time firmly grasping the piece of chain that connected his handcuffs. After cutting through lines of passengers, and swerving about various aircraft and emergency vehicles, they entered a parking garage that was connected to the airport terminal and began up a stairwell. By the time they reached the third level of the garage, Marcus was drenched in sweat. Three flights of stairs and a pounding anxiety had done nothing to squelch the unmerciful heat of the Columbian air. Up to this point, there had been no more words exchanged with the officer.

The third level of the garage was completely empty with the exception of one car, parked alone near the center. It was a jet black luxury model sedan, seemingly German. The windows were blacked out with heavy tint. It looked expensive. Marcus's stomach turned. Something was not right. The officer opened the back door and placed his hand on Marcus Pratt's head, gently assisting him into the rear bench seat of the vehicle. After slamming the door shut the officer entered the driver's side and closed the door.

Reaching over into the passenger's seat, the Columbian officer grasped what looked like some kind of two-way radio and turned it on. He spoke into the radio. A Spanish response echoed back. As the officer set the radio back down in the passenger seat, he looked into the rearview mirror and his eyes connected with those of Marcus.

"Mr. Pratt, please relax." The officer reached backwards over his right shoulder and extended his forefinger, on which hung a set of keys. As he tilted his finger slightly downward, the keys fell onto the lap of Marcus Pratt. Marcus accepted the offer.

"My name is Santino. I am a friend, Mr. Pratt. I am one of the Desconocido." The officer was still staring at Marcus in the mirror.

As Marcus squirmed to unlock the handcuffs behind his back, he was busy calculating it all - the emergency at the airport, the guards that the officer had ordered around, the black sedan...

"What's going on? What are all these guards doing? Why the emergency vehicles??" Marcus's mind was racing.

The officer coolly returned, "There was a bit of an accident at the airport an hour or two before you were scheduled to land."

Marcus shot back, "An accident?"

"Well, something exploded," the officer responded.

"Exploded? What??" Marcus was restless.

"Terminal B."

Marcus swallowed and leaned back in the seat, staring at the ceiling of the car. He took a moment to calm himself before he spoke again...

"How many terminals are there at this airport?"

The officer replied, "Two... we're at Terminal A."

Sensing the discomfort radiating from Marcus, the Columbian officer felt the need to expand upon his account of the situation...

"Sir, it is of the utmost importance that your arrival, stay, and departure here in Columbia go undetected by the authorities. You understand that, I'm sure. And I'm likewise confident that you are aware of the fact that all airspace other than perhaps American is strictly controlled by Civicist regulation. This obviously rules out the use of personal aircraft..."

It was all becoming clear to Marcus... "Why wasn't I informed of your plans?"

"We knew that you would be against the idea, Mr. Pratt."

Marcus said, "Santino, let me get this straight - half

of an airport was leveled so my arrival would go undetected?" He was anxious to hear what a reasonable response to the question would sound like.

"Honestly, it was not supposed to happen this way, Mr. Pratt. It seems that our people got a little carried away with the incident. You can be assured that there will be consequences for their straying from the operation's original..."

Spanish reverberated from the radio in the passenger's seat and Santino quickly swiped it up and responded.

Staring into the mirror at Marcus once again, Santino spoke, "It is time for us to go, Mr. Pratt. Please lay down in the seat until I let you know otherwise. It's for your own safety, sir."

Marcus complied, positioning himself on the floor in front of the sedan's back seat. From this position he had no visual reference, but he heard the car start and felt the motion as Santino drove down the ramps of the garage towards the exit. The tires clicked on the cracks dividing the cement flooring as the car descended to the ground level.

After a pause and an obvious card swipe of some sort at the exit of the parking garage, the sedan seemed to creep cautiously along for several minutes. Marcus could tell they were outside now, mainly due to the flickering of lights dancing throughout the interior of the car.

"Mr. Pratt, no movement and no sound please. This is the last stop we make."

The car rolled to a stop and the driver's side window went down. Marcus made himself as small as possible, scrunching his body up and contorting himself in such a way that he lay extremely low on the floor of the sedan. Sweat was running down his face, no doubt a product of both intense anxiety and the extreme Columbian heat.

Marcus could hear multiple men outside of the car, shouting in Spanish... the inflection in their voices growing increasingly impatient. Santino's voice, likewise, grew more and more intense in his responses to their obvious questioning. Marcus heard the rustling of paper as Santino had apparently been ordered to show some identification. As voices outside simmered down, the driver's side window went up.

"Hang on, and stay down."

Santino's words caused panic to pierce through Marcus's body. Before he had a moment to process his emotions however, the car launched forward, throwing Marcus up into the back seat. The tires of the sedan screamed on the pavement, as something heavy smashed off the windshield. Marcus reacted by glancing out of the back window. Uniformed men were scattering like beetles from underneath an overturned rock.

Suddenly the rear window shattered as gunshots pierced the air.

"Get down now!"

Before Santino had even gotten the words out, Marcus was already laying in the fetal position on the back seat.

Once the airport security was thought to be out of range, Marcus sat back up. Santino was driving well over any sane speed limit. One hand was on the steering wheel and the other was tightly grasping the radio as he calmly spoke Spanish into the transmitter. Marcus could not believe the level of composure that Santino displayed. As Marcus turned around, he saw no vehicles following them - which came as no surprise, given the speed at which Santino was now driving.

Santino took the first exit he could from what seemed to be a major highway. The exit dumped them off into a very poor-looking section of town. Graffiti adorned the crumbling concrete walls of the structures that did exist, while the rest of the "housing" consisted of little more than branches, tarps, and garbage, from what Marcus could see. The speeding sedan swerved left and right to miss pedestrians, fruit stands, and cars, which were no more than obstacles amidst the cloud of concentration surrounding Santino. Within minutes, the poor neighborhood gave way to a section of decrepit warehouses, which lined a large river. As the sedan reached the third warehouse on the right, Santino swerved into the parking lot surrounding the building and sped around to the back. This was obviously some sort of industrial loading area for large ships... or at least it had been at one time. The car screeched to a halt, facing the river below, about fifty feet from the edge of the lot.

"Please step outside, Mr. Pratt." Santino's voice was as cool as ever. Marcus opened the door and climbed out of the back seat, while Santino exited the front soon after, slipping the radio transmitter into his back pocket.

As Marcus stood and watched, still in a bit of shock over the sequence of events which had unfolded in the last half hour, Santino walked around to the rear of the car and popped open the trunk. He carefully removed the jack stand which had come standard with the vehicle for changing tires. After closing the trunk, Santino placed the stand under the back of the sedan, just inside of the rear bumper, and began working the small lever as the jack rose to meet the car's frame.

The radio buzzed with static, and a Spanish voice

emerged, prompting a response from Santino. After his reply, Santino knelt back down and continued working the jack stand until the rear of the car was suspended about four inches above the ground.

With a satisfied look, Santino stepped back and removed a pack of cigarettes from the inside pocket of his uniform. Lighting one, he reached the pack out towards Marcus.

"No thanks..." Marcus replied. "I don't smoke."

As soon as the words had breached his lips, a pair of flickering headlights and the buzz of a four-cylinder engine came flying around the side of the building. A tiny red car skidded to a stop beside the black sedan, which now rested with its back end propped up in the air. The red car was an older hatch-back model, almost certainly domestically made, and perhaps most accurately described as "junk".

Two husky Columbian men, both with moustaches and stern complexions, dashed from the car and opened the rear hatch. Santino coolly approached the small red automobile, reached in the back, and removed an old metal gas can. Setting his lit cigarette down on the cracked pavement of the empty lot, he walked to the black sedan, opened the passenger side door, and began dousing the interior with gasoline. Marcus's heart was still pounding. One of the men from the red car approached Santino from behind. Santino turned and traded him the now-empty gas can for a roll of duct tape. Santino then proceeded to open the drivers-side door, lean in, start the car, and shift it into gear. The rear wheels, inches above the ground, slowly spun from the torque of the engine. He then knelt outside the car, and, reaching in, pressed the gas pedal to the floor. Strips of duct tape were torn and placed across the pedal to maintain its floored position.

As Santino stepped away from the sedan, the engine roared and the car was now wobbling slightly on the jack stand. The smell of gasoline was everywhere. He reached down and picked up his cigarette. Taking a long hit, he flung the smoldering stick into the rear seat of the car. Flames touched the sky and the heat made Marcus jump backwards. After just a second, Santino sprinted towards the rear of the car and booted the jack stand with all of his force. It mimicked the action of a kickoff in football, Marcus thought.

In an instant, the car's rear end slammed to the ground smoking, and the ball of flames raced towards the edge of the lot, launching itself deep into the darkness of the river.

Marcus and the three Columbians stared as the last of the sedan was swallowed by the water. Santino then turned and put his arm around Marcus. As they walked back towards the little red hatchback, a wry smile began to form on Santino's face…

"Welcome to Columbia, Mr. Pratt." The men laughed aloud… and, after reflecting on the fact that he was still alive, so did Marcus.

★ CHAPTER 3 ★

After driving a couple of hours, the cityscape gave way to an unpopulated backdrop, highlighted by densely packed vegetation on both sides. Towering palm trees stretched out like arms reaching from the lush tropical floor. The thick jungle formed a tunnel, through which the tiny red car now drove. Since leaving the urban setting, the road had undergone a substantial downgrade and was now nothing more than a winding dirt path. The soft glow of a sunrise began to form on the horizon as the darkness started losing its grip to the piercing Columbian sun.

Only small talk had taken place during the trip thus far... comments from Santino about the Columbian women, the Columbian heat... But the first words that perked up the ears of Marcus came from the driver's mouth...

"We're here..."

As he spoke, the car took a sharp right off the dirt road and onto a smooth blacktop driveway that curved up the side of the hill now in front of them. The car came to a stop about twenty feet from the road at a large fenced gate which blocked the little red hatchback from completing its journey. Razorblade barbed wire spiraled along the top of the gate. Security cameras were mounted on two heavy stone pillars, one on each side of the road.

As the car jerked to a stop, the driver ratcheted up the parking brake and quickly jumped out. He hastily scurried over to a metal panel that protruded slightly from one of the stone pillars. Pushing a button, he spoke into the panel and immediately a loud clunk brought Marcus's attention back to the gate which was now slowly swinging open.

The rest of the driveway was longer than Marcus had expected... more like a road. The car sped along the half-mile strip of blacktop, swerving up the side of a vegetation-filled slope.

As the hill leveled off and the car neared its highest point, the vegetation gave way to an immaculate display of landscaping. Bright green grass was trimmed with the attention Marcus had only seen on fine golf courses, and the lush lawn led up to a structure even more impressive.

The driveway looped around ahead of the building, forming a porte-cochere, like one might see outside of a fancy hotel. In the center of the loop, directly in front of the building, stood an extravagant marble fountain. The fountain was not turned on, however, leaving the beautiful symmetric structure an inactive island within a pool of water so still that it resembled glass.

Sunrise was now in full effect and the first rays of the new morning lit up the side of the white mansion before Marcus. The driver pulled the hatchback alongside the building, and a Latin man dressed like a bellhop was quick to open the car's door and greet Marcus. It was an amiable reception, excluding the quick body search for weapons or wires, which had proved a tad unnerving.

Marcus nodded his thanks to Santino and followed the bellhop to his destination within the mansion. This destination, it would seem, was a large wooden double-door at the end of a hallway on the second floor. With only a quick knock, the bellhop opened the door, ushered Marcus in, and then stepped out, closing the door behind him.

The walls of the room were lined with book cases. In the middle, directly in front of Marcus, was an ornate glass coffee table, behind which, seated on a plush brown leather couch, was undoubtedly the man who he had come to Columbia to see. The man was quite big… obese may be the better term. He was dressed in a white suit and pants. The jacket, obviously a bit small for the man, was pulled back on both sides by his stubby arms, revealing a pink buttoned shirt underneath. He wore a matching white cap… the kind worn by old men who golf.

As Marcus walked towards the man, he noticed that, while still Latino, the man had a lighter complexion than the others he had encountered so far. He also had a few very noticeable scars across his left cheek. Upon Marcus's approach, the man drove his cigarette into the ash tray in front of him and leaned all of his weight forward to heave himself up from the couch. A big smile radiated from his face.

"Well, well, well… Mr. Marcus Pratt! It is my pleasure to greet you in my home today! I am Alejandro Poloma. You've already met my associate, Antonio Benza. He has spoken very highly of you!"

The man leaned forward and clutched Marcus, planting a kiss on each cheek. Marcus sat himself in a leather chair at the end of the coffee table as Mr. Poloma plopped back down onto his spot on the couch.

"It is very nice to meet you as well, Mr. Poloma." Marcus returned the warm smile.

"Frederico, please get some refreshments for our guest." Mr. Poloma was looking over Marcus's shoulder, and, as Marcus turned, he noticed, for the first time, two men standing on either side of the door through which he had just entered. They were both holding semi-automatic rifles.

"Of course, sir," one of them blurted out before slipping out the door.

Mr. Poloma continued, "I heard there was some

101

trouble at the airport. I am very sorry for any inconveniences this may have caused you. The Civicists are animals in Columbia, and we often must deal with them as such."

"I'm fine," Marcus coolly returned. "In fact, I do not wish to seem rude or curt, but I would just as soon get down to business with you, Mr. Poloma. My departure flight leaves in five hours."

"Fantastic! A true businessman. But, I am sorry to say that your departure flight was cancelled, Mr. Pratt. It is simply not safe right now. You will be sailing back to America... We have arranged a spot on a cruise ship that is currently docked only an hour north of here. It will not be leaving until five o'clock this evening. It is heading directly back to your country, as Columbia is the last stop on its schedule."

Marcus, a bit annoyed at the liberties Mr. Poloma had taken regarding his travel plans, continued, "That's fine. Let's talk Panama."

"Mr. Pratt, I understand you have been briefed by my confidante, Señor Benza... Well, there is more to the story than he may have communicated with you.

Surely, we can both agree on the global threats that Civicism poses to the world. Surely, there are millions who can agree with me here on a political level..."

Marcus sat back and listened intently.

"But the finer points - the *realism* of the suppression, Marcus, is nowhere painted in finer detail than it is here in Columbia and in Central America. Sure, in America you have seen it. But you view it through an eyeglass. For you, it is at a distance. You cannot feel the pressure weighing down on you, and you cannot taste the blood of the innocents."

"I agree with your party, Marcus. The Ascendants work for a noble goal. Your ideals are admirable... Your motives just. But you do lack something."

Frederico, the guard who had gone for refreshments, knocked lightly on the frame of the doorway.

Poloma, with a bit of excitement, beckoned the man in. A massive crystal serving dish was gently placed in the center of the coffee table. It was a palette of various cheeses, ranging in size and color. They were arranged with great care and divided by delicate slices of freshly baked breads.

Frederico then stepped out for a moment and reentered the room with two large bottles of wine – one red, one white. He opened them and set them on the coffee table beside the platter, along with two elaborate metal chalices.

"Gracias, Frederico." Poloma motioned the man out of the room, along with the other guard, who had remained by the door until that moment. They closed the door behind them.

As Marcus popped a piece of golden cheese into his mouth, he spoke as if the minor interruption had never taken place...

"What do we lack?"

Poloma, sliding back into the leather couch, was busy devouring a handful of cheeses himself.

"We are lucky to have such a wonderful chef here Marcus. We are lucky for all of this," his stubby arm motioning around the room. "We fought hard for this wealth. We worked for it Marcus, as you did yours. We are actually quite alike, you and me."

As Poloma tossed a handful of cheese into his chubby cheeks, Marcus spoke again.

"But not completely alike. Apparently I and my party *lack* something..."

Poloma sat forward, wiped his mouth with a small red handkerchief, and stared Marcus Pratt straight in the eyes.

"Action without regulation," he replied.

Marcus concentrated on every word. He knew the details behind the purpose of his trip were only now unfolding.

Poloma continued, "The Desconocido operate without detection here in Columbia. And thankfully so... We would not be sitting here in discussion otherwise, Marcus. The Civic Rule is powerful. They are powerful enough to run this country and almost all other countries in the world. If they knew of this place, if they knew of me..." He paused, then continued on, "They are powerful enough to end everything we have fought for. But, Marcus, the Desconocido, while recently growing in size, still remain undetected. Our acts are considered and reported as random acts of the people. And while there is nothing random about them, the other part is correct – we are an extension of the People's will, Marcus. And, just as importantly, we have the *means* to act on behalf of their will."

Poloma slouched back, as a small portion of his energy seemed lost, "But it is a delicate process."

"And Panama is an important piece of it?" Marcus was playing moderator.

"A very important piece," Poloma persisted.

"The people of Panama are like the people of Columbia. They are like the people of the rest of the suppressed world. They are enslaved to a *government* that they did not elect. A *process* that they did not conceive. A *law* they did not write. They are beaten, raped, imprisoned, and executed by a military they do not endorse. It is not the

Panamanian military, Marcus. Not anymore. There is no longer a Panamanian military, no longer a Columbian, French, German, British, or Canadian military. They are nominal. They are a façade. A pretense. They operate under those names. But we both know what they really are. They are *Civicism*, Marcus. It has become a monster before our very eyes. The GCO, its head. The leadership of virtually every country, a tentacle... an extension of its tyranny. America is our remaining light, but the light is fading, Marcus."

Marcus responded, "I see it. It is fading. When I was a boy, it was much brighter. But it is fading." He was looking down. Images of the truths that were being spoken flickered in his mind, confirming the legitimacy of the words that Alejandro Poloma spoke.

Poloma continued, "The people are divided by the lines on the map. They are divided by oppressive laws and the fear of what would become of them if those laws were broken. The Desconocido seeks unity among the people. We are their only voice. They may not know it, but we are. And, until now, we have remained relatively silent, Marcus... Until now, Marcus."

Marcus interjected, "Why am I here? What does the Desconocido need from me?"

"Funding," Poloma fired back.

"Money," Marcus said... feeling a need for more clarity in the semantics.

Poloma leaned forward, pulling himself from the couch to his feet. He turned his back to Marcus and began walking towards the opposite end of the room, beckoning Marcus to follow. The two men exited through a sliding glass door and onto a cement balcony. Poloma, moving aside the lapel of his white jacket, reached into the front pocket of the pink buttoned shirt and removed a pack of cigarettes. Lighting one in his mouth, he began to speak with a tone considerably more hushed than before.

"Panama, while poor and, as everyone else, politically corrupt, holds a golden key. Her canal connects the east with the west. Ninety-five percent of intercontinental shipping is still done in the water, Marcus. Great tankers, while technologically outdated, still move the majority of the world's exports. And a very high percentage of those goods move through that canal."

Marcus stared out into the jungle beyond the closely trimmed lawn of the facility. The midday heat was beginning to show its true colors. The fog, which had graced the forest floor earlier that morning, had given way to a balmy Columbian heat wave. Despite the environmental shock of moving from a cool, air conditioned room into the heat, Marcus was quite focused on what Poloma was saying.

"We need funding to empower Panama. We want to empower her people. We will need their help to take that country back, and take that canal."

"Take?" Marcus's gaze focused on the dark, ambitious eyes of the overweight Columbian in front of him.

"We want the canal under Desconocido control. We will take it. We will charge for its use. We will use our funds to further our cause..."

Marcus could not help himself. All of a sudden he broke out into laughter, looking around him as if waiting for the hidden camera crew to reveal themselves and laugh along. But there was no crew. Only a fat, well-dressed Columbian man, staring with a look of increasing irritation.

Poloma retorted, "There are many details which I cannot share. But there are others that I can."

Marcus, who was just beginning to return to a

conversable state, managed to reply, "And the GCO?? Canada?? Enlighten me on how a band of revolutionaries, warlords, and peasants will thwart their attack?"

Poloma smiled and laid a hand on Marcus's left shoulder.

"You."

The tide of moods shifted as Poloma said the word. What was left of Marcus's smile faded, while a large grin crept across the face of Poloma. With a gasping series of coughs, Poloma began laughing aloud. Bringing himself under control, he spoke again, "Obviously, as you were so quick to point out, the *powers that be* would not sit silently by while such actions were to take place. Not unless there were potential consequences for their retaliation."

Mr. Poloma leaned in and spoke under his cigarette-scented breath, "Unfortunately, Marcus, the world has gone nuclear. As you know, it has been for many years. There is no threat a group of people can offer, no ace up their sleeve, except for the *potential* of a nuclear blast."

Poloma's words were violently sobering. The picture became clear. Marcus knew exactly why he had been asked to come to Columbia. He began to feel queasy. Poloma sensed this...

"Marcus, please do not misunderstand me. The Desconocido will not be detonating nuclear weapons... Well, only one. A precedent. A wakeup call. Something to let the world know that we are here, and that we mean business. It will be clean, Marcus – no fatalities, only a warning... A warning that more will come if there is any resistance."

Marcus replied, "But you said there will only *be* one."

"There will," Poloma was quick to respond.

Marcus was full of questions, "And if they call your

bluff?" He couldn't believe he was even contributing to the conversation.

Poloma, blowing out a column of smoke, spoke with great assurance in his voice, "To say we have a very detailed plan would be an understatement, Marcus. Multitudes of my top advisors have been arranging this revolution for the last ten years. Many men have died in preparation, in information gathering... in getting you to this very room."

Marcus swallowed. His mouth was getting dry, and the heat was beginning to take its toll.

Poloma continued, "We all die, Marcus. Every one of us. But how many can say that they actually made a *difference* with the time that they had on this earth? You are only a piece of this puzzle... albeit a large one. There are many pieces, and we will fail without any one. And our failure, Marcus, is Civicism's success."

"What are your specific requirements of me?" Marcus asked the question with the directness he was often known for.

"We have a cache of small arms spread throughout facilities across Columbia. Enough to place a gun in the hands of eighty percent of all capable men, women, and children in Panama. We have paid independent engineers over the past few years to piece together what is needed for the nuke. We only lack a certain kind of uranium which is obviously not easy to come by. We have a deal lined up with a group of insurgents... in South Africa of all places, Marcus. They understand our goals, and have provided a path towards our success by way of a deal."

Marcus lowered his head slightly, while maintaining eye contact with Poloma. It was really a question in the form of a bodily motion.

Poloma answered it, "Twenty-five million dollars

American."

The wheels in Marcus's head started spinning. Now this was some information that he could really sink his teeth into. Through his entrepreneurial endeavors, Marcus had more experience in people asking him for money than almost any other man in America, and this wasn't even the most he had been asked for. But if he were to give it, it would indeed be the most he had ever approved. And the return was certainly not monetary in nature. This offer would be a completely different kind of investment altogether.

Moments passed, as Marcus's green eyes darted back and forth, giving away the flood of thoughts tearing through his mind.

"We need you, Marcus," Poloma began, "Without your funding, we are lost. You are the final piece of the puzzle that we have been putting together over the course of the last decade. We know about your affiliation with the Ascendants, Marcus. We share the same goals."

Marcus took a few breaths, wiping away some of the sweat that had beaded on his forehead.

"So, what do you say, Marcus?" Poloma sincerely inquired. "Shall we call this a deal and break bread together today?"

Most would consider such a quick decision, on a matter wrapped in potentially devastating consequences, as brash or compulsive (not even considering the twenty-five million dollar price tag). This only meant that, true to form, Marcus's mind was a step ahead of most. The truth was that Antonio Benza's visit to Marcus's high-rise Pittsburgh condo on that overcast summer evening had left a bigger mark than was immediately apparent. His train of thought, his priorities, and his political, and perhaps even *spiritual*, outlook had been altered to some degree by that visit.

As one of America's most successful investors, Marcus was already quite knowledgeable in the matter of sizeable business transactions. He was certainly knowledgeable enough to realize that he needed to be physically in Columbia *with* Mr. Poloma to make such a substantial monetary transfer at any reputable bank. On top of that, as far as Marcus was concerned, once he left the country of Columbia, he planned to never return. It was also evident that Poloma could never travel to America for such an occasion. Either the Civicists would kill him or American surveillance tag him… Chances were that he would never make it. Things began to add up.

Whether it was this blitz of rational thought, or the fact that he was standing in a revolutionist compound facing a relatively notorious Columbian warlord, one will never know what tipped the decision. As close as one may ascertain, however, *these* reasons only laced the true motive behind the next few words to creep from Marcus Pratt's mouth. And *that* motive was that Marcus knew in his mind that he had just been presented his opportunity to change the world for the better.

"I say yes."

* * *

The rest of that day was kicked off with a lavish banquet, filled with a diverse assortment of the tastes of Columbian culture. The feast was held in the dining hall of Poloma's mansion, a room which carried an extravagance and cultural flare that Marcus would never see replicated.

After the meal, an armed escort transported Alejandro Poloma and Marcus Pratt to the epicenter of Cartagena, the closest of Columbia's main cities, and coincidentally the city that Marcus had flown into and been chased through only hours before. Poloma explained to Marcus that his front for the Columbian Civicists was that of a wealthy businessman who owned a coffee farm where the revolutionist compound was actually situated. Apparently, all it took was a few box trucks with a bogus company logo and, more importantly, consistent payments to the Columbian government, based on profit gouging legislation, to keep them at bay. At any rate, It was the only reason that an armed escort could cruise around in such a tightly-controlled environment as Civicist Columbia.

When they arrived at the bank, it became all the more obvious to Marcus that Poloma was a well-known figure in the community. As Marcus followed Poloma and his handful of armed body guards into the massive, chiseled stone building, he witnessed a very subtle and intriguing sort of dance take place before his eyes. With a hug here and a hand shake there, Poloma was ever-so-delicately placing folded bills into pockets and hands... first the armed guards at the door, then the doorman, and so on. On their procession to the third floor of the building, any worker that passed by Poloma received one of these elusive gifts, and if not by Poloma himself, then by one of his armed men walking around him. Needless to say, Alejandro was welcomed warmly at the bank, and if any person in the building had an ounce of dislike for the man, it remained well hidden.

On the third floor, the group was escorted to a room of glass, framed with a dark-stained wood trim. The architecture of the bank was beautiful – inside and out.

Marcus was sure that it was one of the nicest buildings in Cartagena. As they approached the door of the room, Poloma motioned for his guards to stay, and opened the door for Marcus with a warm smile.

Marcus entered, with Poloma on his heels. They were greeted by a very tall and lean man who immediately shook Marcus's hand and gripped Poloma in a strong embrace.

Poloma blurted, "Jean-Daniel! My friend. How is the business of money going?"

The man smiled broadly, "Very good, Alejandro, how is the family?"

Two things immediately struck Marcus as interesting – the heavy French accent of the banker, and the idea that Poloma had a family.

"Great... My wife sends her regards. I would like you to meet my friend, Marcus Pratt. He is on business from America."

Jean-Daniel looked warmly into Marcus's eyes, "Very nice to meet you, Mr. Pratt. I hope your stay in Columbia is a good one. Both of you, please sit down."

Poloma closed the door behind him and sat in the leather-padded chair across the glass desk from the banker. Marcus planted himself in a similar chair to the left of Poloma.

Despite the warm welcome, Poloma wasted no time in getting to business. "As you know we are here to conduct a standard transfer."

"Yes sir, I have been expecting you."

As the banker lifted a heavy-looking metal briefcase onto the glass surface of his desk, Poloma continued, "Jean-Daniel..." He gripped the wrist of the banker and forced eye contact. "This transfer is to be *off* the record."

The man looked up, stammering... "But, Mr. Poloma..."

Gaining a tighter grip with his right hand, Poloma slipped his left hand across his chest and into the inside pocket of his white suit jacket. He withdrew a large cream-colored envelope and sat it on top of the aluminum brief case. "No *but's*, JD, just keep this one under the radar... It will be in your best interest."

The color faded from Jean-Daniel's face and his mouth seemed to be getting dry. As he glanced over Poloma's shoulder, he could see the backs of the armed body guards outside of his office, and no-doubt, he could see the ends of the rifles peeking out from behind their torsos. Sensing the banker's discomfort, Poloma released his arm and sat back.

"The envelope, Jean-Daniel... Please open it."

The statement was enough to snap the banker out of his light trance and back into the conversation. Gripping the envelope, he poked a finger inside and ran it across the length, tearing it open. A quick glance in, and the banker set the envelope down and walked to the walls of the glass office. He began closing the blinds one by one, until the office was visibly private. Returning to his seat, the French banker spoke in a more serious tone than he had carried upon the arrival of Marcus and Poloma.

"Mr. Pratt, your bank in America requires finger print identification, voice recognition, and your PIN number for a transfer of this magnitude. Mr. Poloma's accountant has already called ahead and set up the details. All of the paperwork is done. I only need your confirmations."

He spun the metal briefcase around and opened it towards Marcus. Inside was a screen displaying some disclaimer information and, more importantly, a big number… Twenty-five million. Marcus was very used to making large business transactions, but this one would dwarf them all. His heart was pounding out of his chest.

"Please read the information on the screen. If you agree to this transfer, place your left thumb on the black plate on the left side, say your name, then the word 'CONFIRM'." The banker, who had now walked around behind Marcus and was looking over his shoulder, pointed towards a smooth black surface on the side of the number pad, and pressed a button.

Marcus did as the man said, and with a hard gulp put his thumb in place and spoke, "Marcus Pratt… Confirm."

The banker hit another couple of buttons, and continued, "Now please enter your five-digit PIN number."

Marcus again followed his instructions. Then it was Poloma's turn. The whole procedure took no more than a minute and it was finished. Poloma shook the hand of Marcus and stared into his eyes. "You are truly my brother, Marcus. Today you have done a great thing."

Marcus barely heard the words. He was too busy thinking about the investment returns he could have seen on twenty-five million dollars.

On the way back to the mansion, Marcus leaned over to Poloma, who sat beside him in the back seat of the long, black sedan. "May I ask you a question, Mr. Poloma?"

"Of course, Marcus…" the comment obviously sparking his interest.

Marcus smiled… "How much did you have to pay Jean-Daniel? How much money was in that envelope?"

Poloma burst out laughing. His laugh was a kind of wheezing cackle which almost looked painful at times. It was a full minute before he could compose himself enough to speak.

"They were photographs of him with his boyfriend..." Poloma caught the laugh bug once again. "Civicists aren't crazy about our homosexual friends... Isn't that right, Alfredo?" Poloma jabbed the shoulder of the guard in the passenger seat in front of him.

The guard shot back, "With all due respect, boss, you can be a real asshole."

Everyone laughed.

The rest of the afternoon was spent in preparation for Marcus's return to America. At four o'clock he said his goodbyes, and by a quarter to five, he was at the coastline. It was Santino who drove him there, using the same small red hatchback he had arrived in. It was apparent that Santino was one of Poloma's most trusted men, as there was no hesitation expressed when assigning him the task of transporting Marcus to the harbor safely and on time. The information that Poloma had indicated in his discussion with Marcus earlier that day was confirmed by talking to Santino in the car during the trip. Marcus was to return to America by cruise ship which would dock in south Florida at about the same time the next day. From there, he would fly back to Pittsburgh, arriving in the early evening.

When they had made it to the harbor, the car stopped in an empty parking lot, removed from the scurrying of taxis and vacationers that surrounded the immense cruise liners docked there. Santino shut off the car and got out, motioning Marcus to follow his actions. As they walked around to the back of the car, Santino popped the hatch. In the back was a gray suitcase which Santino had described as including all of the necessary essentials for what was to be Marcus's short trip at sea – a change of clothes, some toiletries, etc. Marcus grabbed the suitcase and extended his hand to say goodbye to his escort.

"Good to meet you, Santino. Judging by our trip in from the airport this morning, I was pretty confident you'd have me here on time…"

Santino smiled and hugged Marcus, "Mr. Pratt, it was all my pleasure. May your return be a little less… eventful… than your arrival."

The two laughed for a moment together.

Santino spoke, "Ahh… I almost forgot… your boarding pass and plane tickets."

Digging in his pocket, he withdrew some papers and cards and handed them to Marcus.

"Yeah, I guess we don't want to forget these," …Marcus spoke as his eyes focused on the cruise ship's boarding pass. It was a little booklet, like a simplified version of a passport. On the front was the golden logo of the cruise company… "Seascapes" it read. Marcus opened the booklet and immediately saw a picture of himself on the I.D. portion. He wasn't sure where the picture had come from. It seemed like a cropped and doctored image of one of the various American news articles that Marcus had appeared in. That wasn't the main focus of Marcus's attention at that moment anyway. Instead, his eyes were fixated on the more intriguing portion of the page – the personal information. Name: William Conover, Age: 30…

Marcus glanced up at Santino, who was busy closing the car's back hatch, "William Conover?"

"Oh wow. I'm sorry, I forgot to tell you… Your name is going to be William on this cruise. Man, I am so glad you saw that."

"I see," Marcus returned with a touch of skepticism in his voice.

On the walk to the boarding ramp, a simple question plagued the mind of Marcus Pratt. If he was William Conover, what happened to the *real* William Conover? He wasn't sure if he really wanted to know the answer. The day had been a long one. On top of that, between the botched air travel the night before and his haphazard early morning tour of the Columbian airport and the greater Cartagena area, Marcus had gotten virtually zero sleep. His eyes were tired and his thoughts rather muddled from the fast pace of the day. It was enough to soak the thoughts of his temporary false identity in a warm bath of complacency. Likewise, it was enough to invoke the careless, smooth, unassuming tone that would make the cruise ship guard overlook the fact that his picture looked just a little "off"...

"William Conover?" she asked.

Marcus smiled, "Call me Bill."

Marcus didn't even bother to unpack his suitcase when he entered his assigned cabin. The luggage hit the floor and Marcus hit the bed. He slept like a corpse until the maid knocked on the door around noon the next day. After a quick shower, a change of clothes, a coffee, and a hunk of fresh pineapple from the cafeteria, the announcement had already radiated across the ship that they would be docking in Miami in an hour. Passengers would exit in groups based on the alphabetical order of their last names. Marcus figured he had been pretty lucky with "Conover".

The last hour of sailing was spent on the upper deck of the ship. The warm summer breeze was filled with the smell of the ocean, and the yapping of seagulls indicated their proximity to the coast. Marcus closed his eyes, lay back in the folding deck chair, and breathed a sigh of comfort as the scorching sunlight illuminated his face. He was glad to be out of Columbia and back in American waters. He unbuttoned the pink, flower-filled shirt that he had found in his luggage that day. Marcus had figured it for a joke of sorts, but, at any rate, they were the only clean clothes he had.

"A" through "C" were the first series of names called to exit the cruise ship, and Marcus was near the front of the line. The same boarding guards he had seen the day before manned the exit doors. As he walked by, he followed the routine that he had witnessed the other passengers going through – hand the boarding pass to the guard, they glance at it, and drop it into the slot of a locked metal box. And that was it. Marcus Pratt was back in America. Maybe he had expected more security, more of a hassle, more of something... But as he descended down the ramp to the Miami marina, all he saw were vacationing families carrying luggage - many rushing along, probably worried about missing their flights. Nothing broke the normalcy of the moment. Nothing, until...

"Marcus" ...it was a raspy, heavy voice from behind. Marcus froze, his eyes frantically scanning the premises before him. There was nowhere to go. He was on a large cement docking area at the bottom of the boarding ramp. Three sides led to water, the fourth to a group of tourists standing shoulder to shoulder waiting on airport shuttle vans.

Marcus slowly turned around to face the voice's owner. A dark suit, dark sunglasses, shaved head, cigarette... This was no tourist. The well-dressed man stood an inch or two taller than Marcus. A smile snuck across his face as he removed the cigarette from his lips and flung it off to the side. The grin may very well have been a product of the look on Marcus's face – one of shock, confusion, and even a pinch of fear.

Marcus responded, "How do you know my name??"

"That's not really all that important, but through our future conversations, I gather you will come to a conclusion on that matter all by yourself." The man remained smiling as he spoke. He was chillingly calm and had a way of exuding pure confidence.

Marcus, grasping for a bearing on the situation, fired off another question, all the time looking around, as if to look for any others of this type that may be lurking, "Who are you?"

The man spoke without changing his expression, "Marcus, I could give you a fake name, but really what's the point? It may be easier for conversation's sake, but I just find it..." the man turned his head and stared out into the sea, "...dishonest."

The suited man swung his head back towards Marcus and, though his black sunglasses hid his eyes, there was little doubt that their full focus was on him. "*I* am not important. But what I have to tell you is. As far as you are concerned, for all intents and purposes, I am no one... just a messenger."

Marcus's mind and body bubbled with a sense of hysteria. He kept looking around, unaware of what he searched for. Other suited men? Onlookers? *Witnesses?* Hordes of people were still pouring out of the cruise ship behind him, and while the two stood outside of the main flow of vacationers, the conversation was in no way out of earshot of the families forcing their way towards the shuttle pick-up area. The man in the suit, however, did not seem to care.

"How was Columbia?" he asked flippantly, while

lighting a fresh cigarette.

Marcus knew this was not good. It was time to run. As he began to turn, the man swung his arm around Marcus and stood beside him. To any bystander, the scene would have looked like two close friends talking, but the hold was firm and acted more as a restraint than an embrace of kinship.

"I am not here to harm you, Marcus. Please understand this. I just want to talk." The man looked around with a twinge of disgust... "Let's get out of this place. These people are driving me nuts."

The stranger maintained his clutch on Marcus and led him through the crowd towards a walkway which lined the busy Miami street separating the cityscape from the oceanfront. While Marcus was by no means a confrontational being at heart, he was, on the other hand, not a man to be pushed around... And the forcible actions of this stranger were beginning to eat at his patience. Marcus stopped in his tracks, unwilling to continue walking. He spun around, glared into the dark, black lenses of the man's sunglasses, and spoke in a calm, hushed voice, "Why should I listen to you?"

The man released his grip from Marcus's shoulders and turned to face him. He looked up to the sky as a plume of smoke blew from his lips. Returning his attention to Marcus, he reached up and slowly removed his sunglasses. For the first time Marcus could make out the man's face. He was probably in his mid-forties, with a definitive five o'clock shadow and tiny wrinkles on the outskirts of his eyes which projected a certain aura of experience - experience with *what* one could only guess. His eyes were a cold steel-blue, to match his personality thus far. He responded in a normal conversational volume, as if completely ignorant of the masses of people still streaming around them...

"Well... For one, I represent your government. ...For two, I am carrying a loaded forty-five ACP on my right side..."

The second comment caught the attention of a man who had been passing nearby. Marcus noticed it, which in turn caused the suited stranger to snap his head around and stare at the passerby. He held his stare until the man was out of sight, and returned to the conversation at hand...

"But most importantly, because I think you will want to hear what I have to say."

Marcus, though skeptical, was in no way in a position to question the man's authority. And besides, if he *did* work for the American government, you could bet he was not the kind of employee who carried around a badge or I.D. to prove it. Out of options, Marcus conceded with a quiet nod, and the two continued their walk to the curbside.

The suited man reached into his coat pocket and removed an airline ticket and itinerary...

"I believe we've got a plane to catch. Pittsburgh right?"

Marcus returned, "...*We*??"

Ignoring Marcus's retort, he continued, "It's been a while since I've been there."

As they reached the curb, a white SUV with dark, tinted windows skidded to a halt in front of them. The suited stranger opened the back door.

"After you..."

Marcus, perhaps against his better judgment, climbed into the vehicle and slid across the rear seat behind the driver. The suited man stepped in behind him and slammed the door. Reaching forward, the man pressed a switch, causing a black glass panel to rise up and completely shut off the back seat from the driver. With a tap on the glass, the SUV pulled out and started down the hectic Miami street.

The well-dressed stranger, now once again wearing his dark sunglasses, took little time to get to business. He turned his body sideways and rested his back against the inside of the rear door facing Marcus. Marcus positioned his body symmetrically, his undivided attention on the man seated opposite him in the bench seat.

"Marcus Pratt. First of all, I want to reassure you that I *am* with the American government. Even if you don't believe it by now, you will when I introduce you to some of my associates waiting in Pittsburgh."

"Next, for the record, it would be in your best interest to assume that we are fully aware of all aspects of your recent trip to Columbia. We are well aware of your rough time at the airport. We know about your visit with a Mr. Alejandro Poloma. We even know about the *transaction* that was made. And, obviously, we knew enough about your return to end up here."

To say that Marcus was uneasy would be quite an understatement, and the man was certainly conscious of this. One thing that kept the food down in Marcus's stomach however, was the idea that this was not the reception he would expect from a government who knew the details now being revealed by the stranger. A much more predictable chain of events may have included a face full of concrete and a pair of tight steel handcuffs binding his wrists behind his back. He listened on...

"As a relatively prominent member of the Ascendant movement here in America, you have actually been tagged for some time now..."

"Tagged?"

"Watched. Tracked. We have been monitoring you for years now, Mr. Pratt."

The man glanced down at his watch and then out the window, perhaps concerned with the timing of the flight scheduled for that day. He then leaned in slightly and spoke with a certain directness.

"What I am about to discuss is to never be repeated outside of this car. Doing so would be a breach of national security and could result in great harm to yourself. In other words, Marcus... this is as classified as it gets. Do you understand?"

"Yes, of course." Marcus was on the edge of his seat.

"Our government... yours and mine... is divided beyond what you can see. There is deep separation. So deep that most eyes are blind to it. These are divisions that are not recognized by our people, not seen by most of our elected officials, unknown to even our president... But the lines of division are great, and I wouldn't be at all surprised if you have sensed their presence."

"What I am trying to tell you is that there are more *Ascendants* than you know, Marcus. As surely as our government itself has become infected with the poison of Civicism, there are those of us inside who have seen it, and we realize that a stronger, less tolerant stance is required in this regard. We... those of us who recognize this truth... have recently agreed that the Ascendant party is the antidote."

He paused, almost as if he were thinking about how to phrase what he wanted to say next, "...What we lack is a figurehead. A politician without the politics. Someone who can be trusted to take this party... the Ascendant party... to the next level. And, frankly, we believe that you are our man."

Marcus couldn't believe what he was hearing. It felt like a dream. "Me? ... Are you serious?"

The man moved closer and tilted his head. His chilling blue eyes gazed over the top of his sunglasses at Marcus. "Do I look like I am joking?"

Marcus sat back in the cushioned, rear bench seat of the SUV and stared out the window to his left. A blur of pavement and palm trees painted his vision. His mind was once again burning with questions. There were too many for him to prioritize in any reasonable way, so he just asked a couple of the more important ones...

"You seem pretty set on me 'being your man'... What if I say no? I pay my taxes. What do I owe my *government* anyway? What is my motivation?"

The stranger sat back and rolled his neck, ending with his head leaning all the way back and staring at the roof. He let out a sigh, and, still in this position, began to speak again...

"I feel that you don't understand fully. I *work* for the government... yes. But the government I work for is on the verge of an internal revolution. The side that I fall on is the side of the Ascendants... It's the side of Robert Nochman... It's *your* side, Marcus. We are asking for your help. You want to make a difference? I think that your trip to Columbia speaks volumes towards that end. But funding men like Poloma is not the real answer. Honestly, I am personally not thrilled with your decision to pay money to that rat... But, fortunately for you, Nochman does not oppose your newest splurge of venture capitalism... if that is what you want to call it. Is that what you call it?"

Marcus had stopped listening at the mention of Robert Nochman. The stress of the weekend was taking its toll. He was feeling more and more reckless and cared less and less about that fact. Marcus wore the stress on his face as he fired back at the man seated across from him, "How do *you* know about my relationship with Robert Nochman?? What is going on here?"

"Like I said before, there are more Ascendants than you know, Marcus." The man removed his dark suit coat, loosed his tie, and quickly unbuttoned the top three buttons of the white shirt underneath. He gripped the right side of the shirt and pulled it away from the center of his body revealing a massive tattoo on his right pectoral. It was a large, bold letter "A" with a thick, vertical line through the center. The symbol resembled an upwards arrow. The marking was familiar to the eyes of Marcus Pratt. It was the mark of the Ascendant party. It had made its debut on the cover of Robert Nochman's literary masterpiece, which had first carved the lines of the party into the grains of modern day politics. The symbol had later been officially adopted by the group when they applied for official government party recognition... And from there it stuck.

Yes, Marcus had seen such body art before. It was not uncommon to see these markings on some of the more serious campaign activists, or "camps" as they were known. This was a group who ate, slept, and breathed Ascendacism. They lived and died by her words. Marcus had been the beneficiary of the work of a handful of these activists. They had been paramount in getting him elected as a local official a couple years back. And although Marcus had never thought it was necessary to brand his flesh in this way, even if it were for a cause he would gladly defend with his life, there was something oddly comforting to know that some people did.

"Marcus, you made a call to Nochman before you

left on your trip to Columbia... Do you remember?" The man slowly pieced his outfit back together as he spoke.

"Yes, and I am interested that you do as well..."

"Like I said, you're a tagged individual." As he adjusted his tie, he continued on, "During that conversation, you expressed an interest in a political career. Mr. Nochman was very happy to hear this news, and began rallying support among some of the strongest party advocates in America. I speak as both an employee of a weakening government and as a lifetime backer of, and believer in, the Ascendant party when I say... You have our unconditional support in your political endeavors."

Almost on cue, the SUV jolted to a stop, and as Marcus looked up, he realized they were at the terminal drop-off curb at the Miami airport. It didn't give him even a moment to respond to the man, but it seemed fine, as the stranger concluded with, "Let's go... We have a lot of business to do. We cannot miss this plane."

There was mutual silence on the walk through the airport, and even throughout the plane ride home. While the back seat of the SUV had been a place of privacy, Marcus and his new found accomplice were now in a much more public setting. There would be little discussion until their arrival back in Pittsburgh. And honestly, Marcus was perfectly fine with this, as it provided for some shut-eye on the flight home.

The airport security checkpoint was bypassed with a few abrupt words from the suited man. Upon boarding, Marcus quickly realized that every single first class seat on his flight had been vacated, such that he sat alone with the stranger in the front quarter of the jet. This was an interesting point, since Marcus's seat was still based on the original itinerary he had received in Columbia. Interesting, but not surprising, as he realized that the American government no doubt had the power to make such arrangements. A quick gin and tonic to relax the muscles and Marcus was out cold. He was awakened by the clunk of the landing gear coming down in Pittsburgh airspace. Marcus had no reason to be nervous anymore. He had convinced himself that the man with him was, if nothing else, an ally.

It was about five o'clock in the evening by the time they stepped out of the airport and breathed in the Western Pennsylvanian air. Marcus felt a level of comfort in being back in his hometown - this despite the uncertain circumstances of his arrival and the unknown agenda which awaited him. A silver luxury sedan was expecting them at the pick-up curb along the airport terminal. Once again, both Marcus and the man sat in the rear seat while the driver seemed like he knew where he was going. Upon exiting the airport, Marcus broke the silence...

"So, what's the plan? Where are we headed?"

The driver looked at the man in the back seat through the rearview mirror, as if to redirect the responsibility of the answer to him. It must have worked, since he was the one to answer...

"Are you hungry?"

"Actually, yes..."

"Well good. Tonight, you're going to have dinner with some important friends."

Marcus looked down at his clothes, "Important enough that a pink flowered shirt would be considered a tad informal?"

The man's stare followed the eyes of Marcus down to his shirt. His face frowned slightly as it seemed that this was the first time he had even noticed what Marcus was wearing… "Yeah…" He glanced down at his watch. "Do you have something that you could throw on at your place?"

"Sure."

"Great, then we'll stop there first. Tambellini's isn't far from there anyway."

Tambellini's. Marcus knew the restaurant. He had been there once or twice, but it was years ago… which was kind of amazing since, as the man had implied, it was only a couple of blocks from his high-rise condo, and he very much enjoyed Italian food. What he did know was that it was a very formal joint… but with a shower and a black tuxedo, he would be ready for whoever it was that awaited him there.

Marcus was told he had twenty minutes to shower and get changed, which was a little tight considering he wanted to include a quick shave, but he got it done. Twenty minutes after entering the tower that housed his downtown condominium, Marcus stepped out - looking like a million bucks. His dark brown hair was just long enough that it could be styled into the fluttery, controlled-messy look which was not an uncommon trend for fashionable young men like himself. With his face freshly shaven, Marcus looked a good five years younger than his twenty-eight years, but the piercing wisdom of his deep green eyes dissolved any doubt that his mind was among the most mature. His usually-pale skin had been brushed with the slightest touch of tan from his weekend in Columbia, and the tuxedo he bore did not deceive with the fact that it looked like it cost more than the silver sedan he was now climbing into. The bottom line was, Marcus was looking good.

As their car pulled up to the entrance of Tambellini's, the streets were bustling with people. The restaurant was, like Marcus's condo, located in a rather upscale section of Pittsburgh's downtown area. Luxury cars were the norm, and the sidewalks were alive with the likes of young, well-dressed couples hurrying to make their dinner reservations. As he stepped out of the sedan, the smell of warm pavement and fine Italian cuisine combined to send a tingle of Pittsburgh nostalgia through Marcus's body. The murmur of conversations and laughter on the streets took audible precedence over the sound of cars honking their horns and rubber rolling on cement. It was at this time that the man who had been with Marcus ever since his arrival in Miami said his goodbye. He had done his job. An oblivious Marcus, who had stepped off a cruise ship in Miami, was now an informed Marcus, entering a fancy Italian restaurant in Pittsburgh that same day. The briefing that Marcus had received, mostly while still in Florida, was just enough that he was comfortable, yet curious as he approached the door of the restaurant. Marcus would never know this man's name and would never see him again after that day. A job well done by government standards. In fact, other than a word of praise and encouragement, all Marcus was left with was the name that his reservation was under... "Nochman".

Upon reiterating the name to the restaurant's host, Marcus was led through three rooms towards the rear of the building. Entering the fourth, he noticed that every linen-covered table, about ten in total, was empty... except for one. In the geometric center of the room, at a small, round table draped in white cloth and delicately set with sparkling silver cutlery, sat three very well-known people. The first, seated on the left, Marcus recognized right away. She was a senior legislator, one of the most powerful politicians in America. As a direct advisor to the president and an active member of the People's Congress, she was also one of the most well-known faces in American politics. Her name was familiar in almost every household... Rachel Lorrett. Marcus was quite taken aback by her presence, and the mere fact that she was in the room automatically compounded the gravity of the situation. Sitting opposite Miss Lorrett was a less commonly recognized figure in the American government, though Marcus was completely aware of who he was. Fully clad in a pressed, navy blue American military uniform, with a veritable wall of medallions and badges, was the man known as Admiral Mason Bedford. He was the High Commander of American military forces, both domestically and overseas. Basically, he was the most powerful military figure in America who didn't get the publicity that his boss, the Secretary of Defense, did... This despite the fact that he probably wielded more control over America's troops. At the center of the table, seated between the two and facing Marcus was an old, familiar face. Robert Nochman, the long-time friend and mentor of Marcus, released a glowing smile as they made eye contact. His seventy-three year old frame still housed a full head of now-gray hair. The well-trimmed beard and stylish little glasses resting on his lower nose spoke volumes of the sharp mind and keen sense of insight that came imbedded in his being. Marcus knew Robert Nochman to be one of the wisest men he had ever met.

"Marcus! Welcome..." As Mr. Nochman spoke, all three at the table stood and turned to greet Marcus.

"As I'm sure you know, this is Admiral Mason Bedford... And, of course, Congresswoman Lorrett..."

Their greetings were warm and courteous. Although Marcus's past correspondence with Robert Nochman had been consistent, it was typically by phone or e-mail. In fact, as he now scanned Nochman's person, he realized that it had been years since their last face-to-face meeting. It had been at Robert's home in Seattle...

"It truly is a pleasure to finally meet you, Mr. Pratt..." The congresswoman was the first to speak, as the group seated themselves. "...I take it you've been thoroughly briefed by one of our agents?"

"For the most part... yes. And let me say that it is certainly a nice surprise to be sitting here talking with the likes of you three today. When I woke up this morning, I could never have imagined that I'd end up here with you before the day was through." Marcus knew how to be the most formal and polite of conversationalists when the setting called for it.

Nochman responded, "How was your vacation in Columbia?"

"Short..."

The admiral, who had been tentatively listening until now, interjected, "Hah! ...That's the best type of stay you can have in a place like Columbia..." His chuckle was hearty, like his upper body.

Not fully knowing who at the table knew exactly what, Marcus decided it was best not to voluntarily divulge any more information about his stay in Columbia than he had to. The strategy seemed to work, as Nochman shifted gears in the conversation...

"I'm going to get to the point. Miss Lorrett and Mr. Bedford are on pretty tight schedules, as you can imagine. They are flying back out of Pittsburgh tonight, so our time is limited."

The waiter arrived at the table and took everyone's order. Marcus ordered something light, as his appetite was overshadowed by the circumstances of such a high profile engagement.

Nochman continued, "We're here to talk about Ascendacism, Marcus... And perhaps more accurately, your involvement in it. Now, you and I have discussed this before... But this time, it's the real thing. What I am getting at is this... How would you feel about getting more serious about American politics?"

As Marcus began to process what Robert Nochman was saying, the councilwoman chimed in, "We are searching for a fresh face in the American government, Marcus. We need a marketable visionary to lead what we all believe is the only real solution to the ever-growing problem of..."

"Civicism." Marcus finished her sentence for her. He admired the passion that laced the voice of the councilwoman. He felt a true connection on her part with the party that he had forever sought to advance. And Robert Nochman... not a more firmly-planted political mind existed in the eyes of Marcus Pratt. His words could not be taken lightly in any sense.

Despite these things, Marcus realized that there was a knowledge which they all lacked. The knowledge that, in spite of their passions, the injustices they may have seen, or the lack of a proactive response to Civicism on America's part... Despite all these things, the fervor and resolve of Marcus Pratt for the progression of the Ascendant party in his native country could not be matched by any man. This was perhaps the quintessential "preaching to the choir". And it was time for Marcus to let them in on his answer... an answer that they only *may* have been able to predict...

Marcus sat up in his seat and slowly eyed every person at that table. They were all silent, knowing it was his time to speak. In reality, they knew he had more to say on the subject of Ascendacism than them... even Robert

Nochman. Nochman, while the genuine founder of the Ascendant movement, could by no means deny that Marcus was one of the big reasons for the party's recent increase in popularity. For even in sports, everyone eventually forgets the name of the one who created the sport itself, but the names of the players that made the sport famous are forever enshrined in history.

"I am by no means a perfect man..." Marcus began, "...And, while still the best on earth, this is by no means a perfect country. If it were, I imagine there would be no need for this meeting today. As I see it, we are sitting together in this restaurant, this evening, because each of us understands that America, as is, remains an ineffective match for the spread of Civicism around the globe. And this presumes our understanding of what Civicism really is... and *that* is, at the very *least*, a forced limitation on the rights of human beings, while at worst, a serious threat to global security. When a people lose all control over the decisions that their country makes... historically speaking... they suffer. I'm sure no one at this table would disagree with me in saying that every man, woman, and child on this planet is given certain rights at birth. And no matter their age, economic level, intelligence, social standing, race, or nationality... not disease, nor war, nor famine, nor *death* itself, can take away the single fundamental birthright of man..."

Marcus glanced around the table at his company... "It's *freedom*."

He took a quick gulp from the glass of ice water in front of him and continued on...

"We still cling to that right here on American soil, but, as you have expressed with your visit here, you too realize that *clinging* is not a solution to the problem. Rather, it is a temporary delay tactic. I seek victory – not a delayed defeat."

"You have probably read some of my writings... Robert, I know you have..."

Nochman gave Marcus a quick nod.

"...I too believe it is time to take action in this country. We have been granted such a tremendous power among nations... but with it a grave responsibility. Our political strategy as a nation has failed. We have watched our neighboring nations, our *allies*, fall to Civicism. We have sat by and watched as their people suffer at her corrupt hand... All of that must come to an end. And although *you* have called this meeting with *me*, I want to make something crystal clear to you now. I want to be plain as day with this... You asked me if I want to be involved in politics... if I want to be involved in taking the Ascendant party to the next level. My answer is this. I *am* taking this party to the next level. I *will* do everything in my power to crush Civic rule on this earth. I will do it at the expense of our current political system, and I will do these things with or without your help... as harsh as that may sound. If you are here to suggest to me that the best way to do that may be through the political system, then I am here to agree with you. If you are here to propose that I am the man to lead the effort, then I am here to say *yes*."

Nochman was looking left and right, surveying the reactions of the admiral and councilwoman as Marcus spoke. They were hanging on every word. To both, the statements were like a rush of fresh air into a stagnant political grave. The admiral had not heard this kind of rhetoric since the early days of Civicism's birth in Western Europe and its subsequent spread to neighboring Canada. With time, the power of Civic rule had grown, and America's staunch criticism of her ways faded. But the words that this young man now spoke lit a flame in the admiral's heart that had long ago burned out. The councilwoman too, though having read many of Marcus's ideas in his various articles, now sat speechless as her own past political failings were under review in her mind. Nochman only sat back and smiled. Something was cooking at Tambellini's that warm summer night.

★ CHAPTER 4 ★

Two years had passed since the summer that Marcus had decided to make a difference with his life. Two years since his trip to Columbia and that fateful meeting at Tambellini's. The path to political success was not a simple one in America. Popular elections and a system of checks and balances resulted in a rather long road to the top. It was nothing like Civic rule, where deep-seated corruption could crowbar a figure into power in a matter of weeks.

The original political strategy was this – if Marcus could acquire a spot in The People's Congress as Pennsylvania's Representative, and if it could be done within two years from the inception of his campaigning, he would be lined up for candidacy by the next presidential bid. Still, it was not quite as easy as it sounded. While his political savvy, public speaking, and charming charisma would go a long way to benefit Marcus Pratt, the fact remained that he was running as the first ever Ascendant to be officially elected to such a high role in the American government... a circumstance which would certainly prove a worthy obstacle in his path. To this end, after only a small period of research, it was determined by his team of Ascendant "camps" and advisors that the state of Pennsylvania was not the optimal host for Marcus's campaign. Instead, Florida would act as the catalyst.

It was only months after that meeting in Pittsburgh when Marcus made the move south. He had to establish residency in the state for a year before he gained eligibility to run as its Congressional Representative. But the move was necessary. Florida was the perfect setting for the launch of the Ascendant movement in America. This was largely because of the number of Civicist refugees living in the state. Latin America was by far the most unstable Civicist region on earth. *Unstable* in the sense that it was the part of the world that the tentacles of Civicism had most recently reached. Therefore, while the governments were more established in countries like Canada and France, in Latin America the people under Civic rule had not yet accepted their roles, and, largely due to poverty and oppression, were not yet loyal to their countries' new governments. This often led to the phenomenon of mass exodus. Civilians would hide themselves on cargo ships, sail their own undersized crafts by night, and even sometimes accept aid from American mercenaries and entrepreneurs (oftentimes Ascendants) who would frequently fund their seaward escapes. All of this despite the GCO assisting Civic-ruled countries in the attempt to cut down on such activity. In any event, as a matter of geographic and political convenience, the bulk of the escapees wound up in Florida. And an overwhelming majority of these refugees were certain to do anything in their power to undermine the corruption that they felt had polluted their native countries. This included voting for a newly established political party that was founded on flatly opposing the Civic movement.

But, one balmy night in South Florida, the world changed.

It was the night that Marcus was to hold a fundraising banquet where he would officially announce his plans to run as the Representative of Florida in the People's Congress. The event was a portrait of luxury, located in Fort Lauderdale's newest convention center known as the Triplex Plaza (due to its distinct three-wing architecture). The building's exterior was one-hundred percent glass, allowing a crystal clear view of the ocean from anywhere in the wing that extended eastward, hundreds of feet out over the blue water. This section of the convention center housed the conference room and banquet hall that were currently rented out by Marcus's campaign.

It was only minutes before Marcus was to give his keynote address. He was in an area that could be considered a "backstage" division of the banquet hall. The room that Marcus stood in was some sort of small training room, one side of which was a wall of glass. The wall was part of the south side of the convention's east wing which stretched out over the Atlantic. The view was magnificent. As Marcus stood at the edge of the room and stared out along Fort Lauderdale's southern beaches, he watched the lights of the cityscape take form as the sun had only moments ago fully disappeared from sight. In his right hand, Marcus held a crumpled paper containing various notes and key points that were to guide his speech to his supporters. In his left, he gently gripped a wine glass, half full, and took a sip. He was ready for his address. He had done several like it in the last couple of years of campaigning, and while perhaps none had been this important, he was not in the least bit nervous or even concerned. Marcus actually enjoyed these moments by himself, as he peacefully awaited his turn to speak. He could hear the barely audible voice of Congresswoman Lorrett addressing the room, accompanied by sporadic episodes of muffled applause and cheering. Miss Lorrett had become one of the key backers in the campaign to elect Marcus into a position within the federal government. This was a big night for her as well, as she had only moments ago announced her allegiance to, and eventual re-filing with, the Ascendant party. It was quite a statement for a politician as well-known as her, and certainly one which had the potential to put her career on the line.

As Marcus cleared his head and stared blankly out the window into the darkness of the ocean, something caught his eye. Looking straight down the southern beachfront, but slightly out into the water, a dim light was growing on the horizon. Marcus squinted and pressed his face against the glass wall. The soft light became more defined over the course of only a few seconds, then quickly faded. A moment later, everything went black. Everything. Power outages were not uncommon in southern Florida, but as Marcus fixated on the scene outside, the entire coastal region was black. Off to the right, the lights which had been shining, defining the downtown Fort Lauderdale region (and beyond that Miami), were gone. It was complete darkness, except for that fading glow on the horizon which had become the only source of light, until even it disappeared into the darkness. It only took a second for Marcus's brain to process what had happened, and when it did, it hit him like a sledgehammer to the face.

The backup generator kicked on and the lights in the convention center were restored, causing a faint cheer to radiate from the banquet hall, but Marcus's ears did not sense it. As he collapsed to his knees, the wine glass fell from his hand, shattering on the tiled floor. Marcus slouched forward and planted his head against the glass wall, his face vacantly gazing at the floor. He didn't even notice his personal security guards scurry into his room to check on him. He didn't hear their beckons for a response. The thoughts that were racing through the head of Marcus Pratt only moments ago were now eclipsed by his mind's fixation on one single word...

Panama.

Welcome to the pain, its glorious hour. Say hello to hate, tap into the power.

- Suicidal Tendencies, Tap into the Power

STORY III

EMPOWERMENT

★ CHAPTER 1 ★

After you kill a Canadian judge - the cornerstone of the justice system - that system tends to treat you... *differently*. This was a truth that Vincent Laymon would soon have no trouble testifying to, despite the familiarity of the hospital in which he now lay. Indeed, Vincent was making his second appearance at Saint Andrew's Medical facility in Thunder Bay. Yes, it was here only months ago that he had been admitted for head injuries sustained from the blow of a rifle's stock. This time around however, the setting was not quite as amiable.

The security detail that had been dedicated to Vincent's initial transport from St. Andrew's *to* the Transrek prison was no match for the one that accompanied him upon his exit. Instead of a civilian train with a single car isolated for his confinement, Vincent's newest road trip would call for a Canadian armored personnel carrier. And, instead of a couple of Canadian officers, a full detail of troops in jeeps and vans were escorting the carrier. Undeniably, within the confines of the Canadian armed forces, Vincent Laymon had earned quite a reputation. Had offenses equivalent to that of killing a Canadian Captain and Judge of the Global Civic Order been carried out in civil society, "Vincent Laymon" would no doubt be a name uttered in every Canadian household. He would be at the forefront of the media and would be at the top of every most-wanted list. But while, due to the secrecy of the Canadian government, no civilian knew his name, indeed Vincent Laymon had become quite the infamous figure within the tightly-woven fabric of Canada's military sect. Whispers traced the air around Vincent's envoy...

"Is Laymon really in there?"

"Who else would justify a security detail like this?"

"What are they going to do with him?"

This last question had certainly consumed the bulk of Vincent's own thoughts as he lay sprawled out on the dirty, steel floor of the personnel carrier. And now, with ankles and wrists cuffed tightly to the bed posts of the hospital bed, the question still remained.

The shot that was fired at Vincent in the courtroom had entered his back behind his left shoulder blade and exited his chest just under his right rib cage. The doctors would later marvel over the path that the 5.56 caliber slug had taken. All vital organs were spared, though the exit wound in Vincent's torso had required serious emergency treatment at the scene. The prison's medical staff was able to curtail the majority of the bleeding, and once stabilized, Vincent was released for his military parade to the hospital. Now heavily drugged, the pain in Vincent's body had been reduced to a dull throb... almost like a very minor heart attack every second or so. But despite his current predicament, Vincent was fully capable of counting his blessings.

Though the hospital setting was certainly not new to Vincent, the room he was now recovering in was starkly dissimilar to the one he had been in the first time. The most obvious difference was the smell. A fragrance of stale mustiness lingered about, while the dim lighting did little to lighten the mood. Two Canadian infantrymen were on guard outside of the door. There was very little inside the room. Some sort of I.V. dangled from Vincent's left arm, connecting him to a small electronic box on wheels... no doubt regulating the rate of *some substance* flowing into his body. There were no windows, and this, combined with the heavy musk in the air, led Vincent to believe he was somewhere in the basement of the medical facility. It was all Vincent could do to take in his surroundings before drifting back into a drug-induced sleep.

Four days went by in a terribly predictable manner... Wake up to the sound of the door opening... mean-looking guard sets plate of bland hospital food on the floor... unlocks wrists... stands and waits for Vincent to eat... while eating, nurse comes in and checks vitals... replaces I.V. bag... guard locks wrists back up... picks up plate, and both walk out. Rinse and repeat around dinner time. By the fourth day, Vincent could no longer tell which meal was breakfast or dinner. The pain in his chest, however, had subsided a good bit, and, following the previous meal, the nurse had removed the tube from his arm.

It was on this fourth day that the chain of repetition was broken. Instead of a mean-looking guard with a plate of food, four mean-looking guards entered the room. But it wasn't about the guards... It was about what they were guarding. Striding a step ahead of the soldiers was a man known not only by every person in the hospital room, or even by every person in the hospital, or Canada... It was a figure known by virtually everyone in the *world*. Andrew Marcell – the President of Canada and de facto leader of its military. Obviously, Vincent was hallucinating... he scrunched his eyes tightly and slowly opened them. The President was still there... no hallucinations here...

"Vincent..."

Now, Andrew Marcell was a fairly short man, whose frail appearance did little to testify of the terrifying notoriety that he carried with him throughout the world. He was essentially one of the founding authors and leader of modern Civic society in the world… in a dingy little hospital room… here to see *Vincent Laymon*. Andrew Marcell was 71 years old, and looked older. His left hand gripped a smooth black cane on which half of his body weight was supported. True to form for a President of a Civic nation, a press-fitted military uniform adorned his frame. The uniform was tan… almost brown in color, and the amount of pins, medallions, and badges that hung from the left side of the President's chest almost seemed like a burden on the old man's legs. Despite the war-torn, seen-it-all appearance of the man, however, a spark of youth glowed in his countenance. It was this spark that was now most prevalent as Vincent listened in anticipation…

Andrew Marcell, now at Vincent's bedside, leaned forward, peering into the young man's eyes. He studied Vincent like one would look at a long lost friend… almost scanning for familiarities. Vincent had lost some weight while in the hospital, though his arms, still stretched out to the corners of the bed, remained solid. The reddish-brown hair that had been shaved from his head in Transrek was sprouting back in, and his eyes were still a cold gray. Though a touch more pale than usual, largely due to the malnourishment bestowed upon him by sup-par prison and hospital food, not to mention the fact he had been out of the sun for a while, Vincent's face still had a passionate radiance about it. The President spoke…

"Your father is Terrence William Laymon?"

Confused by the President's curiosity with his family tree, Vincent answered…

"Yes…"

A welcoming smile lit up on the old man's face. The

President tapped his cane on the floor and spun around it to walk out. With a snap of his fingers, one of the guards rushed to Vincent's bed and began to unlock his ankles and wrists from the cuffs that bound him. Vincent's focus was still on Andrew Marcell. As he reached the door, the President turned around and looked back.

"I'll see you soon, Vincent. We're getting you out of this..." He looked around the room with disgust... "...place."

"You're alright now... everything is going to be OK."

With that, he whirled around and made his exit.

To say Vincent Laymon was treated differently at this point would be an understatement. The change came instantaneously and the contrast was staggering. As soon as the President left the room, a backflow of medical and military aides rushed in to fill it. As the shackles were delicately removed from his wrists and ankles, hospital staff began examining him rigorously and calling out orders for ointments and medications. Two men, who seemed like Canadian Special Forces escorted him from room to room, as he showered, shaved, and ate his first hot meal in weeks. He was able to determine that he was in fact in a hospital by chatting with medical personal who were decidedly more open to conversation than they had been prior to the President's visit. Although Vincent's stay was quite short.

After spending the midday in a room that would be considered nothing less than luxurious when compared to his recent accommodations, Vincent was ushered to a military post by way of armored carrier. The drive took almost an hour, during which Vincent was able to ascertain his location from road signs. He was apparently somewhere in northwestern Ontario. While no soldiers sat in the rear of the personnel transporter with him, at least three jeeps could be seen accompanying the vehicle. Something was very different this time around though. Vincent Laymon's hands and feet were unbound. A bottle of purified water rested in the console to his left. No one was watching him as far as he could tell. Even the driver of the machine could not be seen from the rear portion of the carrier. The doors appeared to have no locks. This was a different type of convoy. They were not restraining Vincent and guarding against a possible escape. Instead, this was a *security* detail. They were guarding *him*.

* * *

It wasn't until the next morning that Vincent would speak to the President again. Upon arrival at Fort Matane, a desolate military outpost apparently unknown to the Canadian public, Vincent was given a tour of the President's Quarters, a colossal structure embedded in sheer rock at the base of a pine-covered mountain. There had been multiple checkpoints heading into the base, each of which required Vincent to exit the vehicle and be frisked by soldiers. At every stop, it was the same scene - guard shacks, guns, and razor wire. Looking around now, Vincent understood why. It appeared as though he was getting a sneak peak at some scenery that not many in the history of his country had been tapped to see.

A beautiful blonde, probably in her mid-twenties, was tasked with showing Vincent around. Her hair was pulled back and a tight tan uniform was molded to her model-worthy build. She was polite but curt. Some of the more notable sections of the compound included a full service bar, a bowling alley, and an Olympic-sized swimming pool. Other levels (the base descended many floors down into the mountainside) were a bit more sobering. Command centers, conference rooms, and weapons caches that were not necessarily part of the tour were all too evident to Vincent. But for him, the "wow" of the tour was stifled by the "why" of the circumstance.

Vincent's little sightseeing outing ended in the office of the President. As the girl steered Vincent into the room, she quickly slipped out behind him, quietly closing the door. President Marcell was standing to the side of the room, staring into an aquarium that lined the entire wall and talking on a cell phone.

"Brian… I gotta run. I'll have Michelle set something up with you. OK, thanks. Bye."

The president turned and greeted Vincent with a handshake as his face seemed to beam with excitement.

"Vincent. I want to apologize for the lack of intel you've been provided. I normally would have had you briefed back at the hospital, but the truth is… No one really knows why you are here except for me."

Vincent's curiosity was overwhelming, "How do you know me??"

"Let's go for a walk." Andrew Marcell turned and slowly walked towards the exit, his cane tapping on the mahogany floor. As he opened the door, he pressed a button centered on a small white panel to its right, and while beckoning Vincent to follow, he spoke. "Pierre… Vincent and I are going to walk up the trail."

"It's cold out there, Vincent. I suppose you don't have a coat…"

Vincent lightly shook his head in response.

"And get a jacket for my guest. Size…"

The president's eyes scanned the torso of Vincent Layman...
"Medium."

"Yes, sir." The sound emanated from what must have been a speaker system built into the ceiling.

The president leisurely guided Vincent to an elevator, up a few floors, down a hall, and then took a right, placing them in a small lobby with a desk. Men in black suits and ties were standing at nearly every corner along the way, and only now Vincent noticed that two of them had been walking closely behind him and the president – probably the whole time. At the desk sat the same girl that had shown Vincent around only moments ago. Two brown fur coats hung on a dark metal rack on wheels. The girl quickly handed Vincent one of the jackets and began helping President Marcell put his arms through the other.

"Thank you, Molly." The president's polite nature was in stark contrast to his reputation.

As the glass doors slid open, Andrew Marcell turned to Vincent. With a casual smirk he said, "Here we go!"

The bitter cold air slapped Vincent's face with a stinging sensation. Just through the door was the edge of a beautiful pine forest, rising up the side of the sloping mountain and disappearing into a foggy mist about five hundred meters ahead. Snow was lightly falling, each large flake meandering down through the atmosphere and finding its place on the ground. The forest floor was covered in about ten centimeters of the powder, and the branches of the surrounding pines gleamed with white. A small, paved path, perfectly cleared... in fact, only wet, cut through the woodland ahead. On his way into Fort Matane, Vincent had noticed a dusting of snow, but he was now at a significantly higher elevation on the mountainside, and the view was stunning.   Vincent bent his head back and let out a controlled breath of steam.

"Call me Andrew."

Vincent snapped back to reality as the two began walking up the trail. The sound of the president's cane was a constant tapping, and the grinding of salt between their shoes and the pavement completed the rhythm. Looking back towards the compound, Vincent saw no men in black suits, no soldiers, no guards.

Vincent couldn't help himself, "Sir... err Andrew... Do you go on unguarded strolls through the woods with murderers a lot?"

The old man started laughing, "I'm a lot tougher than you think, young man. Don't try anything."

Vincent loved it. He chuckled as the president paused and knelt down. Picking up a tiny, smooth stone, he spoke...

"Vincent, your father and I fought together in Peru."

Vincent was engrossed.

"We led an infantry unit from the tip of the Amazon to the Pacific."

The president tossed the rock to the side and continued walking.

"Ha... that son-of-a-bitch was one of the best soldiers I've ever seen. You know he was the Army's top marksman at the time?"

Vincent's eyes were tearing with emotion. He knew so little about his father.

"He left that country with over one-hundred confirmed kills on American and Peruvian military personnel."

The president glanced at Vincent, sensing his emotion.

"You don't know much about your father, do you, Vincent?"

"No, I do not, sir. I remember him in the hospital..."

The president's face cast a grim look towards the ground.

"That pig... shit 'judge' got what was coming to him, Vincent. I would have done it myself if I had found the bastard."

Andrew Marcell stopped and, after brushing the snow off with his cane, sat on a log which had fallen down alongside the path. Vincent followed suit.

"His real name was Cedric Redsford... not *Brenson Terat*. He apparently changed it years ago... before I had any power to do something about it. It's why I was never able to find the piece of garbage. After you killed him, one of our administrators matched his records in our database. And when I read that he was killed by a man named *Vincent Laymon*... I knew it couldn't have been a coincidence."

The president placed his hand on Vincent's right shoulder and continued... "Peru was a hell hole..."

Andrew Marcell gazed blankly at the drift of snow near his feet. "Towards the end of the war it got messy. Funding was dwindling... Your father and I were posted at one of the most remote Canadian outposts in the country. The officer in charge was a real asshole. Jack Brenamann was his name. This guy would never have made private second class, let alone captain, had his uncle not been on the Canadian High Court at the time."

The president shook his head. "I mean this kid was a true piece of work. I don't think a night went by that the bastard didn't get drunk. He would send some of the new guys out every weekend to raid the local villages for any booze they might have. He was dangerous and reckless.

151

Your father and I of course wanted none of it. We were professionals."

Andrew Marcell stood up and the two continued their walk through the winter wonderland.

"One night, Captain Jack ordered your father and I into his barracks for a game of cards. By the time we sat down at the table, Jack was already plastered. There were a couple of fresh recruits there too... also pretty well on their way. We were against the whole thing, but we were not about to disobey a ranking officer."

"As the night went on, your dad and I played along, though we never touched a drink. About two hours in, I won a big hand. Jack immediately accused me of cheating. It was an absurd claim. Your father and I didn't even really want to be there that night, let alone care about winning. We were playing for cigarettes and change anyway... I denied the charge, showing everyone my hand, but that asshole was incessant. Out of nowhere he draws his sidearm and points it at my chest. I was across the table and all out of options. He pulled the hammer back and began shouting something. I'll never really know what he was yelling though, because the next thing I saw was the bayonet of a rifle sticking out of the front of his throat. It was your father's."

"They would have executed Terrance were it not for his impeccable record of service. Instead, the sentence was fifteen years. Fifteen years taken from his life to save mine. We exchanged letters every week."

The president slowed to a stop and looked up. A network of branches formed a neurological-looking silhouette against the evening sky. He was visibly shaken from recounting the whole matter, as was Vincent. Andrew Marcell breathed in deeply...

"If only I were president back then... This could all have been avoided. You know, your father suspected he was poisoned. He told me in his final letter. It was the last correspondence I had with Terrance. The judge had him discharged from the prison and apparently sent back to you and your family in Drayton Valley. I never knew where the military had your family relocated during his sentencing. Even after I made it into the political system here, I couldn't find it on record. That judge... Cedric Redsford... He really went to great lengths to cover the whole thing up. I mean... What did the doctors tell you and your family??"

Vincent was staring ahead without a trace of expression on his face...

"Cancer."

The president squared up to Vincent and looked him straight in the eyes.

"I made a vow to your father, Vincent. I promised him that if I ever found your family, that I would take care of you like my own."

A grin made its way across the old man's face and masked the tears that had welled up in his eyes.

"And here you are, Vincent. Here you are."

The president extended his arms and pulled Vincent Laymon to his chest, embracing him. It had been years since Vincent had felt such an act of... love. Memories of his mother quickly turned his attention to the fact that he needed to contact her... a luxury that, until this moment, had not been so feasible. And now another thing came to the attention of Vincent. He was crying. Yes, with his face buried in the fur coat of Andrew Marcell, tears flowed over his cheeks. And he was not the only one. So was the president of Canada.

***

For the first few months it was definitely awkward. A ditch digger in the presence of virtual royalty. Vincent was quick to follow up on his decision to get in touch with his mother, and, after explaining the whole situation, President Marcell took great care in moving her into a government suite in Calgary, while making sure her every need was met. Various attempts at contacting Frank, however, were unsuccessful. Word was that he had left Canada altogether, a story corroborated by mom. As for Vincent, the transition that lay ahead was neither easy nor natural. President Marcell placed him in a breathtaking living area, just a floor below his own quarters. The beauty and extravagance of the place was something that Vincent had never seen. His private living space consisted of a kitchen, bedroom, bathroom, and lounge. The floors were some sort of smooth, black stone, and crystal light fixtures gleamed above. Exquisitely carved walnut and hickory furniture displayed a level of detail that Vincent could never have dreamed possible. Gold and crimson floral patterns stretched around the perimeter of the ceilings. Artwork was hung in every room, some of which Vincent could have sworn he had seen once in a book. Vincent was afraid to touch anything, often to the amusement of Andrew Marcell.

Before coming to Fort Matane, Vincent Laymon knew next to nothing about Canadian politics. The truth was, no one did. No one except those who were a part of it, really. As the president brought Vincent into the "War Room" on his second day there, however, Vincent quickly realized he was in for a crash course.

The War Room was bustling with activity when the two entered. A flurry of dark suits and tan-colored uniforms swirled together like some sort of controlled turbulence. Here, maps and flat-screen monitors replaced the expensive artwork that was common to other parts of the compound. There were probably twenty to thirty people in the room when Vincent entered with Andrew Marcell, and with a single word from the president, everything stopped...

"Attention..."

All of a sudden, twenty to thirty pairs of eyes were focused on the two, and twenty to thirty mouths were zipped shut. You could hear a pin drop. As Vincent scanned the room, he did notice an exception here and there. Indeed, more than one of the suited men had their mouths wide open. And *their* eyes were affixed on none other than Vincent Laymon.

The president continued, "I would like to introduce you to someone."

Seeming to notice the reactions of some of those in the room, he added, "...though I'm sure some of you already know who he is." Andrew Marcell placed his left arm around the shoulders of Vincent and rapped his cane on the hard floor.

"This is Vincent Laymon."

A subtle murmur rapidly swept through the audience of government workers and then faded.

"A killer? Yes. He is. But more importantly... like his father before him... A hero. And now a friend. I want him to feel welcomed here. Vincent will be a member of my Personal Advisory Staff, effective immediately."

Vincent hastily glanced at the president, moments ago unaware he was being given a job. The president, still staring at the men in the War Room, gently squeezed his shoulder.

"Carry on."

Andrew Marcell motioned to two of the suited men, "Alex, Jonathan... you two, come with me." Both men set down the papers they were holding on a large, round, stainless steel table at the front of the room and followed Vincent and the president out to the hallway.

"Vincent, this is Alex Zanderberg, head of the Executive Council." The taller of the two men extended his hand and shook Vincent's. The man seemed surprisingly young to Vincent, perhaps only a year or two older than himself. He had light blonde hair which was pulled back into a tight little pony tail, and bright blue eyes. His countenance was one plagued with curiosity and a hint of distrust.

Alex smiled. "Nice to meet you, Mr. Laymon."

Turning to the other man, the president spoke again, "And, of course, Jonathan Nester. He's in charge of the security around here..."

The president grinned, "National Director of Security... Isn't that what they're calling you these days?"

The man laughed along. He was much shorter than Alex and considerably older too, as was evidenced by his well-trimmed, gray-flecked beard. He wore a sleek little pair of frameless glasses which gave his thin facial structure a kind of modern look. Vincent initiated the greeting this time by reaching out his hand. "Hello."

The small man responded in kind, "My pleasure."

Andrew Marcell spoke, "I want you two to make Vincent feel completely welcomed here. He's a good friend and he has, as you both know, been through quite a lot lately." Both men chimed in with a "Yes sir."

The president's cell phone rang and he answered. Cupping his hand over the phone he quietly excused himself, "I'll catch up with you fellas later." As Andrew

Marcell disappeared around the corner of the hallway, the taller, younger Alex turned directly towards Vincent. His expression had quickly morphed from one of curiosity to one of... disgust.

"Look, Vincent." He almost instinctively glanced down the hall to where the president had disappeared a moment earlier, then looked back at Vincent.

"I haven't quite figured out exactly why Andrew just nominated a murdering, ditch digger... *nobody* like you to his Personal Advisory Staff... But if you've got a gram of intelligence in that peasant head of yours, you should understand this..."

Vincent, delightfully amused by the little monologue, was already grinning from ear to ear. In fact, he had stepped back and now had his arms crossed, as if enjoying every word.

Alex continued, "The Advisory Staff has no authority in this place. You may have the president's ear, but we have his guns, his laws, and his trust. Just stay out of the way, and perhaps we'll attempt to coexist."

By this time Vincent was doing everything he could to keep from breaking out in laughter. He could barely get the words out to respond...

"Whew, for a minute there I thought you were going to steal my lunch money..."

Vincent slapped Jonathan on the back and motioned towards Alex with his other hand.

"I don't know about you, Jon... but this guy seems a little high strung."

Then, composing himself to almost a chilling sincerity, Vincent took a step towards Alex and whispered in his ear, "Look, blondie... I don't care about you, your title, or your politics. I'm just along for the ride."

Alex turned and stormed back into the War Room, leaving behind Vincent and Jonathan. Jonathan, staring at the door which had just slammed shut, spoke calmly, "I'm sorry about that, Mr. Laymon. Alex isn't a very *welcoming* fellow."

He then followed suit, leaving Vincent alone in the hall.

* * *

And so it was... Vincent was not interested in the intricacies of Canadian politics, nor the drama tied to her internal power struggles. But as days turned to weeks, and weeks to months, things changed. It wasn't Vincent's character, personality, or interests that changed. It was merely his situation. And when the same man is placed in a different situation, it results in a different outcome.

Slowly, Vincent's eyes became opened to the lesser known workings of the Canadian government. He was indeed now a member of the president's Personal Advisory Staff, a group he learned consisted of only four people, including himself. At times it almost seemed like a gentlemen's club of sorts, and no official power had been delegated to its members. Rather, the president gathered these constituents merely for unofficial advice, in a way granting them a type of power sometimes more influential than those of the Executive Council, which was the president's right hand when it came to the creation and execution of legislation, as well as control of the military. Certainly, the Advisory Staff were among the most trusted and befriended members of Andrew Marcell's empire. But why was Vincent Laymon included among them? It was a question that loomed largely unanswered, and one that infected the back of Vincent Laymon's mind.

Now, a year and a half into his stay at Fort Matane, he was beginning to think the whole thing must have been a tremendous act of faith, loyalty, and a hint of foresight on the part of Andrew Marcell. Ever since his arrival at the compound, Vincent's friendship with the president had grown deeper and deeper. It was certainly odd in a way, partly due to the age gap, and partly due to the drastically different backgrounds of the two... but it worked. Their personalities clicked. And while the other three members of the Advisory Council were apparently there for their expertise, vast knowledge, and broad portfolios of experience, Vincent found his role to be primarily one of a good friend.

★ CHAPTER 2 ★

Needless to say, a nuclear event at the epicenter of commercial trade routes during an already-stormy geopolitical atmosphere was a disaster. The headlines were filled for months in America and in the Civicist-ruled countries abroad. The most dominant Civicist countries, namely France and Canada, were quick to tie the explosion to a growing political movement in America known as Ascendacism, although a substantial connection had not yet been made. In the meantime, American politicians scrambled to deflect responsibility to a purely autonomous extremist group whose name was now engraved in all of the world's memory... "The Desconocido". The Unknown were now a staple of dinner table chat. It seemed that, in the tumultuous aftermath, there were only two things that America and the rest of the world could agree upon. One... this event was undoubtedly an act of terrorism, and two... it was time to spend more money on the military. As for the GCO... they issued a statement.

Unfortunately, there were no such voices or opinions left to be heard in the region of Panama. Panama, as it so happened, was a real radioactive milkshake. The blast radius had encompassed the canal and middle third of the country, while gamma rays, alpha rays, a slurry of radioactive isotopes... you name it... wreaked havoc all the way through Costa Rica and even into parts of neighboring Columbia to the south. Hundreds of thousands of people were disintegrated. Millions of people were dead. People. Men, women, children, babies – whole families. Dead. This wasn't the first time in history a nuclear assault had taken place, but it *was* the first time a group not associated with a specific government had obtained and utilized such a weapon. Not to mention the sheer magnitude of the affair. The largest published nuclear blast in history had occurred during a war between France and Peru (the last major country to fall to Civicism) nearly four decades earlier. The Panama detonation was approximately one hundred thousand times its size. It was clearly an act comprised of one part motive and one part pure insanity.

And the direct loss of human life was one thing... But it could be argued that the impact that this catastrophe had on international trade was even more devastating. Ninety-five percent of the world's trade was conducted by sea-faring vessels, and sixty-five percent of *that* relied on shipments which passed near or through Central America and Panama. Within weeks, countries were running out of food. Many smaller economies were on the brink of collapse. Starvation was creeping in. People began revolting around the world, and as a result, Civicist governments were clamping down even harder and reinforcing their suppressive power over the populous.

In the weeks following the Panama Event, Marcus Pratt himself barely survived a near mental breakdown. His prior involvement with the Desconocido plagued his conscience, and the fact that he had been lied to regarding the results of his funding did very little to quiet the sounds of screaming families in his head at night. Despite his mental anguish, however, Marcus's initial reaction had been one soaked in self-preservation. Marcus changed all of his personal information – phone numbers, P.O. Box, bank accounts ... anything that had been or could be used to connect him to the Desconocido. He developed a solid alibi for his impulsive trip to Columbia. He even bought a stake in a small software company based in the region to make any of his past communications less suspect. And apparently, either the precautions of Marcus were effective, or the investigations of the American government were not. Months went by without an authority knocking on his door or calling his phone. In fact, if anything, the whole incident had readily aided him in becoming Florida's next Representative. The Ascendant party took a vehement stance against the act of terror, claiming the apparent lack of oversight from the Civicist Panamanian dictator was to blame. This in spite of the Ascendant's pro-military, nationalist stances rapidly growing in popularity in the wake of the catastrophe. In fact, the election ended up being a blowout, and Marcus, with all of his emotional baggage, was simply hanging on for the ride.

While the rise to political power was certainly exhilarating, it was not enough of a distraction to offset the suppressed remorse. The weight of guilt hung like a lead robe on Marcus's shoulders, the effect of which was magnified at night, alone, in an unfamiliar hotel. As the new face of a growing political movement in America, Marcus spent half of his time in session, debating bills and legislating, and the other half flying from New York to Los Angeles to Miami, appearing on talk shows and acting as an expert opinion for news programs. The public exposure made him both a celebrity and a target, and it definitely wore him out. Marcus had to hire an entourage of advisors and representatives just to deny, deflect, and counter-accuse. A sort of media meat-shield, as it were. But this night, lying on the plush carpet floor of a luxury hotel suite in New York City, Marcus was ready to give it all up. As he lay, staring at the marble ceiling, tears were rolling from the corners of his eyes. Every fleck of ivory-colored stone in the marble was a face of the dead. Every granite swirl was an innocent family.

There was no choice but to turn himself in as an aide to terrorists. It would end his political career – maybe his life. But it was the right thing to do. Marcus considered calling his parents – something he knew he didn't do nearly enough. They were so proud of him, and besides news of family and friends, it was Marcus's success that they mostly spoke about. No. Not tonight. That conversation would have to come later… In a half-daze, Marcus grasped the telephone line and yanked the whole phone, base and all, to the floor. The phone itself rolled under the bed and, in his depressed trance, Marcus reached under and grasped it. He dialed.

"9-1-1… What's your emergency?"

Marcus gulped and opened his mouth to speak. At that moment, he felt something on his right side. A vibration. He placed his hand into his bath robe pocket and retrieved his humming cell phone. The screen was lit up with the name "Robert Nochman".

"Hello? Is anyone there??"

Marcus realized he was still on the phone. He cleared his throat… "Did you say this was 9-1-1? I'm so sorry, I was trying to dial out from my hotel. My mistake." Click.

He quickly answered his cell. "Hello?" Marcus hadn't spoken to Robert since before the election… before Panama.

"Marcus, are you OK? You don't sound good. For a second there I wasn't sure if you were going to pick up… "

Marcus began to compose himself. "I'm fine. Wow… Robert. It's been a while."

"Congratulations!" spurted Robert. "I had meant to get in touch with you sooner. But it seems that you are increasingly difficult to get a hold of these days."

Marcus chuckled, wiping his eyes, "Heh, yeah... I guess that means my staff is doing a good job."

For the next hour, Marcus and Robert caught up. Family, friends, politics, you name it. The familiar voice of his mentor, Robert Nochman, along with the warm memories they shared, was enough to pull Marcus's mind far from where it had been just moments before. But there was an elephant in the room – Marcus's involvement with the Desconocido. And after the small talk and catching up had been exhausted, Marcus couldn't bear to ignore it anymore. He knew that Nochman was aware of his little excursion to Columbia over two years ago, but had no idea what the man's feelings were.

"Robert..."

"The whole Panama thing..." Marcus paused, but Robert remained silent on the other end. "I'm thinking about turning myself in, Robert. I was just about to turn myself in..."

"Marcus - listen to me." Marcus was surprised at the resolution in Robert's voice. It was almost as if he too had been waiting for this part of the conversation. The old man's words couldn't have been more clear and crisp.

"You can never do that. You must *never even think* about this. Look... Marcus, are you listening?"

Marcus, a bit taken aback by the devotion in Nochman's voice managed, "I'm here, Robert."

Robert continued... "Marcus... Do you realize the opportunity you have right now? Ascendacism is on fire. The American people are ready, Marcus. Tell me... What is better for your countrymen – for their only political hope and inspiration to be placed in prison... or worse... or for that same man to grasp the reigns of fate and make a difference in this country? In this *world*, Marcus. Now more than ever, what the American people need is *hope*. You did not will this terrible tragedy. This was never part of your plan. So... instead of giving America another political scandal, and even... giving the Civicists the ammunition they need to bring our party... and country... to its knees..."

"Give us *hope*, Marcus. Give the people *hope*. And believe me... In doing so, you will deal a deadly hand to those who would rather see this country buckle to Civicist rule. And don't forget our little dinner in Pittsburgh. I have been keeping in touch with Admiral Bedford, and I know you have remained close with Congresswoman Lorrett. Ascendacism has more backing than you know, Marcus, and her numbers are only growing."

"Look around you, Marcus. See what is happening in Europe... and on our own continent! Understand that the freedom this country was founded upon has never been in greater danger. Realize that. ... *Remember that*."

Marcus knew the words coming from the old man's mouth were true. The Ascendant movement was poised for something special. Congresswoman Lorrett was now positioned for a win in her upcoming election to become the second Ascendant member of Congress, after Marcus, and a quiet murmur was drifting across America regarding potential candidates for the next presidential election, still two years out.

Marcus Pratt did not turn himself in that night. In fact, the next morning he began drafting what would be his defining piece of legislation as America's rising political star. It was an idea that would give America hope, reopen international trade, and extend an olive branch to her Civicist superpower to the north. An olive branch that would last just long enough for America to build its military might to full capacity, so that finally the only *real* avenue towards a free world could be pursued.

That morning Representative Pratt began his work on *Article 126.12 – The American-Canadian Canal Act.*

★ CHAPTER 3 ★

Frank Laymon stood on the balcony of his apartment, peering down into the darkness of the streets below. It was pouring outside, but he was shielded from the water by the balcony of the next floor up. The headlights of the cars hissing by were gleaming across the wet roads, and, fourteen stories down, water was pouring into the storm drains alongside the street. As Frank watched the tops of umbrellas meandering around below, he thought of his brother, Vincent.

Despite his efforts to see his sibling, Francis Laymon had been denied visitation rights by the Canadian Army. In the weeks that had passed since the incident at the canal in Michigan, he had quit his job as a Union digger, and spent most of his time trying to figure out a way that he could see Vincent. He had been allotted a fifteen minute phone call to the hospital, which had been spent telling Vincent how much he loved him, and reassuring him that he would lay it easy on mom. But now, after receiving a letter from a General Martin W. Rachtman, and the devastating news of another killing... in a military court room no less, it was becoming clear that the two brothers would probably never see each other again. Everything that had happened he blamed on himself.

Frank thought about the story he had been told of what he considered his older brother's bravery. Unlike Vincent, Frank had always carried a particular hatred toward Canada, especially its military. And now, with the accounts of his brother's actions replaying in his brain, it seemed like a good time to act on what he had been planning ever since he was able to convince Vincent to come to Michigan as a digger. That night, Francis Laymon decided to head home and inform his mother of what had happened, and of his decision to immigrate to America.

* * *

With the exception of refugees fleeing a few certain Latin American countries, America had made it quite difficult for would-be immigrants to gain access to the country. This was, at least in part, based on the typical war-time mentality that tended to promote isolationism from enemy nations (which, in the case of America, had become pretty much everyone else). Canada was certainly no exception, as tensions along the border were reaching an all-time high. By the time Frank had left his job, the GCO's military courts, like the one his brother had recently torn apart, were teeming with trials over incidents of minor conflicts surrounding the Canal Project.

A loophole did exist in the immigration policy, however... and it was this avenue that Frank was looking to exploit. It seemed that no matter how bitter a nation's relationship with America grew, she was still more than willing to accept foreign dissenters into her own Armed Forces to passionately combat the system that drove them from their home soil. Contracts were available to immigrants that granted permanent residency based on time served in the American military. While this might seem like a conflict of national security interests to some, the issue of spies and traitors entering the service was squelched by the fact that immigrant soldiers rarely gained any considerable rank in the military, and were never grouped together in large numbers unless necessary. The reality was that the strategy was designed to play out rather brilliantly were a full scale war to develop, as Canadian dissenters who crossed the border could be immediately turned around to charge right back into their home countries with American weapons in their hands. A recyclable, foreign-born army.

Francis Laymon's immigration contract landed him in a division of the American military that was under serious development at the time he joined. The group was a high-risk, high value target team designated as X44. The X44 flew well under the radar of the common American citizen, and was even hidden from most of the military. The team consisted of only twenty-four soldiers when Frank began his service. The concept was that this would be an extremely agile team of troops that could perform some of the "less-clean" jobs for the American military, while operating in seclusion from the public eye. Immigrants were perfect candidates to fill the spots, as they were excellent spies in their home countries, and were frankly easy to "cut loose" if something went wrong. No significant paper trails.

The bulk of the positions in the X44 were reconnaissance-based, while eight of the men were assigned to sniper training, which focused on the elimination of single, high-value targets. Based on Frank's biometric and psychological profiles, he was assigned a position on the sniper squad.

The job of a sniper ended up suiting Frank quite well. It wasn't a position that required great looks or even an abundance of physical strength, both of which had always been more evident in his brother, Vincent. Instead, patience, a steady hand, and an unnatural kind of endurance were the key. The training was downright grueling, however. For six months after his contract was signed, Francis Laymon would wander about the frozen tundra of northern Alaska learning the tools of both survival and killing... the means to both maintain and destroy life. And he ended up being quite proficient at both.

Not only did Francis Laymon lose contact with Vincent, but for the half year during his intense training, he was out of touch with the world. There were no politics, no media, no talk of war among the frost-ridden army bases of Alaska's northwestern coast. All that mattered was the next mission... the next target. There were times, like fourteen hours into a watch, lying face down in the snow, at a whopping twelve degrees Fahrenheit, at four in the morning, that Frank questioned whether American citizenship was worth the price. But then he would remember the injustice he witnessed firsthand along the trenches of Michigan. Visions of GCO and Canadian officers treating workers lower than the dirt they dug in... The story of his brother's friend, Saul, and now the tragedy that was no doubt unfolding in Vincent's own life. It was certainly more than enough to keep Frank going.

Sometimes, the sniper training targets used in the mock training missions were dummies, like you would expect to see behind a storefront window at the mall. They were often dressed and decorated to quite a level of detail so as to, over time, numb the soldier down to the idea of taking a human life during what would be, in effect, a rather personal encounter. Any moment of hesitation or sympathy expressed by a sniper at crunch time could easily result in a failed mission. A second look, an extra breath, a brief moment of self-doubt or even a gentle tugging on the strings of one's conscience... These were the true enemies of the X44 sniper. And by the fifth month of Frank's training, they had been all but eliminated from his chilling routine of *the hunt*.

It was early March... twelve days until Francis

Layman's scheduled redeployment into active duty. Frank was in the middle of one of his final training exercises, and what was undoubtedly considered the most difficult in the X44 sniper training regimen. Soldiers were blindfolded and flown by helicopter to various locations in the Alaskan wilderness. They were dropped off with nothing but a day's worth of food, their rifle (loaded with only a single bullet), and a large skinning knife. No compass, no GPS... Only what was kept in their memories from studying topographical maps for days prior to the exercise. The mission was to locate and eliminate a single target without detection. The "without detection" part referred to the swarms of trainers camped throughout the landscape, whose stealth rivaled that of the X44 sniper, and who were equipped with high powered spotting scopes and radios ready to report the location of a detected soldier back to base.

Frank was motionless. He was a natural part of his surroundings. The smell of the mossy vegetation covering his camouflage uniform permeated his senses as he lay face down on the frozen ground. The terrain was wooded, and Frank had just reached the peak of another tree-covered hill. A light dusting of snow coated his body, further hiding his outlines against the snow-spotted forest floor. The drop off had occurred at noon the day before, and Francis Laymon had spent the entire night and early morning hours inching and crawling forward towards his best estimate of the target's location. He was quite confident of two things: one, none of the other soldiers had reached the target (largely due to the fact that he had yet to hear that single shot ringing across the landscape), and two, he knew he was getting close. The latter was confirmed as a slight upward movement of his head revealed the tiny trail of green rooftops lined up in the valley below. This was the target – a simulated Canadian military convoy with government-marked personnel carriers, tanks, and all. It would be another half an hour of slow and subtle movements before Frank could position himself to see the true mark… a silver SUV. Without any magnification, the stationary line of vehicles looked like tiny beetles frozen in time. With his spotting scope, Frank estimated the distance to the silver SUV was around twenty-five hundred feet – almost half a mile away. The stinging tightness in his fingers was a harsh reminder of the brutally low temperatures that he had been exposed to the night before while inching through the darkness. Another look through the spotter convinced Frank that he was not positioned at an optimal angle for a fatal shot on the dummy that would be lounging in the vehicle's back seat. He was too high up, and would have to make his way further down the hill to level himself with the target.

"Snap!" It was only a stick breaking, but it might as well have been a twenty-one gun salute going off just behind him, and slightly off to the right. Francis Laymon lay motionless, holding his breath and waiting for the sound of an officer calling out his name on the radio. Instead, just another light rustle, and then another… Whatever, or whoever it was… was getting closer. Frank buried his face in the cold, leafy earth and tentatively shifted his eyes to the right. He peered out from under his moss-covered hat through a small sliver of light that separated it from the ground. "Crunch!" A black hoof landed what seemed like inches from his face, followed by another. Even the heightened senses of the Alaskan black-tailed deer connected to those hoofs were oblivious to the assassin lying beneath. The revelation did little to calm Frank, however, as he recognized that every training officer hidden throughout the valley had probably just positioned their scopes on the big buck that had emerged over the horizon. What bad luck, Frank thought... This would ruin his position for another hour or so, until the deer was well out of the area.

Time passed. Enough, Frank determined, that it was safe to progress down the face of the hill. About forty yards beneath him, Frank had spotted a collection of massive rocks, each easily the size of an automobile. Such terrain was not uncommon in the Alaskan wilderness, as large glaciers were known to have left even greater formations than this behind. It was lying in the darkness under one of these boulders that Frank would take his shot. His belly crawl down the slope might have been best measured in inches per hour, but eventually, and probably a half an hour or so before sunset, Frank had reached the black crevice separating one of the massive stones from the sloping ground. It was beginning to get very cold again, a condition magnified by the frozen, dark pocket of space in which he now lay. Nuzzled down underneath the snow-dusted rock, Frank could finally afford to move around a bit more freely. Time was of the essence, however, with the sun beginning to fade, and with a swift wipe of his rifle's scope and rub of his eyes, Frank rested into position.

A light breeze, maybe five miles an hour from the left... Sight adjusted for windage... Deep breaths... flashes of the setting sun glimmered off the windshield of the silver SUV as Frank panned his rifle's scope, resting the crosshairs on the dim face of the well-dressed dummy officer in the back seat. Frank pressed his thumb firmly against the rifle's safety switch until he heard the dull "click" that let him know it was time. The shot was at least seven hundred yards... not a short poke, but Frank was ready. Deep breath... half way out... and then... IT MOVED.

Francis Laymon almost dropped his rifle as he rolled back under the rock. His heart was pounding out of his chest. After a few seconds, he began to regain his composure and peered through his spotting scope for a better look. He had now been in the woods for well over twenty-four hours... Could he be hallucinating? As Frank stared at the seated figure, he saw it again. This was no target dummy. The form seemed to be wriggling from side to side. Frank strained his eyes trying to ascertain more detail from the facial area. Something was over the person's mouth... what... was... that...

"POW!!!" The report of an American sniper rifle ripped through the tree tops, filling the valley. As the rear passenger side window of the SUV shattered, a red mist coated the inside of the front windshield. Frank was horrified... something was wrong... someone was just killed... A real person. He was not ready for what he would see next. One of the tanks in the "dummy" convoy fired its engines, swiveled its colossal head and angled the cannon, snapping into position. The massive barrel was aimed about ninety degrees off to Frank's right, in another corner of the valley. The blast that followed was deafening. The valley shook. Once the smoke and dirt had cleared, only a crater remained where one of Frank's fellow snipers must have positioned himself for the shot. Immediately, the convoy came alive. Jeeps and personnel carriers flew through the woods, the crashing of leaves and branches barely masking the sound of men on radios. While the convoy consisted of the same captured and retired Canadian vehicles and weapons that the military had always used for these types of training exercises, the operators were different. These were actual Canadians. The training exercise had turned into a real-time battlefield.

Of all the sounds that had pierced the ears of Francis Laymon so far that day... from the snapping of sticks behind him, to the thundering clap of a Canadian-occupied tank... the one whispering in his ears now was by far the most disturbing. It was the faint, trailing sounds of dogs barking. Hounds. Frank knew he had to move... and fast. The dark crevice beneath the mossy boulder was no longer a safe haven. It would be only minutes before a dog would catch his scent. At that moment Frank gathered himself together to force his body to do what every X44 sniper-trained ounce of it told him not to... stand up and run.

Frank didn't bother to look back into the valley. The rattle of machine gun fire and the splintering of nearby trees was enough to keep him sprinting at full speed. He was gambling that he'd make it back over the crest of the hill before the giant revolving turret of the tank below could hone in on his position. The bet paid off. Frank was a third of the way down the other side before he heard the piercing echo of the tank's artillery fire. The shell glanced the peak of the hill behind him, sending a shower of dirt and leaves across his back. Frank was never the athletic type, but the adrenaline pumping through his veins now drove him at a blazing pace. Now hurdling over stumps, jumping streams, and tearing through the brush... No one would have second guessed him as a most decorated track star.

After minutes of running, the terrain began to rise again and level off, and the barking, yelling, and buzz of engines began to fade. Climbing over a large, rotting oak tree lying across the ground before him, Frank plopped down on the other side and gasped for breath as he lay staring up at the tree tops above. The branches overhead resembled a network of arteries and veins... very organic. A gray squirrel scurried around one of the trunks, disappearing out of sight. Snapping out of it, Frank swung his rifle up over the damp log and scanned the terrain for any movement. Nothing. The woods were open enough that from his elevation he could see all of the way back to the scarred earth that the tank's artillery fire had left as he was making his escape. As Frank slowly panned the scope, tracing his path, he could see no soldiers in pursuit. But as he set his focus on the horizon of the adjacent hill from which he had come, a flash of light filled his vision. It was the reflection from a windshield. A moment later, the feint hum of a diesel engine accompanied a jeep, as it took its full form over the horizon. As Frank steadied his rifle across the cold, damp oak, he made out a single driver and another man standing in the back, manning a swivel-mounted machine gun which was attached to the roll bars. The jeep seemed to be traveling quite fast – almost recklessly so – as it bounced over rocks and dodged trees in hot pursuit of Frank.

It was now clear that this was some sort of Special Forces group that had been sent out by the Canadians. Probably a team that operated without the stifling clouds of bureaucracy - much like the X44. They had obviously overtaken the training unit, if not the local base. And Frank had seen at least one of his fellow snipers meet his end. Surely the others were being chased or killed at this very moment. Frank also had established that the "moving dummy" had likely been one of the X44 trainers tied up as a live decoy. However, despite the tactical efficiency and execution of the assault... and the undoubted elimination of a large portion of the X44 sniper team... there was one thing these two Canadians in the jeep had overlooked... They were in pursuit of one of America's best snipers... and he still had a round chambered in his rifle.

It wasn't reasonable, and certainly not a part of his training, but the swell of emotions that filled Francis Laymon could not be doused by the forces of cold logic. One bullet. One shot. As the jeep bounced through the woods, down the adjacent slope, Frank's crosshairs traced the head of the driver. It was about four-hundred yards. Frank moved his aim ahead of the jeep to a lightly wooded clearing and waited. As the jeep entered the frame of his view, Francis Laymon fired. The wheels of the vehicle cut sharply to the right, sending the jeep into a barrel roll down the hill. The soldier who had been standing jettisoned through the air and slammed head first into the trunk of a maple. The jeep continued its clumsy roll until it reached the bottom of the valley, where it rested upside down in a small brook. Steam rose as the cold mountain water doused the engine and exhaust of the jeep. It had been a perfect shot. Frank was certain that the driver was missing his head, or at least a fair portion of it, and the machine gun operator was squirming. It was not clear whether the subtle movement was "just nerves" or if the man was conscious... but Frank knew that, even if his rifle hadn't been empty, he would not have afforded the soldier the privilege of being put out of his misery.

★ CHAPTER 4 ★

The Canal Project was nearly an overnight success. Ascendant-backed groups loved that the canal, another physical barrier of separation, would no doubt help secure the northern border. On the contrary, pacifists saw it as an opportunity for Americans and Canadians to work side-by-side and hopefully use this common ground to strengthen ties between the two opposing ideologues. Though not much grease was needed for the political skids due to the irradiated status of Panama, these points perhaps provided just enough. The GCO was satisfied as long as they, of course, maintained a significant level of oversight.

But then it all went to hell one Sunday morning...

It was a morning that would carve a spot in the memory of Marcus Pratt forever. The phone rang at four-thirty A.M. Marcus rolled out of bed and picked it up.

"Marcus, this is Eric."

Coming to his senses, Marcus realized he was on the phone. "Eric" was Eric Harbison, one of the advisors closest to Marcus within his staff.

"Get up. Something's happened in Alaska. It's not public yet, but it will be by the time the sun comes up."

Marcus, still a bit groggy from his slumber, fired back, "What are you talking about, Eric? What happened?"

Eric's voice grew quite serious for his reply, "Marcus. I just got a call from Admiral Mason Bedford. He was trying to get a hold of you. Canada has invaded Alaska, Marcus."

The words were like a shot of caffeine that no amount of coffee could deliver. Without even realizing it,

Marcus was busy putting clothes on and looking for the cell phone that was already planted against the side of his head.

"Why is he calling me?? Shouldn't he be on the phone with President Drake??" Marcus was baffled at the thought that the leader of the American military, who he had only met briefly at a restaurant in Pittsburgh, was trying to contact *him* only hours after what might be the largest invasion of American soil in history.

Eric replied, "He *has* contacted the president. Look… Marcus… I think you should call him now. He left this number…"

"What did he say?!?" Marcus was losing his cool a bit, as the whole scenario was a rather unpleasant way to start the day.

"He said the president was planning on taking no action, Marcus. He thinks the president is going to let Alaska go…"

Marcus Pratt was not an angry person by nature. In fact, very few things in the world had the capability of arousing the sense of rage that was now flaring up in his chest. The idea of his country turning the other cheek to Civicism, however, was one of them.

"Let it go???" Despite Marcus's skills in mathematics, this combination of three words simply did not compute.

"He wanted to talk to you because he's not sure what is going to happen when this gets out to the media this morning. He said he needs you to keep the Ascendants under control. Just call him. Write this number down… 389-423-9002."

Using all he could find, which happened to be a black magic marker and his bed sheets, Marcus jotted down the number and hung up. As he began punching this new number into his cell phone however, Marcus paused and reflected on the gravity of the situation at hand. President Arnold Drake had always been known as a pacifist. Marcus, along with the rest of the Ascendant party, were vehemently aligned against his tendencies towards a harmonious existence with Civic society. But this was taking it to a whole new level.

Marcus collected his thoughts. After all, he was about to call the top American commander at a time of unprecedented national crisis. Marcus dialed. The phone rang…

"American command. What is your purpose?"

Marcus, realizing now that this was obviously not a personal cell phone number, quickly replied, "This is Representative Marcus Pratt. I am trying to reach Admiral Mason Bedford. He wanted me to call this number."

"One moment, please." Marcus found the voice eerily calm and unemotional for a time of crisis.

After a serious of clicks and beeps, the phone began ringing again.

"Marcus?" It was a voice that Marcus had heard before, however the strain of the situation made its way through.

"Admiral… A member of my staff briefed me a minute ago… But what is going on?"

"There's a lot of intel rolling in right now, but here is what we know for sure. Marcell has ordered a full scale assault on Alaska, aimed at first taking down our military outposts in the region, and we think… next moving into the southern areas populated by our civilians. Juneau, Anchorage…"

Marcus was straining his ears to make out the Admiral's words over a barrage of shouting and what sounded like radio transmissions buzzing in the background.

"What are we doing? You've spoken to Arnold?"

"Marcus... our President..."

"What is it, Admiral?"

"My orders are to pull out our boys from all remaining outposts in the region and begin evacuating American citizens safely to the lower forty-six... We are retreating, Marcus. Alaska will soon be theirs."

Marcus swung his left arm around, sending an eight hundred dollar lamp crashing to the floor. Continuing his blind rage, Marcus fired his foot through the wall.

Obviously hearing the racket, Admiral Bedford barked, "Marcus! Are you OK?"

Admittedly, it was hard. The words that were now tracing through his ears were not easily digested. Marcus had studied history and the traditional patterns of Civic imperialism. But America was different. And maybe more importantly, it was really the last stronghold of a truly free society. He was not ready to watch it be swept away by the tides of indifference.

"Look, Marcus. I know how you feel. We all feel the same way. But we *must* show restraint right now. If the Canadians sense any unrest from within our country they will see it as weakness... And maybe as an opportunity to push further."

"Admiral... You know the tide is shifting in this country. You know the Ascendants are poised."

"Marcus. I know. And the time is coming when we can raise the gate. But that time is not yet here. We must stabilize this situation first. President Drake is going to make an announcement this morning about what happened and our course of action."

"Or inaction..." Marcus interrupted.

"Admiral... I *may* be able to mobilize the Ascendants to show restraint, but if I were you, I'd be more worried about the American people right now."

After a long pause, the top commander of the American military spoke...

"I am."

For the next few hours, Marcus and his staff scurried frantically in a race against the clock. The objective was that all of the political leaders, camps, and outspoken proponents of Ascendacism had to hear about the Canadian invasion and, more importantly, the American retreat, from a fellow Ascendant, rather than from Arnold Drake's presidential address at nine o'clock in the morning. Passed along with the news was a sense of the need for at least temporary restraint, which went over better with some Ascendants than with others. All of this time, the media was catching up with the story as well. Newscasts were beginning to stream and websites were being flooded with articles on the Canadian offensive.

By eight-thirty A.M., Marcus was happy with the progress of his team, although the effectiveness of their message remained unknown. He had the few members of his local Pittsburgh staff working out of his high rise office, while others were being mobilized in countless cities around the country. As a precaution, Marcus had also taken efforts to beef up the level of security at his Pittsburgh condo.

At eight forty-five A.M., Marcus was handed a cell phone. It was Congresswoman Lorrett. He knew that she had surely been just as busy as himself, if not more so, based on the seniority of her position within American politics and her recent realignment with the Ascendant party. For these reasons the call was not really a surprise.

"Hello, Marcus. How are we doing?"

"I think OK. You know… All of this… It's really beyond our control now."

The congresswoman replied, "I know. We can only try to hold things together. Remember, this is only temporary, Marcus. The time of the Ascendants has come. But we must be very wise about this. If the goals of our party are going to be realized, we must show restraint right now."

Marcus repeated the words, "Right now."

"Be safe, Marcus. I think this is going to be a busy day for you."

"Thanks, you too, Rachel."

It was almost nine o'clock. All televisions, radios, eyes, and ears, both American and Canadian, were now tuned to hear the words of President Arnold Drake. The world was watching. And even a patriot like Representative Marcus Pratt could only sit back, watch, and wait.

The President's address was being recorded live from the press room at the Executive Office. At exactly nine A.M., all national broadcasts snapped over to the scene of a thin black podium with a backdrop of American flags lining the wall. A lush bouquet of microphones bloomed from the top of the podium, displaying the emblem of just about every cable network you could think of. Moments later, President Arnold Drake entered from the left side of the screen accompanied by a flurry of flash photography. As the president took his position and squared himself up to the camera, Marcus Pratt's high definition flat screen television caught every sign of strain on his face from the day's events. Every nugget of body language, every nuance, would surely be studied and debated for years to come.

He began... "My fellow Americans, early this morning, while many of our countrymen slept, the nation of Canada launched an unprovoked, unprecedented invasion of our homeland."

The president paused for just a moment, almost as if he couldn't believe his own words.

"Intelligence is still being collected, but what we know for sure is that sometime around two o'clock Eastern Standard Time this morning, thousands of Canadian soldiers, heavily fortified and accompanied by mobile armored weaponry, crossed over the eastern border of Alaska from Whitehorse, and marched inland, hundreds of miles into our sovereign territory. The towns of Tok and Delta Junction have been invaded. All efforts at communications in this region have been unsuccessful, as phone and satellite infrastructure has been disrupted. The overall purpose or goal of this strike remains unknown, but attempts at a diplomatic solution are being made..."

The president grasped a short glass of water that was resting on the podium, raised it to his mouth and gulped.

Setting the glass back down, he continued, "In the meantime... I have ordered the first and second battalion of the American military to begin evacuating the highly populated southern regions of Alaska, and urge any and all citizens located anywhere in the state to leave immediately for the lower forty-six. Emergency vehicles are being sent to the area and all grounded American passenger jets and empty flights are being ordered to land in the cities of Anchorage and Juneau to assist in the evacuation. The remainder of the military is on high alert, as we make attempts to engage the Canadian administration while continuing to collect intelligence on the situation at hand."

"While this initial address has been very brief, I will be holding press conferences to communicate with the American people every twenty-four hours, indefinitely, until this situation is resolved. I will now take a few questions."

Marcus's blood boiled. He now understood why his morning's mission of trying to keep a lid on a potential overreaction by the Ascendants had been critical. Even he could hardly contain the disgust swelling in his being over the impotence of the president's response to what was an unparalleled disregard for American sovereignty and freedom. But what really beleaguered the mind of Marcus Pratt was the current mindset of the American citizen. Surely the emptiness and weakness of the president's comments had not been lost on the average American. And if it had, the very first question fielded from the press corps cleared things right up.

As the camera zoomed outward from the podium, President Drake pointed to a reporter in the second row, "Question... Yes?"

The reporter stood to his feet. The camera angle flipped to a view that captured the front of the man who now stood amidst a sea of seated journalists and correspondents. The man was old. Very old. Marcus did not recognize him, and thus determined he was from a local branch of the media. The man was frail, with a bent back. Most of his weight rested on a stick in his right hand. His other hand, trembling with age, clutched a thin black microphone which he raised to his mouth. As the man began to speak, the camera panned in and captured a glimpse of a set of golden wings pinned to the lapel of his worn gray overcoat. Marcus knew it to be an emblem of valor – one only received for over thirty years of service in a branch of the American military. The president must not have seen it.

"Mr. President..." The old man's breathing was heavy and his voice quiet enough to cause a hush to ripple through the room. With eyebrows raised, his gaze shot over the delicate pair of bifocals resting on his nose.

"I would like to clarify your statement. Are you saying that we are retreating from Alaska and thereby accepting Canadian occupation of American territory?"

It was the question heard around the world. The president started to speak, but the buzz of commotion sweeping through the room was beginning to drown out any chance of interpreting his words. A moment later, the old reporter slammed the butt of his cane repeatedly across the back of the metal chair in front of him. The hammering sound drew another instant of silence.

"Mr. President... Are you saying that you are willing to let the lives of our fallen comrades over the course of hundreds of years be wasted due to the inaction of your presidency?"

The president began to respond, but the man persisted, "Civicist!!" He hurled his old, worn cane through the air. The stick harmlessly glanced off the front of the podium, and suited men rushed in to subdue the journalist. The old man grasped his chest as he was violently forced to the floor. Reporters began to run out of the room, starting a chain reaction of panic. The camera momentarily flashed back to the now-empty podium, before suddenly switching to local programming.

As Marcus stared blankly at a shampoo commercial, his mouth hung wide open. Before he was able to close it, his phone was ringing off the hook. One thing was clear... A very, very bad situation had just become much worse.

The next couple of days played out like a horror movie for the American president and his administration. In the twenty-four hours following President Drake's address, Marcus's staff was busy taking calls from constituents, friends, reporters, and politicians, while Marcus met with some of his closest advisors to discuss the situation. It seemed like just about every talk show on every TV network wanted to know what the most popular Ascendant had to say about the president's position. But things in the private sector were also becoming very volatile, very quickly.

News reports of rioting and looting began to spread. Localized pockets of citizens began coalescing, fortifying themselves with whatever weapons they could find. Ascendants took to the streets armed with various means of propaganda, including fliers that gave times and locations of political rallies. The internet became a real-time source of strategic awareness for the concerned citizen. It seemed that no one had even tuned in for the president's follow-up address on the second morning. The American people were quickly coming to the conclusion that their government was no longer willing or able to protect them, and that this duty now fell on the common man.

At nearly midnight, on the day after the president's initial address to the nation, Marcus received another call from Admiral Bedford. While the admiral's voice seemed more controlled than the last time they spoke, there was a distinct sense of gravity that accompanied it.

"Marcus... As we speak, tens of thousands of American citizens are mobilizing and travelling towards the capital for the president's speech tomorrow. Projected estimates, by the time the president speaks at noon, are between one hundred and twenty thousand and one hundred and fifty thousand people." Marcus Pratt was aware that, over the last two days, many of the Ascendants had propagated plans for such a rally. But while Marcus had caught the buzz about the assembly, he had no clue that the turnout would be so immense.

The admiral continued, "A lot of these activists will be armed. The nation's military is currently on the highest level of alert, with the White House surrounded."

The admiral paused, then added, "President Drake has given me the orders to use any and all means necessary to protect the infrastructure of our government and its members... including lethal force."

Marcus could see where this was going. He knew enough to realize that a shot from a government-issued weapon at a political rally as charged as this one would be like toasting marshmallows in a fireworks factory.

"Whatever you do, Admiral, *do not* let that happen. You don't want that fight on your hands."

The admiral recognized the truth behind the words. He was no greenhorn. But while this situation was more complicated and paradoxical than any he'd ever been in over his forty years of military service, he had the sovereign duty of defending his country. The real problem was that Admiral Mason Bedford was beginning to question what exactly that meant. Was his country his government? The President? Or was it the American people? The questions penetrated his conscience that night. By the time the sun cracked the horizon the next morning, the admiral hadn't gotten a minute more sleep than Marcus.

It was raining that day. A rainy Wednesday. It was the Day of the People.

The projected estimates were all wrong. A hundred thousand people quickly turned into over half a million. Cars lined every major highway to every back road within twenty miles of Philadelphia. Many who were drawing near to the capital, close to the time of the presidential address, had abandoned their cars and gone ahead on foot. News coverage was rampant. Helicopters swarmed overhead, shooting wide-angle views of the emulsion of humanity forming around the White House. Many held up signs and banners, but it didn't matter what they said. Everyone knew the common message. They knew why they were there.

Security was doing their best to quell any outbreaks, but the numbers were beginning to overwhelm the uniformed military police. The White House itself was fortified by some of the nation's best. It seemed Admiral Bedford's unit had spared no expense. Tanks and massive armored guns were accompanied by rows of armed soldiers, rifles gripped tightly across the chests of their navy blue uniforms, their countenances unaltered by the rain dripping from their berets.

But as Marcus watched the drama unfold from his Pittsburgh high rise, nearly two hundred miles away, he noticed a definitive trend to the flurry of activity. Boundaries were quietly being redefined, laws were becoming strong suggestions, and overt signs of military might on the part of the American armed forces were starting to look like a big mirage. As the events unfolded, Eric, Marcus's top advisor, leaned leftward across the couch and glanced up at Marcus...

"What do you think?"

Marcus leaned back and stared at the ceiling, gulping down the last of his glass of red wine. Setting the empty glass on the end table to his left, Marcus rolled his head over his right shoulder and gazed smugly at his friend.

"I think *this* set of dominos is already falling..."

Looking back at the flat screen TV, Marcus finished

his thought, "And all the king's horses and all the king's men are not going to be able to stop it."

* * *

Go-time was approaching. It was only minutes before the president would take the podium overlooking Freedom Square. A group of suited men carried out a series of what seemed to be very heavy glass panels, and surrounded the platform completely. As the crowd encompassing the area surged, the first two rows of soldiers locked arms, forming a human barrier. A loud speaker introduced the president, and a skittish-looking Arnold Drake quickly paced to center stage. He looked drained. Everyone would have noticed this. Surely the situation had become too much for the man to bear. The massive speaker system whose components were haphazardly placed around the White House lawn projected his first words...

"My fellow Americans. As I have promised, this address is a part of my continued focus on the national crisis our country is currently facing in the northwest..."

The boos and jeers began drowning out even the amplified voice of the president. The crowd made another concerted push towards the platform, seemingly breaking through the first line of guards in spots. It was obvious that President Drake could see what was happening around him, and likewise apparent that he was rather shaken up by the whole scene. What happened next, however, he did not see coming at all.

From somewhere amidst the body of humankind swelling before him, an arm reached out of the crowd and fired what appeared to be a flare gun. With an almost divine guidance, the flare's trajectory arched perfectly over the front of the mass, over the lines of soldiers, over the tanks and artillery, and passed just barely above the upper edge of the protective glass surrounding the president. President Drake had already been thrown to the ground and covered by secret service agents by the time the impact sent sparks harmlessly showering the entire platform.

The crowd sensed weakness and fed off the excitement, screaming and surging forward into the yoke of the military's finest. Automatic weapon fire broke out, as the fortified rows of soldiers began firing in the air. The crowd pulled back several yards in response, and the American soldiers dropped their rifles such that they were now pointed directly at the multitude of their fellow citizens before them. It was now a true standoff, and the president, still lying face down under his body guards on the wet stage, knew there was only one thing left that could help diffuse the situation. Ordering, almost pushing, the men away from him, President Drake made his way to his feet and approached the podium again. This time, there was dead silence. It seemed that even some of those soldiers, whose muzzles were now aimed at their own countrymen, were curiously glancing back to see what would happen next.

And what happened next was, well, the only thing that could happen. The president's words echoed across the White House lawn…

"I can hear you. I hear your discontent. In order to retain stability in our country and protect the doctrines on which it was founded…"

A long pause preceded his last words… "I am hereby resigning from the Presidency."

A roar exploded from the crowd, as the mass surged towards the president's platform. Drake swiftly made his exit stage left, and the soldiers did their best to maintain order, while seceding towards the White House itself. And order was maintained... mostly. The mood had changed from one of retribution to one of rejoicing.

Marcus processed the events in his brain. All of the outcomes of this day had already been considered, this not being the least likely of them... However, the gravity of the situation was perhaps best illustrated by the event yet unfolding on the TV screen in front of him. A member of the massive wave of protestors at the White House that rainy day had made their way behind the first line of defense and was now climbing on the front of the stage where the president of America had stood just moments before. It was a girl. She couldn't have been older than twenty. As she made it up onto the front of the stage, she reached into the pocket of her gray hoodie and extracted a can of red spray paint. The only thing between the girl and the presidential podium was the wall of thick security glass. And it was the glass that became her canvas as she started spraying. Seconds later her masterpiece was complete. Drips of wet red paint ran down across the glass paneling. It was on display before the nation.

It was the mark of the Ascendants.

Moments later, the camera cut to political commentary, and Marcus slid back in his couch. Surely, many of the men and women celebrating on the White House lawn that day knew what Marcus knew. They knew that Article 16 of the Founding Papers stated that the Senior Head of the General Congressional Committee was empowered to lead the nation under emergency situations. They knew that emergency situations included the death or *resignation* of a sitting American president. They also knew that the recently confirmed Head of the General Congressional Committee was Congresswoman Rachel Lorrett. And it was not lost on anyone's mind that Miss Lorrett was an Ascendant.

* * *

The resignation of an active American president was unprecedented. The laws dictating the subsequent legislative procedures, however, had been in place for ages. Though the resignation of Arnold Drake had immediately placed Congresswoman Lorrett in power, her title was not "President", and her powers hung in the balance with the rest of congress. The American founders did not wish to leave the country leaderless for a long period though, and the Executive Regulation reflected this. An emergency populist election had to be held within two weeks of the president's resignation. As one might imagine, this kick-started a frenzy of political leveraging, lobbying, and advertising, as each political party in America elected their candidates for the ballot.

Marcus was a shoe-in for the Ascendant party. His pure convictions and unmatched popularity within the inner circles of the Ascendants made any campaigning a non-factor. Instead, the game became one of prioritizing interview requests. The next week and a half would be one of constant motion. In and out of television studios, radio stations, and airports. Of course, a wholehearted endorsement from the defacto leader of the country, Miss Lorrett, as well as the highest-ranking officer in the American military, Admiral Bedford, didn't hurt. But it was still a long shot in Marcus's mind. Was the country truly poised to elect an Ascendant into the presidency? Only a few short years ago, the Ascendants were considered to be a radical sect born in the wake of an overreaching Civicist movement, rather than a legitimate political party. Times were volatile, however. And while Marcus may have had his doubts about the preparedness of his country, he knew in every inch of his being that it was exactly what America needed, at exactly the right time. If Civicism was the poison, Ascendacism was the cure.

Marcus Pratt had saved the biggest televised event for the eve prior to Election Day. The speech was set for seven o'clock, and would air on every prime time network television station in the country. Every penny had been paid for out-of-pocket, as the fruits of years of entrepreneurial successes had been put on the line for Marcus's convictions. For the three days leading up to the event, Marcus had purposely disappeared from the public eye, leading to speculation upon speculation and rumor upon rumor. The tactic had spun up a media-driven fervor that was peaking at just the right time. More Americans than ever before were tuning in to hear what the man behind the Ascendant movement had to say.

At six fifty-nine PM, Representative Marcus Pratt walked out into the press room at the capitol building in Philadelphia. As he approached the microphones, he was blinded by the barrage of flashes emitted by the media's cameras. On the other end of the airwaves, Americans sat and watched as a different type of politician appeared before them. Marcus was only thirty-three years of age. His complexion was paler than most, but not sickly looking. His choppy brown hair looked like it was cut out of a fashion magazine. His green eyes, on the other hand, burned with a conviction that no model could ever reproduce. Marcus took care of himself, which was made evident by the tailored suit and gleaming cufflinks that adorned his being. This man looked more like a celebrity than a politician... but he spoke like a revolutionary.

"For those of you who do not know me, my name is Marcus Pratt. I have been an elected member of your Congress for nearly two years. I thank you for those two years. I hope I have served the state of Florida and our country well during my term."

Marcus paused, but it was not a moment of hesitation. His eyes closed for a second and then focused directly on the video camera in front of him.

"Tomorrow's election is not only about our country. I want to make this crystal clear to each and every man, woman, and child watching or listening to me tonight. Tomorrow's election is about our world. You have seen, as plainly as me, the infection that is stifling the rights of our brothers and sisters in Europe, South America... Canada. You have seen the suppression, the redistribution of wealth, the expansion of government. And now, in recent days, you have witnessed the blatant disregard for American sovereignty. As I speak, this very moment, I am revolted to say that our evil neighbor to the north pitches her tents on American soil. Whether we like it or not, my countrymen, we *are* at war. And our previous administration has met this challenge with a diplomatic impotency that is simply unfit for the greatest nation on earth."

Again Marcus paused as he collected his next thoughts, "I am not afraid to speak of the world's plague. The disease is *Civicism*."

A hushed murmur rolled across the room. Though these words may have been uttered by millions of bartenders, mechanics, teachers, barbers, pastors, and garbage men across the nation, such rhetoric was unheard of in the political realm.

Looking around the room, Marcus smiled, "And why should this statement be so ghastly a quote?"

Again firing his glare at the camera, he continued, "Are the words more appalling than seeing the blood of your countrymen spilled on your home soil?"

"Are the words more atrocious than an American president ordering a retreat... leaving the very citizens who placed their trust in his leadership to die at the hands of our enemy?"

"My friends, I am sickened to say that, over the past month, our own leaders have committed a more horrific and detestable crime than the invasion by Civicist Canada. Their offense, however, is not one of action, but one of inaction."

The room was silent.

"I have not come to speak to you tonight at great length on the policies and positions that lie dear to my heart. I trust that my countrymen are of adequate intelligence that deciphering my political views provides no challenge. Nor have I requested your attention to make promises I'll fail to keep or lies I'll come to regret. No, America... Tonight I come to you with an offer. It is an offer that is yours to reject, or accept. An offer that enshrouds within it a beautiful thing."

"A choice."

"Tomorrow, by this time, you will have been given a chance to turn the tides of global oppression that now lap at our own shores. You will have been given a chance to undo the political monstrosities of Arnold Drake. You will have been given a chance to ignite a counter insurgency of freedom in our world."

"What will you do with your choice? What will you

say when it becomes *your* chance to speak?"

"War is an ugly thing," Marcus paused momentarily, then continued, "...but not the ugliest of things..."

"The decayed and degraded state of moral and patriotic feeling which thinks that nothing is worth war is far worse."

"I, and the Ascendant party, come before you as humble servants. Should you call on us, we will fight until our last drop of blood has touched the ground and our lungs have released their last breath... to ensure every man, first in this country, and then worldwide, will have his God-given rights unscathed. My countrymen, our *intent* is clear. Our resolve concrete."

"But every revolution begins with a choice."

Bowing his head, Marcus finished, "And the choice is yours."

In an election, forty percent can be a plurality. Fifty-one percent is a majority. But eighty-three percent is a mandate. Call it a landslide. Call it a slaughter. It was an opportunity for the Ascendants to write a few pages of their own in the history books. On Election Day, the first Ascendant State was born. Her name was America, and her leader a man they called Pratt.

The object of war is not to die for your country but to make the other bastard die for his.

- George S. Patton

<u>STORY IV</u>

THE GREAT WAR

★ CHAPTER 1 ★

Vincent Laymon never fully understood man's thirst for power. It was something that simply did not appeal to him. One thing he did understand, however, was friendship. Therefore, if a comrade had power that men were eager to strip from him, well… those men would be his enemies. And Vincent would do whatever it took to keep that from happening.

Alex Zanderberg was leading a growing number of gentlemen in the Executive Council that were becoming rather restless with the foreign policies of Canada. Vincent would hear a conversation or catch a glimpse of an unofficial memo here or there. As a member of the Presidential Advisory Staff, he had access to more personal dialogue with the President than any Executive Council member would ever experience, but was usually left out of the loop on matters discussed by the Council. Though, from what Vincent could gather, the general consensus seemed to be that Canada had become too complacent in its position in the world. Too weak. Too passive.

The mentality no doubt stemmed from the fact that Canada had been founded on a culture of imperialism. It was uncommon for a Civicist country of such strength to rest on its laurels and subsidize things like infrastructure and education. In fact, the country had never gone on such a drought of aggression as it did during the reign of Andrew Marcell. While Marcell had done much to grow the military internally since becoming the leader of Canada, his foreign policy was one of isolationism rather than expansionism. And while his policies were rather populist in nature and his reputation with the Canadian people quite good, there were an increasing number of individuals within the government who were growing restless with the strategy.

Despite the unrest, no one dared voice their opinions around the President. Even those who considered his foreign policies weak, knew better than to test what might easily be the world's most powerful man. Andrew Marcell had certainly witnessed his share of war. He was a military tactician who had seen it all and had merely decided that it was time to settle down. And a man could not stay in such a position of power for that long without burying a few problems along the way. All it took was a single word from Marcell's mouth, and anyone could disappear from the face of the earth. Anyone.

But Vincent could see a different kind of threat brewing from within the echelons of the Canadian regime. It was not the dissent of a single man, which could easily be snuffed out. Instead, the opposition was a slippery one. It showed its face in tones and glances. It made its bed in the shadows of Fort Matane's inner dwellings. Cloaked in whispers and thoughts, the opponent never quite surfaced in any tangible form. But Vincent was beginning to understand that the sentiment was all too real.

The Executive Council met almost daily to discuss everything from legislation to execution dates for notorious Canadian inmates. The meetings were closed-door, but recorded and filed. Neither the President nor any of his Advisory Staff attended these gatherings, and there was no reason to really. A single weekly meeting was in place for the Council to bring forth necessary information or decrees for the president's consideration. The decrees were broken down into categories such as diplomatic, economic, educational, and military. For the past year, almost every set of proposed military decrees included an "opportunity for expansion of natural resources and territory control". These decrees were, not surprisingly, dismissed by Andrew Marcell as overreaching or untimely, and the Executive Council would consequently go back to the drawing board.

And so the routine continued, until one week, Vincent Laymon recognized a change in the pattern. No one else noticed, but Vincent did. That week was the first week in months in which the Executive Council did not include an expansionist proposition in the set of military decrees up for consideration. By itself, this may not have tripped the attention of the President's most trusted Advisor... but there was another wrinkle in the fabric. That same week, Vincent noticed a new meeting on the Executive Council's agenda. It was a late night meeting. And, one could be sure that this meeting would not be recorded. Indeed there were no meeting minutes associated with this gathering.

Weeks passed, and Vincent's curiosity simmered until one day it boiled over. The Executive Council's meeting was at nine-thirty on Thursday night. The gathering was held in a small conference room directly below the War Room. At nine forty-five, Vincent left his living quarters and entered the main section of Fort Matane. Vincent had complete access to the facility at Matane, and thus had no trouble making his way from corridor to corridor until he arrived at the meeting room. As he turned around the corner of the hallway leading to room 304D, Vincent was surprised to see two armed guards standing watch in front of the brushed stainless steel door. Not as surprised as they were to see him, however. Everyone at Matane knew who Vincent Laymon was. Most knew him as the most influential Advisor on the President's staff - the guy who always walked and talked with Andrew Marcell himself. His impression on the guards was certainly no less striking, as their eyes widened and stances straightened at the sight of Vincent. Not a word was said, however. They knew better.

Vincent slowly approached the guards who stood at attention, saluting their superior.

"You know who I am, yes?" Vincent spoke softly. "Do you know the purpose of this meeting?"

One of the guards whispered, his lower lip quivering, "Sir, no, sir."

Vincent was abrupt, "What are your orders, soldier?"

The man responded, "To deny entry to any person..."

His voice trailing off, Vincent interjected, "Does that include the Presidential Advisory Staff? Because I can leave..."

The sarcasm was completely lost on the Canadian soldiers standing guard.

The guard swallowed, "Of course not, sir."

Smiling, Vincent brushed past the two men and placed his ear against the cold metal door. The voices inside were muffled, but he could make out a good portion of the dialogue.

The discussion seemed to be one of hypothetical leadership roles. The funny thing about it was... that the leadership roles being debated and seemingly divvied out were already occupied. One of which was by the President. The more Vincent heard, the more the true agenda of the meeting materialized. This was a coup. It might have been in its infancy, but to Vincent, there was no better time to end one.

Vincent Laymon was not born into or reared up in

politics. Dialogue and political leveraging were not his strong suits. As such, he preferred a much more... *direct* approach to resolving the ongoing situation.

Vincent turned to the gentleman at his right, "Give me your firearm, soldier."

The man stared blankly at him until Vincent reached out his open hand and spoke again, "Please don't make me repeat myself."

The soldier handed him his rifle and Vincent turned to the other man.

"Back me up."

The second soldier simply stood with his mouth wide open shaking his head. Vincent must have figured the response was good enough for him. He reached down, slowly swiping his clearance card, and quietly turned the lever handle. In one motion, Vincent shouldered the door open, lunged into the room, and raised the firearm. It took only a split second to identify his main target. It was Alex Zanderberg, sitting at the end of a long conference table closest to him. Vincent swung the rifle to his head, which had only had a chance to turn around far enough to partly see Vincent's face. A few others dived under the table, causing papers to flurry in the air, while some just froze in shock.

Vincent scanned the room momentarily and was able to identify almost the entire Executive Council. Every man in the room knew Vincent's background and was likely expecting a bloodbath. But Vincent, foremost, wanted answers. Driving the butt of the rifle into the side of Zanderberg's neck, he spoke in a controlled manner, "What is this, Alex?"

"Vincent... Glad you could join us. Sit down."

Unconvinced, Vincent pushed the rifle forward,

pressing Alex Zanderberg's face into the conference table.

Alex spoke again, his words partly stifled by the juncture of his lips and the lacquered walnut finish of the table.

"Look around, Vincent... You can't kill us all. Be reasonable."

Vincent measured the words. He realized that the phrase had little to do with the ammunition-to-person ratio and more to do with the fact that the group of men before him represented over half of the law-making government of his beloved country. Having made this consideration, Vincent slowly relieved the pressure of the gun from Alex's neck and plopped down in a chair in the front corner of the room.

Leaning back, with the muzzle of the rifle resting on his crossed legs and directed towards the table of politicians, Vincent spoke.

"Then, by all means... proceed. Don't let me spoil the party."

Obviously not interested in continuing the meeting with his cohorts, Alex replied, "This isn't what it looks like, Vincent..."

Vincent quickly snapped back, "So it's not a coup then? Oh... my apologies..."

Vincent's head tilted slightly to the side and his eyes narrowed, as they focused on Alex.

"I must have been thrown off by the secret, guarded, nighttime meeting that I wasn't invited to."

Alex turned his chair and faced Vincent, as many of the others in the room were only now beginning to collect themselves. Most of them were back sitting in their seats.

Alex quietly said, "We need to have a serious talk, Vincent."

"Alex, I couldn't agree more," Vincent replied.

Alex continued, "Marcell can't keep this up. These populist policies are not what put Canada on the map. Maybe you haven't been around here long enough to see that, but I assure you, Vincent, every other man in this room has."

Vincent, controlling his emotions, slowly surveyed the sample of men in the room. By his quick count, the group easily made up over half of the Executive Council. Alex was right in that, despite his position, Vincent was fairly new to the political realm. He was not such an amateur, however, that he didn't realize the power of what a fifty-one percent majority of the Council could mean. So, instead of killing every last human being in the room that the high-capacity magazine hanging out of his rifle would allow… he listened.

"Canada's resources are limited, and at the pace that Andrew is spending them, we cannot keep this up forever. And besides, you know as well as I that our neighbors to the south are in the same position. I only pray that they have more patience with our policies than we do with theirs. Vincent… I have tried the normal channels of change. Every week, my Council works on a decree to present to Marcell. Every week our decree is rejected. Canada needs a military victory." He paused. "… And if you don't help us, we'll have to make it happen the hard way."

Vincent Laymon, now staring down at the floor, slowly lifted his head and looked at Alex.

"Do you really pray?"

"What???" Alex was taken off-guard.

"Just now, you said that you *pray* that America has more patience with our policies than we do with theirs. Did you mean that? Do you pray?"

Clearly thrown off, Alex replied, "Vincent, I don't understand. What does that have to do with…"

Vincent lunged forward, grasped Alex's long blond hair, and pulled his head back over the headrest of the office chair…

"DO YOU PRAY?!?"

Alex whimpered, "No… I don't pray…"

Releasing his head, Vincent glared at the room. A flare of hatred lit his eyes, but the tone of his words was as soft as silk.

"You had all better pray. Pray that, if I make this thing happen, if I give you your… *victory*… Your additional resources… That you will end these meetings forever. You will obey your President. You will follow the rule of law."

Vincent turned his gaze upon Alex.

"Because if you don't… If so much as a very thought of yours secedes from your Mother Country in any way… I will personally kill every single last one of you. And if you know me at all, you have every reason to believe that what I am telling you is the truth."

It wasn't exactly diplomacy, but not a man in that conference room took for granted the way things had gone that night.

It was not an easy decision for Vincent, but if he could have thought of a better way to protect the sovereignty and power of President Marcell, he would have pursued it. The truth was that Andrew Marcell had become nothing less than a close friend, and if a war was the only way for Vincent to help him retain his authority, a war he would craft.

Two days went by before Vincent was ready to have the conversation that was needed with Andrew Marcell. But while he knew that the only feasible way forward was to appease the Executive Council, Vincent was going to make sure it was done *his* way.

Every Sunday morning that the president was at Fort Matane, Vincent and Marcell would have breakfast together in the president's quarters. This Sunday was no exception. It was a beautiful arrangement. Spring had sprung at Fort Matane, and sitting at the small round table on the president's balcony was an amazing way to soak it all in. Dark red buds had formed on the tips of the tree branches below, and the first of the year's flowers, mostly violet and yellow, were beginning to coat the edge of the forest surrounding the barracks.

The president was running a few minutes late, but Vincent, sipping his latte and inhaling the fresh mountain air, didn't notice at all. As Andrew emerged from the tinted glass doors separating the balcony from the building, Vincent stood to his feet and approached him. The morning sunlight lit up the president's face, revealing every line and fine wrinkle that had developed on the old man. Even though, with his cane, the president was still more than mobile enough to get around, Vincent grasped his arm and helped him into his chair.

"What a beautiful morning, eh, Vincent?"

"It is, sir." Vincent sat back down and leaned backwards, staring up at blue sky above.

As Andrew poured coffee into his mug, he spoke, "I miss these mornings, Vincent. Winter can be so depressing."

Vincent smiled, "Andrew... I would like to discuss a matter of business with you, if I could."

"Of course, Vincent... any time," he replied.

"You know, Andrew... I could never lie to you. You know that, right?"

"Yes, Vincent. I know that. What is wrong?"

"It's the Council."

"What about the Council?"

Vincent replied, "They've grown restless."

Marcell bellowed out a laugh interrupting the dialogue...

"Of course they have!"

Vincent let out a smirk and took another sip of his latte.

"Andrew, it may be time to appease these guys."

The president's laugh had subsided and he now stared inquisitively at his confidante.

Vincent continued, "And maybe it's not just about the Council. Or even resources. Maybe it's really bigger than that."

"What are you saying, Vincent?" Marcell softly replied.

Vincent sat forward and leaned across the table, looking intently at his friend, "I guess what I am saying is that Canada needs something to rally herself behind again. We need our people to once again pull together for a common cause. We need..."

Marcell interrupted, "A war..."

The words were clearly painful for the old man to produce, and Vincent was glad that he wasn't the one who had to speak them. A minute or two went by, as both men leaned back and soaked in the gravity of the ongoing discussion. Such matters, though perhaps so by the Council, were not taken lightly by Andrew and Vincent.

After some time had passed, Marcell spoke, "Vincent, first off, I want to thank you for having this conversation with me. One of the reasons that you have been such a great friend is your honesty. I know, without a doubt, that you offer your council while keeping my own interests at the front of your mind. And for that I thank you."

Vincent prepared himself for the "but".

"And there is no 'but'," the president continued.

Vincent smiled as he wondered at the thought of how the old man had read his mind.

"In fact, I agree with you. *And* with the Council. I have been thinking deeply about this day in private, Vincent. Until now, I admit that I have not had the courage to discuss such things. I have always shaken off the advice of the Council when it came to the subject of "expansion". For I know what horrors the word can contain, and I often wonder if men like Alex can even comprehend them."

The president hesitated for a just a moment before continuing, "But what I needed was for it to come from you, Vincent. And now I feel that I am seeing things more clearly. What we need *is* a rallying cry. This American regime cannot be allowed to inhibit our control of the continent. The resources, well... The resources are secondary to me. The land... also secondary."

"I can remember when we acted as a country. When our people had a reverential fear of their government, and when their government provided for them so that they never had to fear for their wellbeing. I do want that again. And if it means that we have to face the capitalist pigs once again on the battlefield, then so be it."

Vincent listened intently to what seemed to be a fuse that he had just taken part in lighting. A fuse that had been hidden behind the hazy old eyes of the president for some time. As Vincent immersed himself in the words of his mentor, he became amazed at how this tiny seed of an idea had taken root in Andrew Marcell's mind. And as the president's inspiration reached a full bloom before him, Vincent now realized that its growth was fueled not by the mere opinion of a friend or even the suggestion of an advisor, but rather by a deep-seated ideology that was only now being unearthed after years of cerebral entombment. The idea of war had done much more than taken hold. Vincent may have started the engine, but Marcell was now, without a doubt, driving the car.

"We must meet with Council at once." The president's quick directive broke the moment of reflection and, with a nod and a final swig of his morning latte, Vincent was on his feet and fully aligned. This was not a time to ask questions, but rather a time to answer them.

★ CHAPTER 2 ★

It was almost spring. But March had yet to take on the form of a lamb. While the military strike on Alaskan soil had caused a major bump in respect for Andrew Marcell among his political comrades and most Canadian officers, public opinion throughout the country was divided. As a result, President Marcell began a string of miniature "campaigns" across the countryside, to drive support for what was now being dubbed "Marcell's War" among his political adversaries.

It was these campaigns that ended up bringing Vincent Laymon into the public spotlight for the very first time in his life. The camera shots of Vincent standing at the right hand of the President initially sparked questions, such as, "Who is this guy?", which soon burst into a media frenzy about the young sidekick whispering in the ear of the world's most powerful leader. Of course, the Canadian government had a heavy hand in the media, and the whirlwind of news stories was allowed to persist only because Andrew Marcell believed that it was time for Vincent to step out of the shadows of the administration. And step out of the shadows he did.

Images depicting President Marcell were quite a routine matter throughout Canada. But as the winter maintained its firm grip on the season, the bust of another personage found itself strewn throughout the Canadian cityscapes and countryside. It was a fresh face, usually depicted with a cold, blank stare, made manifest through eyes of frigid gray. It was an image of originality, power, passion, and even invincibility. Soon, the bust of Vincent Laymon could be seen on the walls of buildings, billboards, bumper stickers, and even found itself expressed through graffiti in many of the shoddier urban streets. Those who supported the confrontation with America latched onto the image of Vincent Laymon as their war banner, and within months he had, through no endeavor of his own, become inseparably coupled to the conflict, and to the recently hawkish stances of the Marcell administration.

While the dramatic increase in popularity and public visibility was mostly uncomfortable, if not plain unnatural, to the discreet persona of Vincent, Andrew Marcell was completely satisfied with Vincent's sudden leap into the arms of fame. For it was Andrew who had been nurturing and mentoring this man for a very distinct purpose. The fact of the matter was, that no other human being on the planet had as much of the president's respect or held as much of his trust as Vincent. It was Marcell's conviction that only Vincent Laymon could one day fill his shoes... and with a bit more tutelage in the veiled arts of politics, media manipulation, and image management, he might just be there.

But on one frigid morning, in the waning days of winter, everything was launched into fast forward, in a way that no one could have forecast.

Most would have considered it just another part of the public relations campaigns that came with convincing a populous that war can in fact be beneficial. Andrew and Vincent were to travel to Fort Nestor, a Canadian military stronghold near Saskatoon. The flight was a short one, which was quite fortunate for Vincent, as he was able to get an extra hour of sleep over his usual schedule before waking up at six o'clock in the morning for the trip. Ever since the invasion of Alaska, Vincent's life had accelerated to keep pace with the overwhelming task of helping Andrew

Marcell stay ahead of the public relations curve. Early morning departures on one of Marcell's private jets had become habitual, as Vincent's new journeys took him crisscrossing the Canadian map.

This excursion seemed no different at first. Vincent met the president next to the air strip at Fort Matane. The flight departed at seven-thirty in the morning and touched down in Saskatoon by eight. A convoy of armored vans rushed the two to Fort Nestor. Roads, as always, were shut down for the presidential visit, and bustling, traffic-ridden streets were vacated for the drive from the airport to the military base. The base itself was about fifty kilometers outside of Saskatoon, on a vast plateau amid very mountainous terrain. This day, Vincent travelled in a van with the president, in spite of the typical procedures which would never have the two most prominent figures in politics together in the same vehicle. The day was a beautiful one. Sunlight streamed through the frost-speckled windshield of the van, as Vincent and Andrew sat together in the rear seat. Vincent laid his head back on the seat, looking upwards and resting his eyes, as Marcell sifted through a handful of papers, reading the days agenda under his breath.

"This won't be bad. We get to check out those new tanks today... You know the ones that are supposed to climb walls or something..." Andrew glanced over at Vincent, smiling, but Vincent was on the verge of dosing off. A little nudge got his attention.

"I believe they're capable of a sixty degree ascent... not sure about a wall..." Vincent replied, as a smirk appeared on his face. The relationship between the two men had grown even stronger over the past few months, and, despite the enormous age gap, their images had somehow fused together into one.

The van screeched to a halt on the blacktop of Fort Nestor's weapons test facility. The president was quickly let out first by one of the members of the security detail accompanying the leader on the outing. Vincent followed. As Vincent stepped out of the van, his eyes were hit with the direct rays of the morning sun which were now peaking over a row of perfectly aligned assault tanks, no doubt arranged in honor of their executive visit. All in all, it was an amazing sight, and as Vincent slowly turned around, he marveled at the cornucopia of weaponry on display – anti-aircraft weaponry, tanks, what appeared to be some sort of large communications equipment laden with satellite dishes... but, in that moment, Vincent Laymon's wondrous trance was snapped by what sounded like an enormous bumble bee zinging past his ear. A moment later, a startling BOOM clapped across the asphalt and sent him instinctively to his knees. Vincent quickly spun around to see three of the guards from their security detail lying over the president in a protective posture. Soldiers were blaring orders, but Vincent was more focused on something else - a pool of crimson red slowly creeping from underneath the huddled men. Vincent furiously shoved the men away, who in turn were now trying to protect him as well. Vincent won the scuffle however, reaching the president's side. He was alive, but what Vincent only now perceived to be a gunshot had ripped through the president's upper right torso. The wound was so bad that Vincent thought he could see pavement through the hole. Vincent wept and screamed for medical assistance while he gently held up the president's head. Andrew Marcell's eyes were still open as he had somehow managed to retain consciousness through the event. He calmly peered into Vincent's tear-filled eyes as the color slowly receded from his face.

"It's OK, son." The president let out a weak cough, spattering blood on the white shirt under Vincent's pressed black suit. He then reached up as if to try and clean the specks of blood from the garment, but Vincent grasped his hand and slowly shook his head, still unable to speak. Andrew spoke again. They would be his last words. "Vincent. I love you... You are like a son to me..." He then paused and uttered a final phrase...

"Finish this."

As Andrew Marcell's eyes rolled back, Vincent collapsed on his chest. The amount of time that passed just after these events could have been seconds or minutes. To Vincent, this would remain unclear. But what happened next would be imprinted on the minds of those security guards and military personnel at Fort Nestor forever. Surrounded by the flurry of sirens and loudspeakers blaring and soldiers rushing around, Vincent stood to his feet – a young, handsome man in a black suit, covered in the blood of his best friend. His eyes had gone... blank. Devoid of feeling. He gazed off into the wooded hills surrounding the plateau on which the military base was located. He stared... as if staring right into the eyes of the perpetrator of these actions. The first words from his mouth were a request – a request to speak with the person in charge of security at Fort Nestor. The man happened to be one of the profoundly medaled officers who had lined up in preparation to greet Andrew and Vincent. The man stepped forward and identified himself as head of security. His second sentence began by assuring Vincent that everything was now under control and the... But before the sentence was finished, Vincent Laymon had removed the officer's side arm and emptied the first two rounds from it into the soldier's head. He then released the pistol, letting it fall to the ground. Zero emotion.

Looking at the other officers he again spoke, "Bury your president… and take me to Fort Matane."

Unknown to even the witnesses of these events on the tarmac of Fort Nestor that day, seismic shifts in the political landscape had taken place. To the uninformed, it appeared that a suited man, covered in blood, watched a friend die and executed an officer. What was not clear to the men at Fort Nestor was that, based upon Andrew Marcell's signed and sealed orders securely filed away at Fort Matane, this suited man was now the president of Canada.

★ CHAPTER 3 ★

It was an extreme mission to say the least. Codenamed "Snakehead" (likely due to the imagery of "cutting off the head of the snake"), the operation was largely based on the historical credence given to the effectiveness of risking only a handful of lives and bullets to eliminate the enemy's top leadership. While this efficient act of war was what one could expect from the calculating mind of Marcus Pratt, the resourcefulness of the mission was no comfort for the ones whose lives fell into that elite "handful". In this case, one of them was one of America's greatest man-hunters, Francis Laymon. No one outside of the office of the president and the top military personnel knew the details. Penetrating the borders of Canada would only be a small part of the task. But Frank was a perfect candidate for the operation. One of America's most prolific marksmen, and fresh from his brush with disaster in the Alaskan wilderness only months ago, Frank Laymon was more than ready.

He would be traveling only with his spotter, Jeremy, and another sniper, Anton, who was of equal rank and skill. They had all run missions together before, and, as the most capable group in America's top sniper squad, very little could intimidate the men.

The infiltration of the Canadian border was no small task. What delicate relationship had previously existed along the perimeter of the country throughout the fledgling years of the Canal Project had since eroded into mutual violence and hatred. Both nations had pulled back miles from the actual border and established heavily-fortified lines of defense, leaving the region in between a vast chasm of incongruity. It was a shell of a project that was once a symbol of hope for the future, but had decayed, over time, into a symbol of the irreconcilable differences between two diametrically opposed societies.

As Frank and his team now belly-crawled through the mud which filled the base of the unfinished canal, his gaze trailed across the horizon. It was the middle of the night, but a full moon cast its light across the landscape, illuminating a scattering of rusted and disheveled machinery that had years ago been the life of the Canal Project. Now rust, mud, and debris separated two lines of barbed wire and lookout towers. The team was crossing into Canada only miles from the work site that Frank and his brother had once occupied. Frank missed Vincent and had deeply regretted falling out of touch with him and his mother since coming to America. The communication level between the two nations had fallen through the floor since the invasion of Alaska, and those who had friends or family on the other side could only hope and pray for their wellbeing.

The team reached the de facto Canadian line at four o'clock in the morning... well on pace for mission success. Heavy reconnaissance had ensured that the breach point was at the weakest link in the enemy's line of defense, and after some minor wire cutting and one freshly shattered Canadian vertebrae later, they were through.

The next several days involved a totally different style of travel. The southernmost regions of the Saskatchewan province were densely wooded and sparsely populated, both of which proved to be quite beneficial to the small strike force. Normally under such conditions, the team could masquerade as hunters, except of course, in Canada, hunting was illegal... In fact, so were guns. So Frank, Jeremy, and Anton would have to be much more discrete about their movements.

For the first three days, it rained. Poured actually. Heavy booms of thunder ripped through the air and flashes of lightning provided little glimmers of life in an otherwise dismal landscape. The rain turned to sleet at night, numbing the faces of the travelers with needles of ice. But on the third night, the clouds cleared. The X44 sniper squad was now only three kilometers from the target location. The mission orders put Andrew Marcell, the Canadian president, at Fort Nestor the next morning for a high profile weapons exhibition showcased by a group of top Canadian commanders. Marcell was Target One... the package. Anton would be the one making the shot. Target Two was an unnamed person... a close advisor and confidante of the president who was to be the only other government official traveling in his convoy that day.

The final trek of the soldiers' journey was certainly the most unpredictable. It was the type of delicate dance to which only the most elite American snipers knew the steps. The team woke up from their four hour sleep shifts and set out through the rolling hills directly surrounding Fort Nestor. Ghillie suits decorated their backs as the three warriors began their snail-paced belly-crawl through the high, blowing grass. The rally point was a small, flat hillside overlooking the immense, stretching plateau on which the tarmac of Fort Nestor's runway lay. The bright sun now blazed, making the countryside alive with the colors of spring. The last seventy-five meters took nearly all morning, but by nine o'clock, the three were nestled in the saw grass at their destination and all but invisible... even to the multitude of eyes which now peered through telescoping lenses, scanning the hills surrounding the base. Eighteen security towers were sprinkled throughout the property, serving as the Canadian's own sniper nests for the special event. The closest was a mere one-hundred and fifty meters from the men's current location, but by now those guards were likely peering hundreds of meters behind the team's current position.

Frank could taste the grit of the damp Canadian soil between his lips. The smell of wet grass permeated his nose as his eye followed an earthworm's journey through the basin of the weedy jungle in which he now dwelt. Frank was not lying on the ground... he *was* the ground. Having not even glanced at each other in hours, the soldiers kept their gazes on the tarmac ahead, resting their faith on the validity of the intel that more than one fellow American had perished to collect. Thankfully, the thick fog had lifted during their five hour creep, which now gave way to a crystal clear view of the runway and an orderly line of tanks that rested nearly eight hundred meters ahead.

After another hour, as if on cue, a black snake of armored vans slithered through the security gates and screeched to a halt, as officers scattered into position like ants from a disturbed nest. Frank snuggled his right cheek against the butt of his rifle and peered downrange through the high-powered scope, setting up for Target Two - the president's escort. Anton would be targeting Canada's Number One. Despite having been in many seemingly similar situations throughout his service, the gravity of this particular mission was not lost on Frank, and he imagined the same held true for his fellow countrymen lying beside him.

The sting of sweat in Frank's eyes had no effect on his gaze, which was now affixed on the van which had pulled forward, in front of a line of Canadian officers. As the door of the vehicle cracked open, Frank's crosshairs hovered over the tarmac just a meter from the vehicle. As tremendous as the American intel had been to enable this moment, there was no way to know who would step out first. As a figure emerged from the opened door, Frank could make out the familiar bust of President Andrew Marcell.

As naturally as breathing, Jeremy's whisper was spoken over Frank's right shoulder, "Eight hundred meters. Up two clicks, left four for windage..." followed by Anton's cool response, "Engaging Target One..."

The slam of the .308 rifle's report in Frank's ear was eclipsed by his attention to the second figure which had since emerged from the car. As Frank Laymon's eyes strained to focus on Target Two, time stopped. It couldn't be...

Going against every teaching that had been pounded into his head in sniper school, Frank raised his head and again intensely peered through the scope of his heavy-barreled rifle...

Vincent!

Paralyzed by fear, Frank released himself, flattening to the ground face down. To think that a mere two and a half pounds of pressure exerted by his right index finger would have been enough to end the life of his only brother was a dizzying thought that sent Frank's mind spinning out of control. The knot in his stomach tightened and forced him to momentarily black out. Even the sound of his spotter's voice was at first inaudible to him...

"Frank!" Jeremy's hand grasped Francis Laymon's right shoulder. Another jostle and Frank began to come around. The darkness faded to draw a picture outlining Jeremy's frame.

"You abandoned the objective... Frank... You had

him… What is going on with you, man??"

Jeremy's voice was distressed, but the words of his fellow X44 sniper, Anton, were again calm and controlled as could be…

"Don't worry. I've got him. Initiating on Target Two…"

As soon as the phrase was uttered, Frank lunged into Anton, planting his elbow directly behind his fellow soldier's right ear. The blow was sufficient to knock the rifle out of the sniper's hand, but this was the last thing that Frank would remember before waking up to see the face of none other than his Commander In Chief… President Marcus Pratt.

★ CHAPTER 4 ★

Marcus had long despised the idea of *a traitor*. It was against everything that America stood for – Honesty, Integrity, and Patriotism. In fact, Marcus felt that a man's devotion and allegiance to a cause was sometimes more important than the cause itself. But when the cause was Ascendacism, and its underlying foundation freedom, the act of treason became intensely magnified in the mind of Marcus Pratt.

For hours prior to the transfer of Francis Laymon to the capital, Marcus fixated on the situation. How could this man, who was clearly a Civicist sympathizer and potentially a downright spy... How could he obtain such a high profile position within the American military? What if it had been him on the end of this man's rifle? Could this have been part of a sinister Canadian plot all along? So many questions and so few answers. Within minutes of the news of President Andrew Marcell's successful assassination, the ensuing jubilation had been cut short by reports of the disturbing twist. Every file on Francis R. Laymon had been pulled and parsed. Every detail of his known history picked apart word by word. The problem, which quickly became apparent to Marcus's staff, was that the record of the life of Francis Laymon was effectively a black hole prior to the initiation of his immigration paperwork from none other than... Canada.

It wasn't iron clad, air tight proof of espionage and conspiracy... In fact, many Canadians had immigrated to America during that time frame. But the odds were quickly stacking up in the mind of Marcus Pratt. For not all Canadian immigrants joined the ranks of America's most secretive and elite military wings and attempted to compromise a mission designed to assassinate a figurehead like President Andrew Marcell.

Before the chained, hooded, and unconscious Francis Laymon was whisked through the capital gates under the cover of darkness that night, Marcus had already ordered a team of top counter-intelligence officers to his side. Of course, as Marcus well knew, and as the soon-to-be-quite-conscious Mr. Laymon was about to find out, "counter-intelligence" was really just a fancy word for torture.

Frank's eyes cracked open to see the haze of a bright light shining down on him and three figures seated across an empty, stainless steel table. A cursory scan of the room registered images of concrete walls painted in a light gray color and a white man-door. No windows.

"Do you know who I am?" ... The image of the middle figure coalesced, and now Frank realized it was his Commander In Chief who spoke.

"Sir, yes, sir!" Frank barked out the words methodically, as his instinctive reflexes brought him to his feet. But the chains linking his ankles to two eye bolts embedded in the concrete floor would have it differently. The cuffs dug into Frank's shins, sending pain shooting through his body, as he collapsed on the cement floor.

"Help him up," Marcus ordered, as one of the other men reached beneath Francis Laymon's arms from behind and boosted him back into his chair.

"I'll be brief..." The words of Marcus were those of controlled disgust...

"You need to tell me the truth. I need to know why you compromised the mission. And I need to know right now."

By this time, Frank had no remaining delusions

regarding his ultimate fate. The look on the president's face and the inflection of his voice told the story. It was a tale that would not have a happy ending.

The only door in the small room suddenly cracked open, establishing a radiant strip of light across the dim holding cell. The strip was then interrupted by the silhouette of a head.

"Mr. President... A word, please."

Marcus Pratt turned around and stormed to the door. Though the words exchanged were inaudible to Francis Laymon, the urgency of the conversation was quite clear. Soon the door closed, eclipsing the bright rays its cracked position had provided, and Marcus returned to the table, this time with a manila folder. Marcus sat down calmly and carefully placed the folder before him... the entire time staring into the eyes of Francis Laymon. Frank's gaze crept down to the folder in front of the president. He strained his eyes to make out the text printed on a small white label on the front of the folder...

"Vincent F. Laymon"

Francis Laymon was paralyzed. Though he tried with every bit of his being to act unaffected by the words he read, Frank couldn't help but feel the scrutinizing glare of Marcus Pratt penetrating his every thought.

"Vincent F. Laymon..." Marcus spun the folder around and slid it across the table to his captive. Frank turned his head to the side as if horrified by what might be between the two pieces of manila card-stock now before him.

Marcus continued, "...Son of Terrance and Anna Laymon. Interesting."

A kind of evil sarcasm filled his voice, "*Brother*... of one Francis R. Laymon."

Marcus now stood to his feet, his fiery eyes still focused on Frank.

"Apparently, this brother... Francis... Immigrated to America a while back.

A lighthearted smile fell upon the face of Marcus, "What a coincidence."

He glanced at the officer seated at his right side and pointed at Francis... "His name is Francis Laymon too. And this Frank Laymon here also immigrated to America a while back..."

Marcus snapped his head back and locked eyes with Francis Laymon, "IN FACT," Marcus screamed, grasping the edge of the metal table and flipping it into the adjacent wall... "He has the same immigration case number!"

Even his fellow officers looked stunned by the outburst. Frank's stare remained fixated on the wall to his left. He knew in his heart that, indeed, the ending would in no way be happy. Today, "happily ever after" would have to come second to protecting his own blood and kin.

Marcus, still glaring at Frank, now spoke to his officers, "Get your tools. Leave the cameras rolling. Do what I pay you for." As he walked out of the room, the president paused and looked back... "I want to know everything there is to know about this *Vincent Laymon*. The only way you leave this room is with that information or covered in this man's blood. I hope I've made myself clear." And with that, the door closed and there were only three.

★ CHAPTER 5 ★

In the bustling Canadian city of Winnipeg, one of the lesser-lively areas was known as "Tannerdale"... And in "Tannerdale", one of the lesser-traveled streets was Stallworth Street. And on the very end of Stallworth Street was a line of boarded up, seemingly deserted storehouses. The building on the very end of these abandoned storehouses was a dilapidated structure without a street number. Rusty steel walls, which barely provided evidence of a former coating of battleship gray paint, were garnished with a variety of both green and maroon-colored shutters, while empty wooden pallets rested against the exterior walls. But within this unnumbered and rather unsuspecting accommodation there existed a vast network of high-speed communication cables. On one end of the cables there were state-of-the-art satellite dishes, utilizing technology that ninety-nine percent of the modern world could not even grasp. On the other end of the cables were incredibly advanced servers with monitors streaming an endless flow of information, only an incomprehensibly miniscule fraction of which had any relevance to the men and women observing them from within.

One of these Canadian faithful was Corporal Olivia Saunders. And on an unsuspecting Wednesday evening, she would choke on her chicken and rice soup as the live intercepted video feed of the brutal torture of an unknown man played on her number four monitor. It was a channel that had been mostly blank for months, a trait fairly typical of those feeds which were established to take advantage of inadvertently unprotected communications links utilized by the American government. Maybe once a week... maybe...

you would catch a fifteen minute video conference between two or more military personnel. And because no audio accompanied the video, a team of lip-readers and a small group of individuals selected from the national Canadian television networks produced captions for the video feeds.

But this particular video did not require captions - at least not to capture the attention of Private Saunders's superior officers. When the live feed reached the lip-readers, they sat stunned and wide-eyed, with nothing to report, as the only lips to read were almost unrecognizably situated on what looked like the remnants of a man's face. But he was not dead. And his inquisitors, wearing standard American military attire, were still shouting at him, with their backs to the camera. This continued for several minutes, with an occasional strike of a baton across a knee cap or a cheekbone... Until one of the men decided to walk around behind the seated prisoner to whisper in his ear. The interpreters leaned forward and strained their eyes to make out every inference of the soldier's mouth. It was broken, but at least two of the words were clear as day, and they were repeatedly spoken... "Vincent" and "Laymon".

Immediately the video was escalated, and it was Corporal Saunders who was tasked with debriefing the new president and collecting any more information if at all possible. Because of the sensitive nature of the content, only hard copies of the video would be permitted – no more network-based transmissions. And due to the perceived threat to national security, the urgency of Saunders's mission was unprecedented.

The corporal was on a private jet to Fort Matane within an hour, and within fifteen minutes of touchdown was being ushered onto the premises for an impromptu meeting.

From Vincent Laymon's perspective the corporal's visit amounted to an unusual, last-minute schedule change, which was only accepted due to a convincing conversation with the National Director of Security, Jonathan Nestor. Since Andrew Marcell's assassination two days ago, Vincent had been inundated with a flurry of gatherings within the walls of Fort Matane, but his curiosity was certainly piqued by what could possibly trump the funeral arrangements for Andrew Marcell and the swearing in of several newly-elected members of the Executive Council under an emergency order.

As Vincent entered the conference room, he was greeted by a solemn-looking Jonathan Nestor… and that may have been an understatement. The man's face appeared as if he had just seen a ghost. It was enough to make Vincent more than a little uneasy. The only other person in the room was a young female corporal who didn't look much better.

"Mr. President…"

Vincent had not yet gotten used to the words.

"This is Corporal Olivia Saunders."

Vincent responded with a slight nod towards the young woman.

"We have something I think you need to see."

Jonathan swallowed, "You may want to sit down for this, sir."

Vincent shot back, "I'll stand. Please get on with it," now getting even more antsy over the situation at hand.

The Director of Security looked at Corporal Saunders as she responded by pointing a remote control at a nearby television, resting on a black metal stand near the conference table.

Immediately the screen was filled with horrors. It

was instantaneously clear that the video was of a man's violent interrogation. Two soldiers, dressed in American military uniforms, were taking turns shouting at a figure whose face remained concealed partly because of the camera angle and partly due to the disfigurement which had taken place during the questioning. There was no audio.

As the feed continued to play, an odd familiarity or nostalgia struck Vincent. It was enough to make him momentarily close his eyes and turn his head slightly as if suddenly stricken with a migraine. When he opened his eyes again, Vincent slowly moved towards the monitor, now squinting inquisitively with his head slightly cocked. Then it happened. The man in the video looked right at the screen, as if peering into Vincent's eyes... or soul. It felt like a sledgehammer to the throat.

"No..."

Vincent reached the monitor, now almost pressing his face to the screen... "NOOOO!" Frank's face became as familiar as it had ever been.

It was shell-shock. Over the next hour, Vincent Laymon would not remember many of his actions. He would hear only silence as he tore the speaker phones from the conference table and hurled them against the wall. He would feel nothing as he grasped the edge of that same table and flipped it over onto the floor. His eyes could see only the curtains of pure white rage that had been pulled over them as he sent his clenched fist flying through the front of the television. And now, as he fell to his knees and wept with his hands covering his face, glimpses of childhood memories flickered in his subconscious as the unbearable pressure of compounded grief weighed on his chest.

Vincent Laymon was alone now, as a mixture of common decency and plain fear had led to the timely departure of Jonathan Nestor and the corporal. Positioned on all fours and rocking forward and back, the commander of Canada stared at the floor. As his vision began to once again register his surroundings, Vincent's eyes focused in on the mauve floral pattern on the plush carpet beneath him. A tear rolled off his cheek, striking one of the roses dead center. There were no words. Not yet.

As the memories of his childhood slowly faded, they gave way to images which seared Vincent's brain like a demented slide show. The shredded face of his brother, Francis. The men who were in that room with him. The American flag. The mark of Ascendacism. The corpse of his best friend and mentor, Andrew Marcell. The President of America... Marcus Pratt. And that is where the slide show ended... with that image of Marcus Pratt burning a silhouette of hatred into Vincent Laymon's consciousness.

Yes, the evil conducted by his brother's interrogators was unforgivable. But events such as this did not manifest themselves without a direct order from above. And, for something like this, it would have been an *executive* order... as executive as it gets. But the logic didn't even matter right now. All that mattered was that something... perhaps fate itself... caused the mental slide show to stop on the unmistakable trademark of the Ascendant movement – the symbol of everything that America stood for – greed, power, inequity. That symbol was the bust of a man they call *Pratt*.

Now, it was personal. Did every fiber of Vincent Laymon's soul want to tear down the very construct of free markets, the societal chaos masked as "liberty", and the individual injustices which hid behind the guise of "freedom"? Yes. Unequivocally yes. But how much more would Vincent Laymon give to have only five minutes in a room with President Marcus Pratt. The man who ordered the assassination of his only friend and now the torture of his only sibling. Indeed, politics had given way to a personal vendetta, and reason to reaction.

No one in America, or even Canada for that matter, could have expected what would happen next. In short, a war that had begun as a mere act of aggression with the added benefit of coalescing a country through resource gains, not to mention good old national pride, was about to turn into something quite different. No longer did these trivial matters weigh on the tactical decisions that lay ahead. Only two days after witnessing firsthand the assassination of his best friend and mentor, Vincent Laymon needed no other incentive to unleash his wrath on the American populace. But a man named Marcus Pratt had just given him another one.

It was clear that Vincent would need the support of virtually every willing Civicist nation on the planet. The bulk of reinforcements would come from France, Canada's closest ally, and from there, pressure would be placed on many of the smaller nations to provide what political, financial, and military support they could sacrifice for the greater good. Of course, the communications chatter associated with the nucleation of the most massive and powerful military presence ever assembled would set off just about every alarm in the American intelligence gathering community, but, Vincent reasoned, by then it would be too late. America, though powerful, was now on a veritable desert island of political ideology. There was no nation to come to its rescue.

The offensive would not come without a cost of course, but, to Vincent Laymon, the end of Acendacism and its poster child was as inevitable as tomorrow's sunrise.

★ CHAPTER 6 ★

Marcus Pratt had always been rather proficient in mathematics. He was notorious among his cohorts for expressing his belief that "everything is numbers" - as he seemed to always remind them. And now, wading through a reservoir of steaming blood, it was math that plagued his mind.

"Six pints of this life fluid in every one of our boys... three quarts of blood." General Louis Riccard just listened, as the chief of his country stood before him. The eyes of Marcus burned with passion – green embers amidst an ocean of white. His dark hair ducked out from under the red beret on his head and fluttered in the cold November breeze. As Marcus stood and stared down into the deep tomb that was the Border Canal, his body formed the silhouette of a great statue.

A buzz resonated through Marcus's spine. The reverberations shot into his brain and swelled up behind his eyes. He fell to one knee, his right hand clutching his left forearm with all of his might – a failed attempt to stop the shaking. Flashes of the putrid scenes flickered before his eyes and the air was sucked from his lungs.

"How many men did we send in here today, Lou?" As he spoke, wisps of steam slipped from his mouth.

"Eleven thousand, four hundred and thirty one," the general replied solemnly.

Marcus rose to his feet and lightly swayed the toe of his left boot through the swamp of crimson liquid. Bursts of gunfire and flurries of light on the horizon acted as a grave reminder that the carnage was far from over. It was nearly midnight, but because of a full moon and a light dusting of snow on the ground, the landscape was lit up as if it were only dusk. The illumination was such that lines of aid officers could be seen for hundreds of yards carrying away corpses on stretchers. At thirty four years old, Marcus was the youngest man to ever lead the nation of America, but as the general studied his grave countenance, he noticed the Commander in Chief now looked much older.

"And we only lost what..." the words so lightly formed by his lips.

"Nine hundred and fifty yards, sir."

Marcus admired the general's attention to detail, and, for that slightest moment, a smile of approval may have crept across his lips, were it not for the smell of death around him, quickly thwarting the instance of appreciation.

"Was it worth it, general?" Marcus was not asking with any contempt or cynical doubt... He was truly interested in the general's assessment.

"Sir..."

"Call me Marcus, for God's sake, Lou... This morning I was Sir. Right now... Right now, I'm not sure what..."

The General broke the thought... "Today, American soldiers held a chunk of land that will be critical to the defense of our territory from the hands of the enemy." The general paused, noticing the blank stare covering the president's face. "Wars these days are not easily won, Marcus."

"How did it ever come to this?" Marcus muttered exhaustively.

The question was more rhetorical than anything, but the general graced the president with an answer nonetheless... "No one could have predicted this offensive, Marcus. And the only way to prevent GCO involvement is to play their game. This land war is a mess, but I'm not convinced that there is another way right now with even a shred of hope."

Marcus contemplated the words and replied, "At some point…" He paused, staring into the sky above, while a gentle spattering of snow flurries began touching his face and melting on contact. "At some point, the nuclear option becomes viable."

The general immediately squared his stance towards his Commander in Chief and sharpened his attention.

"I mean, a nuclear war with the GCO is unthinkable, I know… Perhaps unwinnable." Marcus continued, "But it's a war I can manage, General." He grasped the general's right arm and spoke softly, with a level of sincerity which had not yet been exposed during their conversation. "I *don't* know if I can manage sending another hundred… another thousand… boys into these pits to die."

Realizing the lack of good options himself, General Riccard could only listen.

"And if we strike first," he continued, "and with an unprecedented display of nuclear force… it might just be devastating enough to force concession."

"Laymon will never surrender." The general's interjection couldn't have rung more true. "This man is dangerous. Reckless, Marcus. He is not driven by logic. His wartime strategies are evidence of it."

The general's tone became hushed and his countenance purposeful. "Frankly, Marcus, you know as well as I that it is not safe for you to be here, this close to the front lines. And it's certainly not in the best interest of our country."

But these words fell on deaf ears, as Marcus had no intention of "abandoning" the men whose blood filled the very canal in which he now stood.

That evening, Marcus returned to his temporary security bunker, situated only a mile and a half south of where he had witnessed the aftermath of hell alongside the general earlier that day. The bunker was constructed of half inch thick aluminum plates, which were connected at the ends with internal hinges. The structure could fold up nearly flat and be transported from site to site on only a double-axle truck, but when expanded, like now, it resembled a futuristic igloo. The design was not intended for protection from live artillery fire or other combat scenarios, but rather for concealment and portability. This was further evidenced by the camouflage netting draped over the exterior, and the fact that a detail of only two elite American soldiers stood guard at any time.

That night, as he lay on a mattress in the tin can shelter that was his bunker, Marcus's thoughts turned to dreams, which dissolved his consciousness into a saturated state of oblivious slumber. Any adrenaline that had resulted from his day in the heat of battle was no match for the weight of the lives of his men which now hung on the president's mind. It was these things which dragged him down into the subconscious that night. Sleep crept in.

Out of nowhere that subconscious was snapped by the fist of reality. A blast that reverberated through the metal bunker sent Marcus's body hurling across the floor, leaving him huddled against the wall farthest from his tiny doorway. As Marcus hauled himself to his knees, a high pitched shriek echoed in his eardrums. The resonation of the explosion had been amplified by the metal walls of the shelter, causing a deafening barrage of sound throughout. Smoke filled his lungs and eyes, and Marcus's sense of touch was only now catching up with the reality of what was happening, as a wave of heat struck his face.

Instinctively scrambling for his sidearm, which he had kept under the mattress that was now lying against the wall, he froze as a series of red lasers pierced through the smoke, flashing in all directions. The bright dots quickly converged on his center of mass, as four dark figures emerged from the haze. They wore all-black uniforms with reflective masks that seemed to have a mirror-like finish. There was a pause, and one of the men in the rear spoke into a radio. It was French. Another man then stepped forward, pinning Marcus to the ground. All went black.

The smell of musty polyester and the tension of a cord around his neck were evidence to Marcus that he had been hooded rather than knocked unconscious, as was the ringing in his ears that had only partially subsided. Had his sense of vision not been voided by his new head apparel, Marcus may have noticed that the objects which his feet struck as he was dragged out were the bodies of his security detail. The next thing Marcus felt was the sobering sting of a cold needle on the side of his neck. And then… nothing.

★ CHAPTER 7 ★

At one point or another in the lives of most men, they are faced with a choice that will change the course of their lives. Fewer men ever face a decision that could change the destiny of a nation. Rarely does a single man carry the enormous weight of an opportunity to change the world forever. In the mind of Vincent Laymon, the capture of his nemesis, Marcus Pratt, proved just that.

It was a chance to send a dying species into instant extinction. The capture and execution of America's president and global symbol of Ascendacism would deflate any sense of hope remaining for the anti-Civicist movement. More importantly, Vincent was offered the chance to avenge the murder of his brother by providing Marcus Pratt with the same treatment that was awarded Frank. But before revenge was to be had, Vincent requested that his captive be brought before him.

Marcus Pratt had woken up during his unanticipated trip. Though his head covering still impeded his sight, it was clear that it was now daytime, as light poked through the breathing holes which had been made in the bag covering his head. It seemed that barely enough oxygen passed through the tiny holes and, although now fully aware, Marcus was in a constant state of lightheadedness. The hum of an engine and roar of air passing by made the mode of Marcus's transport rather obvious. It was a utility vehicle, quite likely of the Canadian military. For the next few hours there was no speaking, and Marcus Pratt was left only to his thoughts. Thoughts of his parents, his country, and the fate of the war from which he had just been plucked. As the vehicle came to a halt, Marcus was escorted away by two men. Voices were now audible, some speaking French, but mostly English, as Marcus was clearly being brought through a series of security checkpoints.

Vincent leapt to his feet as he received the call from Fort Matane's security command. Four armed soldiers rushed to keep up, as Vincent stormed through the corridors towards the holding room of his adversary.

Marcus's hood was now off, and he sat in a chair within a completely empty room, with the obvious exception of four heavily-armed Canadian soldiers. The room was lit by six fluorescent flood lights, recessed into the ceiling. The floor was dingy cement, and the walls an equally uninviting dark brown plaster. The only way into or out of the room was through a tinted glass door which now violently swung open.

As Vincent entered the holding cell, he finally laid eyes on his prey. President Marcus Pratt stood to his feet as their glares met. This was not a cat and mouse game, but rather two vicious lions, pacing about the corpse of a fresh kill, both ready to die for a bite of its flesh. Every rifle in the room was pointed directly at the captive's face. Vincent ordered the soldiers to stand down, and he now stepped forward to analyze the man who stood before him. The American president was younger than he had imagined, though he had seen much footage of Marcus Pratt. Vincent's countenance fell dead as he approached his arch rival. Every heart wrenching memory of his father, Saul, Andrew Marcell, and his brother, Frank, was stacked layer upon layer and now acted as fuel for the raging fire building up inside.

The face of the man who appeared through the doorway was one familiar to Marcus, though the leader of

Canada appeared younger in person than the intelligence photos would have had Marcus believe. Despite his relatively youthful appearance, however, a dark hatred emanated from the determined gray eyes of Vincent Laymon. This was the face of the world's problems – oppression, abuse of power, big government... everything that Marcus so despised.

It is not important what was said in that room, on that day. It is sufficient to say that there were two men sharing a stage that had room enough only for one, and that both were willing to die for their country and kill for their cause. No word ever spoken in earth's history could change these things. And to think that the leaders of the modern world could exist in the same space and communicate verbally, while the soldiers who fought for them disemboweled each other on the battlefield at the same time. But we should not forget that only one of the two men was there by choice. And that man's, Vincent Laymon's, sole purpose was to gain closure over the matter of his brother's death. But there was no closure. There never really is. The harsh words spoken to his captive, Marcus Pratt, did not bring it. The insults he hurled at the American president and his infantile pursuit of Ascendacist ideals did not bring it. Nor did the look of indifference in Marcus's eyes when Vincent explained that he was preparing the same fate for the president that had been reserved for Vincent's brother, Frank. Indeed, if closure was not a realistic objective, at least Vincent could watch his arch rival suffer incredible anguish in his last hours, as Frank surely had. And not only would Vincent Laymon watch, but the whole world would be given the opportunity to share in the graphic extinction of the last legitimate leader of the so-called "free" world.

The details of the event had already been conceived. There would be seventeen high-definition video cameras with direct-line access to Canadian state television, and from there to the world. A massive stone table, nearly a half a meter thick, with ten centimeter wide leather straps looped through slots at the four corners, and three down the center. A galvanized steel bucket full of rusty razor blades. Twelve different types of pliers. Four liters of undiluted hydrochloric acid. A fire ring full of coals with several long, steel spikes leaning in on the periphery. And honestly, the setup had only just begun. The venue would be an abandoned university stadium in northwestern Canada, chosen for its relatively unrecognizable setting, along with its ability to seat the nearly ten thousand strong live audience of Canadian military "invitees".

In Vincent's mind, while no reason beyond revenge was really needed, the brazen public torture of Marcus Pratt would come with the added benefits of demoralizing the American military force and sending a message of Canadian strength and resolve to the ends of the earth. This second point was surely one learned from Vincent's experiences with the late president, Andrew Marcell.

* * *

Ironically, the last weeks of Marcus Pratt's life would be spent at Transrek - the same facility that had given rise to the man who now arguably replaced him as the most powerful ruler on the earth. There could be little doubt that prisoner number H093 was the only Ascendant in this place. And despite the fact that nearly every inmate had been in some way wronged by their Civicist government and held against their will, there was little love in the air for Marcus

Pratt. Being held in the hard lined east wing of the penitentiary meant that a walk through the corridor came with a shower of bodily fluids, the most desirable of which was saliva. Word had traveled fast within Transrek, such that not a soul was left without knowledge of the identity of their newest guest. And it was for a similar reason that Vincent knew he must act quickly towards Marcus's execution. While a headless American military would be inadequately slow in converging on their next move, the final act could not wait forever. Word would travel quite fast in the intelligence community. But Vincent was careful in his planning. He needed this. Surveillance on the American military forces had been ramped up to an all-time high. Not the slightest move was made under an American flag without Canada's (and Vincent Laymon's) knowledge.

All the while, the president of America was left to the fate of a living-decomposition. After another week of not showering, not eating, not talking... Marcus resembled something far from a powerful leader. A scraggly brown beard had begun to form on his now-filthy face, and his physique had thinned out. The hours passed by in his dark chamber as Marcus brushed his bare toes across the dirty gravel floor in the only region of the tiny room that was visible, thanks to the dim glare that made its way through the seam under the door. His time was spent thinking of his home and his friends. Marcus wondered what had happened in America following his capture. Surely there was much confusion and uncertainty surrounding the event, and his status was likely labeled "missing in action". Though it was undoubtedly the headline of every major news source in the world by this time, Marcus knew there was no hope for a counter strike. With an immediate transfer of authority to the partisan leaders of Congress and an emergency election not something that could be manufactured overnight, Marcus knew that by the time his country had begun to form anything resembling a plan of action, they would be watching him be dismembered in high definition. There was simply too much bureaucracy. Too many cooks in the kitchen with different recipes in mind.

The cell was cold and damp, and Marcus Pratt held only the company of sewer rats and cockroaches in those final days. For a man used to multitasking and prioritizing every last second of his day, the long lingering hours of captivity were a constant shackle on his mind. Only the faint gleam of light from under the door could be used to differentiate between day and night. But as disoriented, gaunt, and weak as his state may have been, Marcus knew who he was and that he had done everything in his power to free his fellow man.

As the day approached, unknown now to Marcus since his concept of time had dissolved, the rats bravely scurried closer to him, as if they could sense that there was somehow less of a human life in their presence to fear. Marcus had found himself scribing characters into the dirt near the door to his chamber. A closer look would have revealed that they were Greek letters. It was an act only made more bizarre by the fact that Marcus didn't know a thing about Greek. But nine days of disorienting darkness can do strange things to a man.

The next morning (or at least *day* – it was really hard to tell sometimes), Marcus was awakened from a rare spot of sleep by the sound of distant shouting. He rolled himself over and positioned his ear as close to the bottom of the rusty steel door as possible, while still lying on his stomach. Slowly, the shouting became increasingly loud, and an array of clanging sounds were added to the mix. It was the clamor of prisoners who were privileged enough to be in possession of a tin cup, or other various forms of metal, smashing them against the bars of their jail cells. Marcus could hear boots pounding the floors of the hallway as Canadian soldiers were clearly moving somewhere in a hurry. The clanging symphony of disorder grew and grew, then... WHAM!!! A flash of light blazed through the bottom of the closed door, and in that moment was even bright enough to find its way through the thinner cracks around the door's border, making a fleeting silhouette which faded as abruptly as it had formed. The flash brought excruciating pain to the eyes of Marcus, which had seen no more than a dim glow in over a week's time. The reaction of his body was to roll away onto his side, as Marcus's fingers grasped at his eye sockets. No more than two seconds of dead silence passed, followed by what could only be described as *force* in its purest form. A force so intense that it drove Marcus's body violently against the back wall of his cell. In a fraction of a second, the door to Marcus Pratt's cell was peeled back like a ripe banana and the concrete ceiling overhead was torn off, showering nature's sunlight down, along with chunks of cement block that barely missed Marcus, but for one which shattered his right ankle.

With this wall of pressure came a wall of sound, but who could notice with concrete and rebar raining from the sky. Exactly three seconds ago, Marcus was straining to hear the apparent disruption stirring at the Transrek facility, and now he lay in a mist of dust and debris. The calming effect provided by the rays of sunlight, which now tore through the haze, was interrupted by a barrage of gunfire and small explosions. Bullets buzzed overhead like supersonic cicada, and Marcus Pratt could do nothing but cover his vitals and make himself as small as possible on the ground. The gunfire died down minutes later, and the decay of its commotion was found to be inversely proportional to the sound of men shouting, which now became more and more prominent. Though the words were still indistinguishable, there was something unique... something *foreign* about their tone. That much was clear. These were not Canadian voices, nor were they American. Instead, the words being screamed were in Spanish... with a distinct Columbian accent.

★ CHAPTER 8 ★

A gentle hand pulled on Marcus's shoulder, guiding him to roll onto his back. The dust had begun to settle but remained dense enough that, when Marcus laid his eyes upon the man to whom the hand belonged, the heavenly traces of light piercing through established the visual of a godsend. The figure inclined his head to his right shoulder, reached across his body with his left hand, and flipped a switch on his radio, which was attached to his vest. Marcus recognized the first word… "Aqui…" The man removed his camouflage mask, which seemed to be no more than a knit hat with a strip cut out for the eyes. As Marcus began processing the situation, more and more masked figures converged on what was left of the room that had held him. The attire of these people varied as much as their weaponry. A semi-automatic rifle hanging on the back of a man with a red bandana across his face here. A vest of grenades dangling like Christmas ornaments on an otherwise shirtless man there. Another, clearly a hooded woman wearing a black, sleeveless undershirt with a pistol in each hand. All exposed features were those reflective of a Latin descent. And now a tall figure emerged as the rest took a couple of steps back. The man knelt down and looked Marcus Pratt in the eyes, but it was his voice that Marcus recognized first…

"Marcus…"

"Santino??" Marcus stuttered. It couldn't be. But it most certainly was. Any doubt evaporated with the emergence of that familiar smile…

"Marcus!" Pure joy spread across Santino's face as, still kneeling, he leaned in to hug his old compadre. The cluster of mercenaries surrounding them raised their weapons and cheered, some firing off rounds overhead, others shouting "Viva Desconocido!"

Marcus slowly fell out of his trance and cracked a smile of his own... It was the first that had crossed his face in weeks.

"Santino... what is...?" Marcus couldn't even finish the sentence, but the message was nevertheless received.

"This is the beginning, Marcus." More cheers and gunfire erupted.

After another minute or two of nothing but pure emotion, Santino stood up and took a step back... "You look like shit!"

Marcus laughed, but it was primarily because he knew the words were likely quite true. His capture, interrogation, and eight night stay in the luxurious accommodations of Transrek had left his usually-dapper appearance filthy and emaciated. Santino reached out to help Marcus to his feet but then paused, obviously taken aback. "Oh, shit," but Santino wasn't commenting on Marcus's slightly sunken, yet still passionate, green eyes or the beard that had begun to form on his now dust-covered face. Instead, his eyes had tracked downwards towards Marcus's feet, and now Marcus's gaze followed suit.

Adrenaline is clearly a funny thing... A truth not lost on Marcus Pratt, as his stare became focused on the ragged bone jutting out of his malformed ankle. Until that moment, Marcus hadn't even sensed the injury, and now the swell of excitement that accompanied the euphoria of freedom was taking over as an emotional anesthetic. Santino ordered two of the Desconocido to help Marcus to his feet, careful not to allow pressure on the mangled lower leg. As they began to make their way through the rubble, something on the ground caught Marcus's eye. It was the

Greek letters that he had been, days before, scribing in the dirt. Despite the now-apparent obliteration of the entire prison, a portion of the small patch of ground he had used as his ad lib parchment remained pristine. As he was led by, only two of the letters were untouched...

"A Ω"

The attack had been initiated at daybreak, and only upon his extraction by chopper later that morning would Marcus begin to grasp its full extent. Not only had the entire Transrek facility been leveled, but the strike had been accompanied by a far greater purpose. As the helicopter gained altitude, Marcus's focus shifted from the ashes of Transrek to the giant mushroom cloud towering before him. Turning his head towards Santino in astonishment, he caught a glimpse of another such cloud on the far horizon before he could even utter a word.

But there were no words. Marcus's mental state had been sharpened now, as he absorbed every syllable that came from Santino's lips... "Poloma sends his regards."

He paused. "We did it, Marcus."

Santino's countenance was now glowing, and a warm grin appeared that he couldn't have held back if he tried.

"How many..?" Marcus uttered.

"There were seven targets in total, Marcus. I have it on good authority that six strikes were successful."

Marcus Pratt's mind flashed back to that fateful scene in Ft. Lauderdale years ago. But if Santino's words were accurate, this would make the Panama Event look like a box of sparklers. As the chopper banked right, Marcus could now see the grease spot that was once one of Canada's most notorious military prisons. The significance of what was happening began to saturate Marcus's sense of reality. "How in the world did you pull this off?"

Santino leaned back on the black vinyl seat, staring up into the network of wiring covering the underside of the helicopter's roof... "Briefcases," he said.

"Briefcases???"

"Briefcases, duffle bags, pickup trucks, and a few split atoms, thanks to a very generous American investor I ran into a while back." Santino transitioned his concentration onto Marcus... "We have much experience operating in Civicist-ruled countries. Many contacts who share the same interests as us. This is a great day for Ascendacism, Marcus."

And no matter how you spun it, Marcus couldn't have agreed more.

"Did I just become the first person in history to incorporate a nuclear weapon in their escape from prison?" Marcus smiled as he stared at the unimaginable sight of *two* mushroom clouds gracing the landscape.

Santino, also gazing at the aftermath, was quick to respond, "Technically... the prison thing was just a fertilizer bomb... albeit a bit overdone, I admit."

"Gee, ya think?" Marcus's sarcasm was not lost on the Columbian... "Is that a Desconocido thing or what?"

Santino laughed.

Marcus continued, "And should I be worried about this?"... motioning towards the remnants of the nuclear blasts.

Santino faced his friend. "We were at least five miles from the nearest epicenter, and upwind. Ionizing radiation from the nuke should be minimal here. But we won't be sticking around too long to test that theory."

Marcus concurred.   "Right, let's get out of this mess."

* * *

And a mess it was. But certainly a well-planned mess. While Marcus's escape had been a fast and furious effort in terms of planning and execution on the part of the Desconocido, the series of nuclear strikes which coincided with Marcus's breakout had been in the works now for months - months before Marcus had been captured, and in some ways even before the war between America and Canada had ensued. The placement of the blasts was meticulous. The coordinates had been chosen based on high population areas, and were narrowed down considering weather patterns and seasonal changes. The Desconocido had learned much from their foray in Panama, and were careful to apply that knowledge to these smaller blasts in Canada.

The coordinated strike had been rushed by a couple of weeks upon receiving intel of Marcus's capture. But the timing was sufficient to ensure that the resulting nuclear winter, though devastating to Civicist Canada, would have little impact on her neighbor to the south.

In the days that followed, the news of the nuclear strikes spread quickly throughout Canada, despite the debilitating disruptions to the power grid. The most immediate effect manifested itself as a mass exodus of Canadian citizens to the southern border, in an attempt to simply escape the radiation, darkness, and chaos which consumed much of the civicist nation. But in this time of war, these people were treated like traitors by the Canadian military, and as invaders by the Americans. As such, there were few that survived the attempted migration. And there is nothing that incites civil unrest quite like the feeling of being trapped in the aura of a nuclear fallout by the action of one's own regime. Even the strongest government facilities were becoming overrun, as the Canadian military was finding it nearly impossible to defend its infrastructure against its own people, while keeping its neighboring nation, whose resolve was now ironclad, at bay.

And now Ft. Matane itself, the stronghold of strongholds, was under siege. From within its underbelly, the President's Quarters, Vincent Laymon struggled to issue orders and portray a sense of control over his military, which was itself wavering with increasing rates of suicide and mass surrenders. And as the masses formed around the fort's perimeter and grew braver by the day, the inevitable began to unfold. Only so many bodies of your fellow citizens can pile up before defections of even the most loyal of soldiers begin to occur. And only so many soldiers need to defect before mutiny, at even the highest ranks, can be ensured. And this is precisely what happened next.

Exactly one week after the date of the planned execution of his nemesis, Marcus Pratt, Vincent Layman was escorted out of Fort Matane under gunpoint by his own Executive Council. And exactly one week after *that* day, his corpse would be found by American forces, hung upside down from a crane over the canal he once helped dig. His intestines hung below – almost far enough to reach the decomposing bodies of Alex Zanderberg and the Councilmen who, only the week before, had led Vincent away from his safe haven in Ft. Matane. Indeed, the common man did not distinguish at a time like this. Government was government.

Someone had tapped into the loudspeakers

surrounding the canal which were once used to issue orders and sound alarms. Now they were being used to play an old Canadian anthem. It was a tune which would have been familiar to Vincent. *"Dum vita est spes est"*... a song that his mother had often sung to him as a young child, while tucking him in at night. But Vincent did not hear it now.

★ CHAPTER 9 ★

Marcus's return to America was celebrated by parades and rallies from coast to coast. In those days following his death-defying escape, morale seemingly could not have been higher. The American war strategy had become one of simply protecting the borders while sitting back and watching her neighbor to the north collapse from within. Marcus's popularity skyrocketed to new heights, despite the fact that the ensuing surge of Ascendant support drove a deep wedge of partisanship between themselves and the more moderate believers in free society.

Marcus's now undeniable ties to the Desconocido, a faction which was still officially considered a terrorist group by even the American government, did not sit well with many people. This, despite the fact that Marcus was sure to downplay the connection at every chance he was afforded. In the wake of the overthrow of the civicist Canadian government and upon word of the death of his adversary, it was time for Marcus to address his nation once again. This time as a victorious leader, rather than a rising political star.

It would be a gathering for the ages, and what better place than where it had all begun for Marcus... Western Pennsylvania. Due to the extraordinary levels of expected attendance, the event would take place outdoors, about fifteen miles outside the city limits, behind an old farmhouse at the outskirts of a rural suburb. The setting was breathtaking... Rolling hills of fields stretched out for a country mile. But by the morning of the presidential address, not a patch of grass could be seen through the sea of humanity which had already amassed for the day's event. Of course it was, logistically-speaking, a thing of nightmares, with only two lane road access and mud-ridden fields serving as parking lots. But Marcus loved every minute of it. He insisted upon it. It was so good to be back home once again.

As the sun peaked over the horizon that morning and began its work burning off the morning fog, a bright red hue saturated the sky. Marcus would be introduced by his mentor, Robert Nochman, and good friend and colleague, Congresswoman Rachel Lorrett, later that day, but that morning he sat across from both in his old office sky rise sipping a cappuccino.

A helicopter was later used to transport the three to the site just prior to the speech. The introductory remarks delivered by the familiar voices of Robert and Rachel were both short and sweet. Then it was go-time.

Marcus Pratt, who had been sitting in a chair to the rear of the podium, stood to his feet and the crowd erupted with applause. It was the first time since his capture that Marcus had addressed the nation in a live format. Looking past the jungle of teleprompters and camera equipment, Marcus could see the swarm of humanity, like a living organism, pulsating with praise.

In that moment, however, the breath in Marcus Pratt's lungs was stolen, and a pinpoint pressure on his chest caused him to stumble backwards. His fingers relaxed, and the papers he had been holding in his right hand were released.

A small circle formed on the floor of the stage, beneath Marcus Pratt's feet. Another drip of blood fell beside it, and then another. An additional bomb of crimson rolled off Marcus's shirt and hit the ground about an inch from the transcript of his speech, which had since fluttered to the earth. Indeed a gunshot had been fired that day. The trained ear may have been able to discern the clap of an American .308 caliber rifle... But Marcus Pratt never heard it.

In his very last moments, Marcus lay prostrate on the platform, his head turned to the side, with his left ear pressed against the surface of the floor. His body's final physiological action was to strain the extra-ocular muscles behind his eyeballs, which focused his vision on a piece of paper. It was the first page of the transcript he had memorized for that day. But instead of speaking the opening words in that moment, he now read them. The words were splattered with the blood of a revolutionary hero... a true patriot...

"The war is over."

And now at last the victory's won
The war hath ceased and hope begun.
Our fate no more lay on the scale
A man's intent can now prevail.

But if his will be not our own
What comes of all the seeds he's sown?
Will not the world trade peace for choice
And join with him in single voice?

For surely hope hath bested pain
And lives so blessed to now remain
Would e'er be ones both safe and jolly
Were it not for... Intention's Folly.

- Sten Rethage